MADE MEN IV

LUCCA

SARAH BRIANNE

YOUNG INK PRESS

Young Ink Press Publication

YoungInkPress.com

Copyright © 2017 by Sarah Brianne

Edited by C&D Editing and Diamond in the Rough Editing

Cover Art by Young Ink Press

Book design by Inkstain Designs

Text set in Centaur.

Connect with Sarah:

AuthorSarahBrianne@gmail.com

www.facebook.com/AuthorSarahBrianne

@AuthorSarahBri

LUCCA

PROLOGUE
THE STORY BEHIND THE SCAR.
A STORY OF SADNESS, GRIEF AND TORTURE

SEVEN MONTHS AGO IN JANUARY...

*P*ulling *his classic black Cadillac* onto the side of the street, he positioned himself to watch the house. Then he looked at the clock, seeing he had timed it perfectly.

School's out.

He flipped his lighter open and closed, open and closed, waiting for her return. Lucca had never been good at sitting still, nor was he a very patient man when he was tired. The night before had been a long one, and his body still felt it. Regardless, he had enjoyed every second of it.

Last night, he had lain Mr. Johnson to rest and held up his promise of fucking the blonde until she regretted it. Both things had satiated his dark side ... *for now, anyway.*

Lucca flipped his lighter closed as a stuck-up BMW pulled into the driveway. He had never trusted a German car. The only thing good about it was its black paint color.

A strawberry blonde exited the car. *Elle Buchanan.* He couldn't help his sneer. His little brother was in big fucking trouble.

Watching her walk to the front door, he believed the girl only got prettier the more you looked at her.

It's going to be a shame when I have to strangle the life out of her.

One thing was for sure, the girl was going to die, and nothing could save her. It was unfortunate she had been there when the trigger had been pulled, but some girls were just born unlucky; this one in particular. She only had another month to her eighteenth birthday, and then ... *the end.*

The stuck-up-looking car reversed, drawing his attention back to it. He wondered who would drop off a girl in this neighborhood, driving that car. Truthfully, he was a little shocked this was the address, considering the girl had come from a prep school.

His gut told him to follow the car. Anyone Elle hung out with could possibly be collateral damage if her fucking mouth blabbed too much.

Looking at the clock again, he noticed there was a bit of time before Elle left for work, so he started his car, deciding to follow the BMW.

He kept a good distance from it, following in a direction he hadn't been expecting. This part of town was mostly owned by the city, along with some expensive restaurants and shops.

Watching the car pull into one of the most expensive shops in town, he parked on the street and pulled out his cell phone, texting the license plate number to a friend. Then he waited in anticipation, curiosity slowly eating away at him, only growing worse when the car door opened.

He immediately knew it was a woman when tall, black boots and black jeans hit the ground. The next thing he noticed was her long, silky hair. It was the blackest hair he had ever seen.

He desperately wanted a glimpse of her face, but she never turned around. Therefore, Lucca found himself turning off the car and getting out, wondering how this felt more important than anything else he could do with his time.

His instincts kept him going, following her into the store.

Lucca prided himself on being able to go unnoticed. His appearance of dark jeans, black shirts, and black sweatshirts allowed him to do just that, plus his scruffy face and hair. He could go places no one in the family could. Made men demanded attention with their suits and immaculate grooming, whereas he didn't need that kind of attention. *I have other ways to get the attention I demand.*

Entering the store undetected was easy with all the expensive shit it held. He navigated the store, finding the girl in all black who seemed to be looking for a particular piece. A slight glimpse of the left side of her face revealed her soft porcelain skin. He stalked closer.

Have I seen her before?

Another small glimpse revealed her young age.

Stopping, he was about to turn around—*She's too young*—but then the girl turned and went back to a table she had already passed.

His heart stopped for a beat when he saw the whole left side of her face and a striking gray eye. The other half was covered by a veil of hair. He wished he could reach out to feel the pure black strands of silk and move it to reveal the rest of her face.

Leave now. Nothing good would come of this. He should have left the moment he had noticed she was just a teenage girl. However, though he was unable to place it yet, something about her called to him; kept him from looking away from her and leaving.

The whole thing felt so wrong, yet so right. He was being pulled in different directions. His mind told him to leave, but his body kept him patiently waiting.

Watching her hand go up to her face, he felt his breath catch when she swept her hair behind her ear.

Fuck . . . His heart skipped another beat at the sight of her face in its entirety.

His eyes traveled down the right side of her gorgeous face that held a scar from above her eyebrow down to the hollow of her cheek. Another one graced above and below her luscious lips.

The instinct to let his fingertips glide down each mark was so strong he thought he might break his cover.

Her gray eyes held the story behind the scar, a story of sadness, grief, and torture. It was like staring at a perfect porcelain doll that had been dropped one too many times. Others would see a flaw in the cracked doll, making her no longer perfect, but he saw only beauty.

She was the most beautiful creature he had ever seen.

The gold, ornate piece she was infatuated with was unfamiliar to him until she opened the egg-shaped object and music began to play. Her eyes danced as she watched a ballerina twirl to the music. He wondered what it would feel like if she looked at him that way.

"It's a beautiful piece, isn't it?" an older woman who looked to be the storeowner asked as she came up to her.

The girl startled, shutting the music box.

He wanted her to go back to the way she had been a moment before. He could watch her study the delicate piece with gentle hands for hours.

When her tongue peeked out to lick her lips, he eagerly waited to hear her voice.

"Y-yes." She went back to looking at the box, avoiding the woman's gaze. "H-how much is it?"

"Three thousand dollars."

She removed her fingers from the piece. "Oh."

The woman kindly smiled. "I know Christmas just passed, but you could always ask for it for your birthday, maybe. I could hold it."

She shook her head. "Thank you, but it's too much."

The lady continued to smile. "Well, you could always come back if you talk your parents into it."

"Thank you." The girl took one last glance at the music box before she left the store.

Watching her leave was harder than he thought it would be. He wouldn't be able to come out of the store until she pulled out. Therefore, he had to watch her go to the car through the display window, and that wasn't close enough for him.

A vibration in his pocket had him pulling out his cell phone. He didn't say a word when he accepted the call.

His friend Sal came over the phone. "The BMW is registered to Maxwell Masters."

That wasn't what he had expected, though it explained why he felt like he had seen her before.

"Girl?" Lucca spoke into the phone carefully, watching her approach the driver's side of her BMW.

"He's married to Elaine Maste—"

"Younger," he cut him off.

Sal paused. "Scars?"

Lucca's eyes traced her markings. "Yes."

"That's Maxwell's daughter, Chloe Masters."

He ended the call with the push of a button.

Time stood still for him as he soaked in anything and everything he could about her before she disappeared into the car.

There was always a moment one faced in life when a choice had to be made, and this was his.

Her tortured soul called to his dark one, whispering for him to save her. His heart was now slow and steady, finding its purpose—*Chloe Masters.*

Taking one last look at the scars on her face, he couldn't wait for the day he could run his fingers across it. *Beautiful.*

MINE

Lucca sat at the desk in his home office, running his hands through his hair and trying to take deep breaths. The image of her had yet to leave his mind. His fingers still itched to trace her gorgeous markings. He wanted her, regardless of her age, *and nothing is going to stop me.*

He had very seldom wanted anything in his life. The first had been becoming a made man, and the second had been becoming the underboss. Both things he had accomplished at a very young age.

Being just twenty-six years old, he was the youngest underboss in the history of the Caruso family, and had become made at the age of seventeen, which was also the youngest anyone in the family had ever been made. What he had done to become made was something that would send most grown men to the psych ward, but not Lucca.

Lucca was born with a dark side. He had realized at a young age he wasn't like the rest of the world. The only emotions he ever felt were when he caused pain. At first, it didn't take much, just simply pinching another kid until he cried. It brought him joy and contentment. Slowly through the years, though, he needed more and more to bring those feelings back. Now, twenty-six years later, he was a full-blown monster, craving nothing but blood and chaos.

Turning on his computer, he searched the Internet, putting in the name that called to him. When an image of her popped up, his heart began to hum in his chest. It was a picture of a much younger her; the scars much fresher, bright red and unlike the faint pink he had seen today. To put it simply, they looked gruesome on her perfect porcelain face.

Zooming in, he gripped the mouse tighter, seething with pure anger. He knew all too well they were caused by a knife. The cuts were clean and precise, at a calculated depth to cause immense pain in those sensitive areas, and to scar her for life.

Whoever the fuck touched her better be dead.

Going back to the search, he looked for who had marked her, but the only thing that came up was a car wreck from three years ago. Reading the old newspaper article, he found out that her father, Maxwell Masters, was the one behind the wheel that night, and that her scars were blamed on the windshield glass breaking and hitting her in the face. *Bullshit.*

Lucca went back to the photo of Chloe, now zooming out to reveal her father getting sworn in as the mayor of Kansas City, Missouri. Not a single scratch was on him, confirming what he already knew.

The thirst for blood now coursed through his veins. He was going to do anything and everything to find out what had happened to her. Anyone who had anything to do with it would be buried six feet under by the time he was done.

Looking at her bitch of a father and mother, he had a feeling the list was going to be quite long. *They will all die.*

He went back to his search of her, wanting to learn everything he could.

Seeing a much more recent picture of her at some function, he stared at the image, his heart humming even louder, somewhat satiating his blood thirst. Fuck, he wanted her more than he had wanted to be made or become the underboss.

His gut twisted at thinking about how long he was going to have to wait for her to become eighteen. He wasn't sure how he was going to keep himself from taking her, unused to these strong feelings. Her tortured eyes seemed to be screaming at him to save her, only making his urges worse.

Putting a cigarette to his lips, he flipped open the lid to his cold, metal lighter before burning the end and taking a long drag.

Smoking always gave him something to do and focus on when his sick, twisted urges came upon him. He only hoped it was going to help him stay away from Chloe as well.

Flipping the lid close, he placed his Zippo back on his desk before looking at the recent picture of her once more.

One single thought entered his mind.

Mine.

IF SALVATION IS WHAT YOU SEEK, VIOLENCE IS NOT THE ANSWER

ucca waited in the tiny, dark room, wondering why his feet brought him here in the first place. The only times he had come here were when he thought about his mother. However, not since his mother had died had he ever sought penance. Penance was for those seeking absolution. He wasn't that type of man. Lucca only sought retribution.

A swiping noise had him lifting his eyes to the intricate window where hardly any light filtered through. He could see the shadow of the older man on the other side of the wall.

The thought of leaving entered his mind, but instead, words came out like it had been just yesterday since he had last spoken them. "Forgive me, Father, for I have sinned. It has been a long time since my last confession."

As Lucca sat there quietly, unable to find words past that, the figure behind the wall said, "Yes, my son?"

"My mother used to make me come here to confess when I was younger, but when I joined the family, she couldn't get me here anymore. I still remember the day I joined. She begged and pleaded with me to come here. I told her there was no saving me after what I did.

"She used to joke, saying there was a demon inside of me. That was the day she realized there really was. I'll never forget the look in her eyes when she saw me for who I really am, when she saw nothing but pure evil." Lucca paused for a brief moment. "Still, somehow, even up until she was murdered, she believed there was a way to save me, that somehow I could still seek salvation after all I've done."

"Is that what you're here for now? To find salvation?" The knowing voice filled the space between them.

Gray eyes stared back at him in his mind. "Yes."

"Then you must repent, my son."

"I'm not looking for God's type of salvation."

The priest went silent for a minute. "Then what kind of salvation are you looking for?"

Now, in his mind, his fingers traced the scar following the path from her eyebrow down to her cheek before travelling down to trace the scar over her pouty lips.

"My salvation comes in a seventeen-year-old girl."

"The rules, Lucca."

"You know very well I'm aware we're not to touch anyone underage."

"Have you …?" The priest wasn't able to finish his sentence, afraid of the answer he might hear.

"I am guilty of the worst sins, Father, but I'm not here to repent any sins I've committed. I'm here to ask for forgiveness of what I might do." *Will do.* It was a question of when, not if.

"You ask for forgiveness for your future but not your past?" Even though there was a wall separating them, the old man's perplexity was evident through his voice.

"The things I'm going to do to her, for her … I'm afraid will be the worst crimes I'll ever commit."

"If salvation is what you seek, violence is not the answer."

Violence is always the answer.

"Like I said, I'm not looking for God's type of salvation. My salvation will come as I lay my hands upon her, the very hands that have taken the life from the bodies of those who have touched her."

Lucca went to leave the room, but the priest's voice halted him.

"I've seen you sitting in my church every once in a while since after your mother's passing when you think no one is here to see you. God has seen you, too. I think you want forgiveness for all of your sins, my son."

"Maybe you're right, Father. Maybe a part of me hoped to find a path to my mother again, but the path I'm on now will only lead me straight to Hell."

As he walked out of the room, he could hear the helpless prayers of the Father and the beads tightening as he gripped the rosary around his neck.

The prayers weren't for Lucca, but for the souls the boogieman was about to claim.

THE BEING BEHIND THE DOOR

PRESENT TIME

*T*he cold metal table underneath her was a stark contrast to her burning face from what seemed like pointless crying.

"Please! Stop!" No amount of kicking and fighting was a match for what felt like millions of hands holding her down.

The laughter from the evil man who held a knife rang through her ears mockingly.

"*Stay still, little girl*"—he drew the knife closer to her face—"*or it'll just hurt worse.*"

Looking at his abnormally large, black eyes, she was sure she was looking into the eyes of the devil.

The silver blade inched closer and closer to her right eye until it was mere centimeters from her pupil.

"*Don't blink.*"

A tear welled up in her eye, making it even harder to keep her eye open. Her body began to tremble. She was going to blink.

"Don't blink, little girl," he warned her again.

The tear fell, and her eye started to close ...

"Chloe!" *Amo's voice boomed.*

A flicker of light entered her mind.

"This way, Chloe!" *Amo pleaded.*

Another flicker of light had her eyes shooting open.

Sitting up so abruptly made her feel lightheaded. The bed, along with the big room, was one she didn't recognize, which made her heart pound like a drum in her ears. The last thing she remembered was pulling up to the airport, so close to her freedom. And then someone came up behind her, and she blacked out ...

No! He's got me, and no one knows I'm even here.

Chloe shakily stood from the bed, going over to the nightstand. She reached her hand out ...

The devil will kill me this time. He promised he would.

Once she opened the expensive gold music box, the familiar lullaby began to play. It was then she realized that it couldn't be hers.

Chloe stepped toward the huge window with a hitch in her breath. She slowly reached out to pull back the curtain.

No one will save me this time.

Pulling back the curtain, she held her breath as she was greeted with a beautiful garden, along with the white gazebo she had found herself under before with ...

The door creaked open, and Chloe turned to meet the being

behind the door.

"Hey, darlin'."

The dark voice made her gasp for air. The blood in her veins slowly turned to ice, freezing her in place. Goose bumps began to trickle down her body from one look of those blue-green eyes. She tried to form a thought, her mouth even tried to form a word she wasn't even capable of thinking, yet nothing came out. The only thing she was left with was simply watching Lucca enter the room, closing the door behind him.

Going over to the bedside table, she watched as Lucca ran his finger over the ornate box that was still playing the lullaby she had been only able to hear in her memories. He then slowly closed the lid, bringing silence to the room.

When he moved again, Chloe found herself still gasping for air as he took a seat in a chair that sat in the corner.

Moments seemed to pass under his unwavering gaze. He didn't speak, seeming content to just sit there and watch her.

With the distance between them and the deafening silence getting to her, she tried again to find words. "H-How did I-I …?" Her voice trailed off, losing confidence when his eyes seemed to trail down her body.

"How did you get here?" he asked, raising an eyebrow.

She slowly nodded.

"I brought you here."

If he hadn't said it so matter-of-factly, she would have thought she misheard him.

"W-Why?"

A matter-of-fact answer didn't come out. Instead, you could see him thinking carefully about his next words. His eyes seemed to turn green while his words began to envelope her, his voice almost warm. "I brought you here ... to save you."

Chloe unconsciously wrapped her arms around herself, trying to keep the warmth from his voice, as she took one step toward him. "S-Save me from w-what?"

With one blink, Lucca's eyes turned back to his strange shade of blue-green, making her feel like she imagined them turning green. The warmth in his voice seemed to have been in her imagination as well.

"To save you from making the mistake of leaving."

What!

"Why would you do that? Why would you care?" Anger coursed through her. She had barely tasted freedom from this city, only for it to have been taken from her.

A smile touched his lips. "I guess you'll just have to wait and see, darlin'."

Her eyes went wide at his cynical tone. She quickly lost any confidence she had gained from her anger.

For a moment, she thought she had seen something different in him, but now she saw only the darkness in him. The smile on his face brought back the memory of the night he revealed his true self ...

Crack.

The sound of broken bones greeted her ears as a baseball bat slammed down onto a limp body.

Snap.

Another flash of the bat making contact with the man's leg, the man who lay practically lifeless on the floor.

He raised the bat once more, pausing only to look her in the eyes. An evil pair of blue-green eyes stared back at her, making her blood run cold. She watched his hands grip the neck of the bat with a force so intense she was positive it was going to shatter before the bat was brought down for its final time.

Crunch.

As she watched the man inhale the air around him, he looked crazed, his appearance disheveled. Then he slicked his overgrown hair back in place, and you could see the slight smile come to his lips . . .

Taking the small step back she had taken forward, she realized the true danger she was in.

"A-Are you going to h-hurt m-me?"

She saw something flash in his eyes, his smile disappearing.

As he got up from the chair, Chloe held her breath once more. Then, as he stalked toward her, she backed up as far as she could with each step he took toward her until her back met the wall.

Lucca stopped when his body was mere inches from hers, leaning down ever so slightly to bring his tall stature closer to hers. "Have I ever hurt you, Chloe?" His voice was an octave deeper, coming out darker than she had ever heard him speak before.

She slowly shook her head, afraid not to answer the demon who had her in his grasp.

His gaze trailed down the scar that ran from her eyebrow to her cheek, making her swear she could almost feel his light caress.

"P-Please, can I-I go?" she pleaded, fearing what her future might hold from this moment forward.

Lucca stared down at her, bringing his hand up close to her face. "I don't think you understand."

Chloe's breath caught in her throat. She desperately wanted to close her eyes, but his wouldn't let her, forcing her to remain looking up at him.

"There is no leaving," he continued, careful not to touch her, though he twirled a strand of her silky black hair around his finger. "You're mine now, Chloe." He dropped the strand, and it fell upon her chest that was now rising and falling heavily.

Watching the demon back up toward the nightstand, she started to realize that the devil was never her worst nightmare.

Lucca opened the music box once more, letting her lullaby fill the room, before disappearing and closing her inside her new prison.

He is. The Boogieman.

Her legs gave out, and she slowly sunk to the floor. She grasped her legs close to her chest as the beautiful melody started to trail off, almost coming to an end.

You're mine now, Chloe.

IF I CATCH YOU, I WON'T BE ABLE TO STOP MYSELF

he devil had been the one to always haunt her, but he never came. In his place was the boogieman, promising her his kidnapping was going to be so much worse than her first by the devil.

Chloe stayed unmoving on the floor for what seemed like hours, now completely numb as she stared at the wall in front of her. It wasn't until the sun rose, shining through the room and warming her skin, that her eyes moved to her luggage that Lucca must have brought in with her.

My cell phone! Quickly going to her bags, she desperately began looking for her phone. *It's gone . . .* It was then that Lucca's words hit her. *"There is no leaving."*

With her bag open, she caught a glimpse of her gold music box.

Reaching in, she pulled out the fragile broken piece, taking it to the nightstand and setting it beside the polished unbroken one.

Seeing them side by side, she realized how much damage the one she'd had since childhood had taken. It had been severely cracked, leaving it unable to play the lullaby she had once heard every night before falling asleep.

Turning the key on the polished one, she began listening to the tune.

How did he get this? How did he know?

As the song played, realization hit, taking her back to seven months ago when she went into a little shop that had the old music box for sale.

Every now and then, she would check the Internet for the piece, seeing if she could somehow find it again, allowing her to hear the tune once more. Finally, her dream had come true when a shop close to where she lived posted it for sale on their website. She had gone the next day, able to hear the tune for just a moment before the owner had told her the price for the piece was three thousand dollars. It was just a little later when she ...

Chloe opened the door to the shop, heading straight to the spot where she had seen the beautiful box just a week before. However, looking at the display table, she saw it was gone.

Figuring it might have been moved, she scanned the shop.

"Hello," the familiar older woman's voice greeted her. She could tell by the woman's features that she seemed worried

"H-Hi."

"I'm so sorry to tell you, but if you're looking for the music box, I sold it just yesterday."

Wringing her hands, Chloe looked down at the floor, covering her face in a veil of hair. "Oh."

"I tried waiting for you, but a man came in right after you left, wanting it. I refused to sell it to him, but then he came back yesterday, offering me more money and explaining why he had to have it. I'm really sorry."

"I-It's okay. I wasn't able to afford it, anyway … I just wanted to hear it one more time."

Closing the music box Lucca had left open, she silenced the room once more as she tried to grasp the fact that Lucca had this in his possession for seven months now. *Why?* Never did she see this coming from Lucca of all people. He was the brother to her best friend's boyfriend, Nero.

He couldn't just kidnap me without anyone knowing, right?

Glancing around the room, she suddenly realized what she hadn't before. She was in their family home, so someone would have to come by … *Maria!* Lucca and Nero's sister lived here. *She will help me.*

Going to the door, she put her hand on the doorknob, taking a deep breath before she slowly turned it, easily pulling the door open. Peeking out into the hall to see if the coast was clear, she tried her best to navigate to Maria's room, which she had only been in once before when she had come over with Elle.

Believing she found the correct room, she quietly knocked on the door. When there was no response, she carefully opened it to find that she had indeed found the correct room, but there was no Maria.

"Come with me," a deep, unfamiliar voice came from behind her, scaring her in place. "Now!" he boomed when she didn't move to turn around.

Slowly turning, she saw a huge man in a suit before he turned himself around and walked down the hall and toward the stairs.

Her feet reluctantly began to move, afraid that the big man would find other means to get her to come with him if she didn't do it herself.

Following him down the steps, through the foyer, and then to the big, open floorplan of the main living room with kitchen, that was when she saw him.

"I caught her going into your sister's room," the big, suited man told him before he stood against the wall, crossing his arms.

She watched Lucca give a slight smile as he poured himself a cup of coffee.

"Come sit down, darlin'," Lucca said, motioning to the stool at the big kitchen island.

With the two men staring her down, she felt like she had no choice. Therefore, she cautiously made her way toward Lucca, taking a seat while he watched her every move.

Letting her hair fall around her face, she stared down at her wringing hands, no longer able to see him looking at her. It didn't help much. She could still feel his eyes studying her.

Taking a sip of his coffee, he spoke, "You look tired today."

Her nails began to dig into her palms.

Setting down his cup, he went to a kitchen cabinet and pulled out another mug. Then he filled it up with the dark liquid before putting it in front of her.

Staring at the cup of coffee, she didn't make a move for it, still digging her nails into her palms. "I-I'm no—"

"Drink," Lucca commanded.

Her lids lifted to meet his eyes that were just as commanding as his demand. When she found herself reaching for the coffee, she couldn't understand why she easily did what he ordered.

After taking a big enough gulp to satiate him, she set the cup back down, finding the warm liquid was much needed to her chilled body.

"Now"—Lucca took another sip of his own—"my family is staying at my father's casino … for a while. I've told them the house is no longer safe, so no one will come here until I give them word that it's safe again."

"H-How long is for a while?" she quietly spoke, once again wringing her hands at his cold words.

"That's going to depend on you."

She raised her head and looked up at him. *Me?*

Reading her confusion, he continued, "When I can trust that you won't run from me."

Chloe blinked at him several times. "Y-You're not going to kill me?"

He smiled down at her; it was obvious he had different plans for her. "No, darlin'."

What does he want from me?

She took another drink from her mug to warm her chilled

body, while she thought about her next few words. "So, I'm your p-prisoner?"

A predatory look came upon him, liking the way she had claimed herself as his prisoner. "Only for as long as you make it."

Now her nails pierced her skin.

"I have to leave," Lucca told her. With a final drink of his coffee, he nodded his head toward the suited man with his back against the wall. "Drago will be your shadow from now on. He will be watching you for me."

Her blood ran cold. She became motionless at the thought of being alone with the unknown stranger all day.

Sensing her distress, Lucca's voice rang through her ears, "Chloe, he will not touch you unless you give him no option. Do you understand?"

The nails in her palms went deeper as she nodded, unable to vocalize an answer.

Lucca took a step to leave but stopped. "If you try to make a run for it, you'll be lucky if he catches you." He paused for a brief instant before his voice turned so dark that it sent every hair on her body straight up. "If *I* catch you, I won't be able to stop myself from taking what I want the moment I saw you."

Blood trickled in her palms. It wasn't a threat he was making. It was a promise.

THIS IS GOING TO END IN WAR

"**D**o *you think you can* tell me now why the fuck my men rushed me and my family out of my home yesterday?" Dante spat at him the moment Lucca sat down in his office in the casino hotel.

Lucca lit the end of his cigarette, desperately needing it for the conversation he was about to have with his father.

"It's no longer safe there."

"What do you mean, it's no longer safe? My home has always been safe."

That's exactly why I need it. However, the details couldn't be given to Dante just yet.

"When the threat is gone, you, Maria, and Leo may come back."

Dante slammed his hand down on his desk. "Fuck's sake, Lucca! Threat? What fucking threat?"

Hitting his ashes out in the ashtray, he figured he was going to have to give up something for now. "I got Luciano's man to talk."

"Shit." Picking up his liquor glass, his father drained the contents, knowing exactly who Lucca was talking about.

The Lucianos were another family who owned a small portion of Kansas City, and up until seven months ago, the two families had been at peace. Recently, one of the casino hotel's penthouses had been under attack when Luciano's man broke in. He thankfully had been unsuccessful in targeting Lucca's sister, Maria.

They couldn't taint the Luciano name by throwing out accusations without any evidence. What they needed was a rat that squealed.

"As your underboss, I'm telling you that the less I tell you, the better. The penthouses are now the safest place for everyone. Stay here until it's over."

Rubbing his temples, Dante finally nodded in agreement. "Does anyone in the family know about this?"

"Two do. Sal"—Lucca took a hit off his cigarette, knowing his father wouldn't be surprised with Sal's name but would likely with the next—"and Drago."

His father's icy blue eyes flashed at him. "Goddammit, Lucca, you're taking him from me, aren't you?"

"Yes," he gave the grave answer his father didn't want to hear. "You will have all the rest of your men protecting you, Maria, and Leo here. I'm asking for just him. I need his help and his protection elsewhere."

He could see his father contemplating on whether he was going to allow his most skilled and deadliest man to leave his side to join Lucca's. Dante, as the boss, and Lucca, as the underboss, both had to have men by their sides at all times; men they needed to command and ask things of they themselves couldn't fulfill.

Lucca's right hand was Sal. Not only was Sal his best friend who was like a brother to him, but he was skilled in different ways than Lucca. Lucca never needed protection, being deadly enough of his own accord. What he did need was information, and Sal was gifted with a brain that didn't work like any others in the Caruso family. He was a highly intelligent individual, able to hack into any computer in under a minute. To put it simply, Sal was irreplaceable. However, Drago was something completely different.

Dante was the highest target on the family tree. He didn't need a man; he needed a tank. A tank that could take several bullets without flinching and still move forward to kill the men who stood in his way. Drago was a skilled killer of the deadliest kind. The kind who had no weaknesses. The kind who would never greet death because … he was Death.

Lucca sat somewhere between those two men, having the skills and intellect, but it was his sadistic, twisted, demented mind that made him the worst of all. With him commanding the two men under him, there wasn't going to be anything or anyone to stand in his way. The three together could desolate all of Kansas City if that was what he wished.

Dante nodded once more, agreeing to let his right hand go until the job was done.

It didn't matter much to Lucca if he had agreed to it or not. Drago was only going to be under his command. And Lucca would have done whatever it took to make it so. Even if he had to put a bullet in his own father's skull, he would have ... *to protect her.*

Putting his cigarette out in the ashtray, he got up to leave.

"This is going to end in war, isn't it?"

Lucca's voice went cold as he looked back over his shoulder. "The war started years ago; we just didn't realize it."

"Where is she?" Lucca asked the moment Drago entered the living room.

"She's still in her room."

Lucca stared at him, dumbfounded. "She hasn't left it?"

Drago shook his head. "No. She's just staring at the wall."

Furious, Lucca went into his office, shutting himself inside.

Fuck! He slammed his hands down on his desk before angrily swiping the contents off and smashing them onto the floor. He was trying to be as nice to her as he could, letting her come out on her own after she was comfortable, but she hadn't come out in two days. The only time she had come out of the room had been on the morning of the first day.

He wanted her to be comfortable here, to be comfortable with him, but Chloe was making it difficult.

A knock sounded on the door.

"Come in."

"Everything all right?" Drago asked, opening the door.

Nodding, he almost let Drago close the door before he stopped him.

"I need you to do something for me."

Taking up the whole double-door doorframe, Drago waited for his order.

"Tell her, if she wants dinner, she has to come downstairs." Lucca paused for a brief second, deciding to continue his order. "Tell her that if she wants to eat again, she has to leave that fucking room."

Drago nodded before leaving, closing the door behind him.

Over the last two days, Lucca had seemed to forget that he wasn't going to baby her like the rest of her little friends had. *Being nice never worked for me, anyway.*

PLAYING WITH FIRE

Chloe sat on the bed, staring at the wall, her stomach growling even louder now. She hadn't eaten since lunch yesterday and had only been able to eat a couple of bites of her sandwich then.

If you're hungry, you will eat downstairs from now on, her mind repeated the words the huge man named Drago had said.

She felt like she would rather starve than have to leave the safety of her room. It was strange, but something in her told her that, as long as she was in the room, they couldn't harm her, like they were giving it to her as a safe haven. She had come to this conclusion over the course of the three days because she hadn't been touched, and now Lucca was trying to draw her out.

Yep, I'll starve.

There was a knock on the door before Drago entered. "Dinner is ready."

Chloe held her arms tighter to her. "N-No, thank y-you."

Hearing him sigh made her look over at him. No emotion had been shown by the man. Every time he had come in, he had simply said in very few words that food had been prepared, only for him to leave right after.

"You're playing with fire." Drago's brownish-red eyes glowed at her. "You'd be wise to realize this door doesn't lock from the inside. Even if it did, it wouldn't stop him from coming up here and beating the door down if you keep disrespecting him. If you're smart, you will get your ass down there while he still has a little patience left."

The door slamming behind him made her practically jump off the bed.

You're playing with fire.

Her eyes moved to the doorknob that held no lock, proving to her that she wasn't as safe as she had thought she was in this room.

She didn't know what to do. She was just trying to figure out which option gave her the best chance of survival. In the end, though, she knew Lucca was going to get what he wanted from her, and it wasn't going to matter if she was on this side of that door or the other.

Taking a deep breath, she followed the path to her captor, taking her time as she slowly dragged her feet. With each step, she could feel the life she thought she was going to have in California slip through her fingers.

Downstairs, she lifted her eyes to see Lucca sitting at the dining room table. With the slight smile he gave through his eyes upon seeing her, she felt that life fully slip away until it was just a dream.

Lucca motioned for her to join him. "Sit down, darlin'."

Looking at the table, she saw two plates already filled, one in front of Lucca, who sat at the head of the table, and the other in front of the chair next to him. Chloe was going to have to sit close to him, and by the look on his face, that was exactly what he wanted.

I should have . . . She realized her mistake then; that her chances were better off in the room.

"Sit." His voice came out harsher.

She could no longer feel possession of her own feet as she walked up to the table, following his order.

His eyes turned green for the briefest moment as she stared down at him, holding her breath, while carefully taking the chair. It was almost like looking into the eyes of a different man. She saw something unusual in them, but before she could figure it out, they flashed and his normal shade of blue-green was back.

She looked down at her clutched hands in her lap.

"Thank you for joining me for dinner. I'm not sure what foods you like, but I hope you like this."

She glanced at her plate of chicken parmesan and noodles, then back up at him. He seemed proud of his dish.

"Y-You made t-this?"

Lucca smiled as he picked up his fork and knife. "Yes. Why do you look surprised?"

"S-Sorry. You just don't look"—her eyes drifted to his black T-shirt that hugged his broad muscles before she snapped her eyes back to her plate—"l-like the cooking type."

"I got sick of ordering pizza after my mother died, so I taught

32

myself to cook." His voice seemed to have turned somber.

Although Nero had told her once that their mother had died, she felt like Lucca had just revealed something very personal to her. *Why?*

"Is something wrong?" he asked.

She realized she had picked up her fork and began picking at her food.

Setting the fork back down, she could barely get the words out, "W-Why am I-I here?"

"I already told you."

I brought you here … to save you. Seeing that he still believed that made her realize he was even more insane than she had ever thought. Lucca needed to be the one locked up, not her.

She couldn't understand the point in keeping her here. She just wished he would do what he wanted to her already and put her out of her misery.

"You're just going to keep me locked in that room forever?"

"I never said you had to stay in that room, darlin'. You can go almost anywhere in the house. Drago will tell you when you can't go into a room." Lucca cut deeply into his piece of chicken. "You can even go in the backyard if you like."

Admittedly, she didn't know that.

"S-Still, you just expect me to stay here and do nothing for the rest of my life?" If she were able to cry, she would have. "I was going to college."

Setting down his fork, he pointed toward the living room's coffee table. "Do you see that laptop over there?"

Chloe turned her head to see the silver laptop sitting there.

"If you had come down today, you would have been told that I got all your Stanford classes changed to online courses. That laptop is yours, and you will find everything to complete your courses on it."

Shock was her only response. *He did that?*

That was when she grasped just how long he planned to keep her here. Long enough for a semester, *at least*.

"So, you do plan to keep me here for a while, don't you?"

"Yes." He told her like it was.

"They're go-going to know something h-happened to me," she whispered.

Lucca shook his head. "Who? Your parents? Elle? You left them behind when you decided to leave early to California. As far as they know, you got on the plane. I saw to it."

She was sure her parents were celebrating her leaving after she had left them a good-bye letter. They weren't coming to find her, but . . .

"Elle. She will know something is wrong if I don't talk to her."

Reaching into his dark jeans pocket, he pulled out a cell phone and set it on the table. Her cell phone.

"I've been texting her for you."

Her nails dug into her palms. No one would know the truth. No one would know that she wasn't a million miles away in California, but instead she was right here, in Kansas City, trapped. *Not my parents. Not my best friend, Elle. Not even . . .*

"He keeps calling you." Lucca's eyes turned blue to match his cold tone. "What does Amo have to be sorry for?"

34

Chloe's mouth dropped open, remembering the first tear that had fallen in years after breaking Amo's heart just nights ago. She had killed their friendship after he had spilled his feelings for her, yet he was the one trying to apologize for something he had done years ago. Something she had never judged him for.

"H-He w-will … He will come for me."

Lucca's eyes got bluer, his tone colder. "No, he won't, Chloe. I promise you that."

Stumbling from the table, she ran as fast as her legs could take her up to her room. With each step she took, she was afraid he would snatch her up from behind until she slammed the door shut behind her.

The invisible tears fell from her eyes, crying for her lost friends, her freedom, and the life she desperately wanted that had been stolen from her grasp.

The darkness in him whispered, Run and catch her. Show her what a real prisoner of yours would be like.

Staring down at the phone, he put it up to his ear, listening to the voicemail.

"*The moment I yelled "fucking freak" through the lunchroom, I regretted it, and I've done nothing but wish I could take those words back ever since.*" Amo's voice seemed to break toward the end before he steadied it once more. "*If I scared you by telling you I love you, I'm sorry. I'm so fucking sorry for everything, Chloe.*"

Lucca squeezed the phone in his hand, making the screen crack.

HEY, DARLIN'

SEVEN MONTHS AGO

When a black BMW appeared on his surveillance camera, Lucca had to do a double take to see if he was imagining it. By the time he watched her walk into the house, he realized that she was very much here. *It worked.*

He had hoped Chloe might come to make sure Elle was okay after the attack. Something told him she would. It had been a long shot to get her here, and an even longer one to get a moment alone with her, but *I had to try.*

Lucca needed her to know he existed. He wanted to see her face when she looked at him for the first time. He constantly imagined how their first encounter would go, and now he was closer than ever to living it.

Taking advantage of the microphone placed on the cameras, he turned the volume up to eavesdrop. More importantly, to hear her voice, which he hadn't heard since she had looked at the music box in the shop.

When she finally spoke, it was just how he remembered: soft and unsure.

Who the fuck did this to her?

Realizing she stuttered out of fear and not because of a speech impediment infuriated him. At the same time, it broke a piece inside of him to see someone had broken a piece of her.

He continued to watch her every move, having to switch between cameras when they went into a different room.

Seeing Chloe inside the house he grew up in only amplified his feelings for her. He began to lose track of time from just watching her. That scary part deep down inside of him seemed to be satiated simply by watching her.

Lost in an almost trance, he barely noticed her eyeing the back door over and over again. Something inside Lucca felt like this was it. *Go.*

When that word popped into his head, he saw Chloe whisper something over to Elle. Then his heart started to pump slowly and steadily as he watched Chloe get up and head toward the big double doors.

This was it. This was his time. His moment was here.

Fuck, what am I? Nervous?

Going out a different back door than she had used, he tried his best to keep his feet light through the little bit of dusted snowfall.

He had to be as careful as possible not to let Elle get a glimpse of him, or worse, scare Chloe away before he even got a chance with her.

Lucca knew he was going to scare her regardless, but he didn't want her too scared to let their first encounter be of her running away screaming. She could think he was scary, but he needed a few minutes with her so she could see something else in him. What a girl like Chloe was going to see, he didn't know.

Going around a corner, he saw her sitting perfectly still on the bench in the middle of the lighted gazebo, making him stop in his tracks. Never had Lucca thought anything like love or soulmates existed, yet now he was sure of it.

All his nervousness seemed to slip away as he looked at Chloe. Finding his purpose, he took a deep breath.

Waiting until the perfect moment to let her know of his presence, he stalked toward her, caging her in like an animal.

"Hey, darlin'." Lucca had anticipated her wanting to run, but she didn't. Instead, he watched her jump at his voice, then freeze. Something about that didn't sit right with him, yet he continued on up the steps. "I didn't mean to scare you."

Chloe still didn't move a muscle.

Leaning against a pillar to block her exit, he took in her appearance. This was the closest he had been to her. Her black dress and tights hugged her body, but her pale, scarred face was what stood out against her black hair, giving him a perfect view of her scare. Finally looking deeply into her eyes, he wished he could say the word out loud. *Beautiful.*

It was almost like she could hear his thoughts as her eyes dashed to her lap, and she began wringing her hands.

"I'm Nero's brother, Lucca. I would shake your hand, but you wouldn't shake it, anyway." He wanted her to know he had been listening to their conversations.

Chloe's eyes darted back up for a second then back down. It was obvious she was silently wondering how he knew that.

"I overheard that you're apparently germophobic." He hoped he had emphasized *apparently* just enough to gain her understanding that he didn't buy it. He had watched her for a week now, not seeing any signs of her caring what she touched, not showing any traits of a real germaphobe. The only thing he saw was that she didn't like human contact.

He could see the slight panic behind her eyes when she looked up at him again, which seemed to increase when she realized she was trapped.

Lucca had in fact finally caught her. Now he was going to enjoy it and see how far he could press his prey.

He slowly reached into his back pocket, watching her hold her breath, not knowing what he was going to pull out. When his pack of cigarettes came out, he could see the relief on her face as she was able to breathe again. Pulling out a stick and holding it with his lips, he put the pack back in his pocket then reached in his front pocket, seeing her give the same reaction and then relief again when it was just his Zippo.

She's scared of everything, isn't she?

Flicking his Zippo open with the flick of his wrist, he lit the end of his cigarette until it flamed a bright red from his inhale. "You don't mind, do you?"

Staring at him, she somehow managed to shake her head.

Lucca had felt the eyes of women on him at even a very young age and knew when they found him attractive. However, as he tried his best to focus on smoking his cigarette, feeling her eyes on him, he realized Chloe wasn't fawning over him like most women did. He could see it in her face that she was simply taking a long look, almost studying him, like he intrigued her.

This is good. Now he was going to step it up a notch.

He made his voice drop an octave as he said, "Aren't you a little cold out here, darlin'?"

Chloe didn't look comfortable with him calling her that in that deep tone of voice. "M-my name is Chloe."

Really fucking good. Lucca couldn't help smiling as he put his cigarette to his lips again, inhaling. Speaking as he exhaled, the smoke escaped more with each passing word, "The mayor's daughter, right?"

A light nod gave him the answer he already knew.

Lucca kept his eyes pierced into hers as he flicked his ashes into the snow, not wanting to miss her expression when he spoke his next words. "You were in that car wreck a few years back. I remember reading about it in the papers. Is that how you tell everyone you got those scars?"

"That i-is how I got them." She swallowed, quickly looking back down at her hands.

Do people actually believe this bullshit?

"No, it's not. I know a knife cut when I see one."

Glimpsing back up at him, he could see she had no idea how he knew. "I-I d-don't know what you're t-talking about."

Because you're the worst fucking liar I've ever seen, darlin'.

Flicking his whole cigarette into the yard, he stared deeply into her gray depths, letting her know she wasn't fooling him, nor was she ever going to fool him. "Yeah, you do."

She quickly stood and took a step forward, clearly stating she wanted to leave and end this conversation.

You're gonna have to come closer than that, darlin', and boy, did he hope she would. He wanted to see her up close, so close that he could reach out and claim her already.

When Lucca didn't move from the exit, she ever so slightly inched closer to give him another hint.

A little bit closer … His body was taut; every muscle frozen.

Another small step forward.

I could claim you right now if I wanted, darlin'. The deep, dark part in his mind whispered, *Do it.*

Chloe's eyes sparked a bit in fear at the small distance between them now. "W-Will you let me through?"

The break in her throat showed him how frightened she was. He could also hear her heels clicking against the wood from her shaking legs.

Fuck. Lucca reached into his pocket again, going for his pack of cigarettes. His darkness was making him lose control, and he needed to keep himself busy.

His eyes didn't move from hers as he flicked the lighter open again before lighting his cigarette. He then expertly exhaled, wanting the smoke to caress her body and face like he couldn't.

Chloe didn't seem to mind, still staring at his silver Zippo that he had already flicked closed.

Taking notice of her interest in his lighter, he flicked it open again, letting the flame shine a bright red. He saw it then—the shine in her own eyes from staring into the flame. He'd had that same look when his father used this same lighter to light his cigars when he was a kid.

"I will if you tell me how old you are." He kept his voice melodic, hoping he could hypnotize her with it and the flame as he slowly began to weave the Zippo between his fingers, watching her eyes dance along with the movements. Lucca needed her to willingly engage with him before he let her go.

"Seventeen. You?" The words seemed to slip through her mouth.

You? Shockingly, she had asked him to reciprocate, letting him know she cared enough to ask. The look on her face told him she was just as shocked.

"Twenty-six." With that, Lucca moved to the side, giving her barely enough room to pass.

Watching her gingerly turn her body to the side, he held his breath as she did, both their eyes not moving from one another's, both seeming slightly afraid he might move even just an inch.

This was the closest he was probably going to see her beautifully cracked porcelain face for a long time, and he wanted nothing more than to freeze time at the exact moment she stood perfectly in front of him. He could practically hear the screams from her light gray eyes, pleading for him to save her. They took his breath away and almost brought him to his knees.

When Chloe finally passed, she began to walk as fast as she could back to the safety of the house, and every movement she made away from him felt like torture. He was letting the most beautiful creature slip through his fingers, and even though the dark part inside of him begged him not to let her go, knowing she belonged to him, he knew he had to, even if it killed him. He couldn't cage her in, *at least not yet.*

"You can't run from the truth forever, darlin'," Lucca warned, making her only run faster and farther away from him.

That single moment, when he had looked down at her, hadn't been long enough for him to savor, but it was all he was going to get.

Save me, Lucca . . . Those gray eyes haunted him.

I'm going to save you, darlin'. You just have to wait for me. You're not ready for me yet.

THE NIGHTMARES THAT
REAPED HER SOUL

Taking a deep breath, he stood, putting the phone back in his pocket. That single crack on the screen reminded him of the scars that graced Chloe's face.

"Drago, can you please reheat and take Chloe's meal upstairs to her?"

Drago nodded.

Being nice never worked for Lucca for the simple fact that he was never nice. Being hard on Chloe, though, was something he wasn't capable of.

Craving a cigarette and some time to think alone, Lucca went to the only place where he somehow found peace.

The quick knock on the door, followed by it being thrown open, had Chloe wanting to scream for her life. For that split second, she knew it was only a matter of time before Lucca took what he wanted. Then Drago appeared, bringing in a tray that held a glass of water and her untouched plate of food that was now steaming.

Watching him set the tray on the bed, she couldn't believe it. She was grateful after being told she would starve if she didn't leave the room.

"T-Thank you, Drago."

His demeanor seemed to be just as sour as before as he nodded toward the window. "Don't thank me. Thank Lucca."

What? She jumped from the bed then walked toward the window as she heard the door slam shut behind him.

She pulled back the curtain, seeing Lucca sitting in the lighted gazebo, smoking his cigarette. From this far away, he looked almost beautiful to her in an obscure way. Yes, he had always frightened her and had made her fear for her life from the moment she had met him, but she couldn't deny the small part about him that appealed to her. She would swear she could almost hear him calling to her at times.

His cigarette's flame grew brighter when he inhaled deeply, causing lights and shadows to dance over his handsome features. Lucca seemed to be deep in thought, a look that suited him, making her wonder what thoughts weaved through his mind.

He was ... *hauntingly beautiful.*

Chloe quickly dropped the curtain, shaking and stumbling back. That single thought coursed true fear through her unlike anything before. For someone who feared everything, she never feared herself. Until now.

The door opening was what broke his slumber, but it was the screams that forced him awake. He ran right past Drago, knowing he had come to wake him up to follow the screams.

His heart began to pound violently. Then it broke into tiny pieces from the audible pain in the cries. It was unlike anything he had ever heard.

The screams only grew louder the closer he got to her room, and when he opened the door, the sight he came upon almost brought him to his knees.

Lucca had always thought himself invincible in many ways, but the shrills that escaped her and the shaking that racked her body proved him otherwise.

He was afraid and was being ripped apart and torn in two. He wanted desperately to wake her up by holding her close, to forever erase the nightmares that reaped her soul. No matter how much he wanted that, though, the other part of him knew he couldn't. It knew she was far from being able to accept the touch he craved to give.

"Chloe ..." His voice came out in a broken whisper. *Please wake up, darlin'.*

She was breaking his heart, and if her nightmare lasted much longer, he was going to break.

Taking a step closer, his voice began to rise with each cry of her name. "Chloe … Chloe … Chloe!"

The blood that trickled down her face burned into her skin. She knew, even then, she would never forget the feeling when her tears met the blood to scorch paths of bloody tears down her face.

"Please, just kill …" It was hard for her to whisper her plea through her hoarse voice, but she had to try, hoping for mercy.

The maniac began to laugh while he caressed the edge of the blade over her skin. "Little girl, this is only the beginning."

Closing her eyes, another tear fell, mixing with the hot blood. Mercy wasn't going to be given tonight, leaving her with one final hope. To be saved …

Her eyes slowly opened at the repetition of words.

"Chloe, wake up and everything will be okay."

Fully opening her eyes to the dark room, she saw a shadowy Lucca a step away with a glow surrounding him from the hallway light. The fear of her nightmare remained, having awoken only to see her other captor.

Lucca could sense the fear she exuded toward him now, but he remained calm, telling her, "See? Everything's okay. I promise you, I'm not gonna hurt you."

Chloe relaxed into the mattress. His voice was soft yet strong, somehow making her feel safe, something she had never felt upon awakening from a nightmare. She also knew he meant his promise just by the way he had said the words.

Lucca took a step closer to her. "That wasn't just a nightmare, was it?"

Wrapping herself tighter in the blanket, she solemnly shook her head. There was no point in denying it. One look in Lucca's eyes told her he could see the truth.

"Go back to sleep, darlin'."

She thought his hand was going to reach out before he quickly disappeared into the dark room. It wasn't until he spoke again that she realized he had gone to sit in the chair in the corner.

"I'm here …"

It must have been the complete nonexistent sleep she had gotten since being here, but her eyes slowly drifted away and into the night.

"… right here, Chloe."

It took Lucca an hour before he unclenched his fists and relaxed back into the chair. It had taken all he had not to hold her, not to touch her to make sure she was all right. Being able to watch her sleep showed him how haunted she was by her past, even in dreams.

This had been the last straw. He had waited long enough. Tomorrow, his and Chloe's life would change, colliding together into one.

One thing was for sure; those had been far from nightmares. *They were memories.*

I'D HATE TO HAVE TO PUNISH YOU, DARLIN'

t took everything Chloe had to walk down the steps after last night. Elle had been the only other one to witness her nightmares, besides her parents. With each person to see it, it was like the curtain had been pulled back, showing her true self, the damaged goods she was. The fact that it was Lucca who had seen it meant he was going to have a part of her now. A deep, dark, locked away part of herself she was never going to get back.

Her father, her mother, her best friend, they all were a major part of her life, and now she had this overwhelming feeling like Lucca would be, too. *Like our lives have now intertwined.*

What she found strange about it was how … *kind* he had been. Even stranger was how much she appreciated it.

Scanning the downstairs, she looked for any sign of Lucca, but when there was none, she figured he had already left for work.

Seeing the laptop on the coffee table reminded her of why she had braved coming down in the first place.

Chloe sat down on the couch and grabbed the laptop, booting it up. Several things popped up, including detailed instructions of her classes and how to submit her coursework. Someone had already taken the time to set up her account and must have written out the instructions since it didn't appear to come from the school. *Did Lucca do this?*

Logging into her school account, that was when it hit her that she was hooked up to the Internet. She could get help!

She quickly tried to go to her email, but the site said "blocked." She then tried to go to her other email site, but it was blocked, too. Then she realized she had a new school email for Stanford.

Signing into that email, it worked. She quickly tried to type in Elle's email into the sender box, only for it to backspace and disappear. She tried again . . . for it to disappear once more.

What the . . .? She looked around the house to make sure no one was near.

Now she put in one of her professor's emails, and in the subject line, she typed out: **HELP ME!! I'VE BEEN KIDN-**

The laptop was shut and taken from her grasp.

Her eyes slowly drifted up to see Lucca's big frame standing over her.

"I-I-I was just—"

"I would be very careful not to lie to me, darlin'." The intimidating man took a seat on the coffee table in front of her, intruding on her space. He put his elbows on his knees to intrude even more, getting close to her face. Even though he was hunched over, he was still taller than her.

Chloe tried to make herself as small as possible, pushing herself back into the couch to get any space she could between them. "H-How did you know?"

"Your computer is strictly for your coursework. You will find most sites will be blocked to you, such as social media. However, you will still be able to research anything you might need just fine. The only site that's available to interact on is for your coursework, like your Stanford email. Now, if you type in, let's say, Elle's email address or the words 'help me,' it will automatically notify the man who programmed the computer. He then is able to override your computer and gives me a call to tell me that you're not being a good girl."

"Oh." Chloe bit her lip. "Who is he?"

Lucca smiled. "A friend."

Lucca, Drago, friend. That meant at least three people knew she was here. Honestly, she was shocked he would even call someone a friend. It didn't seem like Lucca had any friends. Not even he and Drago acted like friends.

When she noticed him still smiling as she continued to bite her bottom lip, she quickly stopped and looked down at her wringing hands.

"I'm trying to be nice to you, Chloe, by letting you do your courses online. In order to do that, you have to be able to contact your professors and turn in your work. What happens if my friend is busy when you decide to say help me again?" Lucca rose up off his knees, making himself sit straight up, intimidating her even more. "I'm not sure if I can trust you yet. I'd hate to have to punish you, darlin'."

"I-I thought you said you wouldn't h-hurt me?"

"I wouldn't ever hurt you, but"—his eyes turned the cold shade of blue—"I wouldn't be opposed to hurting someone you care about."

Chloe's eyes widened. *Elle.* "Y-You wouldn't t-touch her. She's Nero's girlfriend."

Lucca leaned forward, putting his elbows on his knees once more, leaning in even closer to her. Her heart began to race out of her chest. His face was so close to hers she could feel his cold breath sting her skin with each word he spoke. "You don't think I would do it"—reaching out, he twirled a lock of her black hair around his finger, like he had done the night he had captured her—"to keep you here with me longer?"

Staring into his cold eyes, she didn't have to look too deeply to see that he would.

"You would," she whispered.

He let the strand slip from his finger. "Then don't make me."

She supposed she shouldn't be shocked anymore by him, but somehow, her mouth dropped to the floor.

Lucca stood, taking the laptop with him. "You'll get this back when I trust you again."

If his eyes weren't still the cold shade of blue, she would have thought he was hurt that she had tried to get help. However, that would be impossible.

Lucca wasn't capable of such feelings. She had just been fooled by his kindness from last night, but *that was just an act.*

SOLD HER SOUL
TO THE BOOGIEMAN

"You are wanted downstairs."

Chloe had locked herself away in her room again after Lucca had left her in the living room this morning. This was the time Drago usually told her dinner was ready, but today he was demanding something different. As much as she didn't want to go, his presence left her with no choice.

Following him downstairs, the wonderful smell of food entered her nose, making her empty stomach growl. When they reached the dining room, she was met with the same vision as yesterday, except for some slight changes, like there was only one plate at the dinner table and Lucca was already eating his steak and mashed potatoes.

"Sit with me," he ordered as Drago disappeared, leaving them alone.

Chloe cautiously sat down next to him, squeezing her hands in her lap, as Lucca cut deeply into his steak, carving off a small piece before eating it.

Once the piece was chewed, he finally addressed her. "I want to make a deal with you, darlin'."

Chills went up her spine. She wasn't sure anyone would come out alive from a deal with the boogieman.

"What kind of d-deal?"

An evil smile appeared on his lips. "You will stay here with me, and if you still want, I promise to let you walk out that front door at the end of your first semester."

"T-That's it?" *He won't let it be that easy.*

"I have rules."

Chloe swallowed the lump in her throat, too scared to even ask what they were. *I knew he wouldn't.*

"The first one's easy, as I will also do the same for you." He began cutting another piece of his steak. "When I ask you a question, you must not lie."

Her brow furrowed. "So, I can ask you anything and you will tell me?"

"Yes, but only ask me if you want the truth."

She had been ready to ask him a question before his warning changed her mind. She would have to think harder about if she really wanted to know certain things about him.

"W-What else?"

"I want to spend the evenings with you. You will eat dinner with me every night, and after, I want to help you overcome"—Lucca's blue-green eyes rose, holding her gaze—"your fear of touch."

Chloe's blood ran cold, not wanting to take part in those plans. "N-N—"

"Then you will stay here for as long as I like," he said nonchalantly, going back to eating his food.

Her nails dug into her palms. He was giving her an ultimatum. She feared if she was ever going to walk out of that door, she would have to give in.

"Is there anything else?" she whispered.

Lucca looked back up at her. "One last thing. When I ask you to do something, you will do it. But know I will not ask anything of you I don't think you can handle."

This was it. She was signing her life away. Lucca was going to take away everything she had clung to, the things she had used to survive.

Chloe solemnly nodded her head. Seeing no other choice, she would be lucky if she walked out the front door alive.

He raised his eyebrow. "Deal?"

This was the moment Chloe would give her life over to Lucca in hopes that one day he would return it back to her. "Deal."

It didn't take long for the impending doom to creep in. She could see he saw it as a game. *A game he already won.*

"Are you hungry?" he asked simply, like the conversation they'd just had didn't happen.

As much as she wished she could run back up to the room, she no longer could. This was a part of the deal now. *You will eat dinner with me every night.*

"Yes."

Using his fork, Lucca picked up a piece of his steak and held it out for her, expecting her to take it with her mouth. His eyes told her this was no offer, but a demand.

"I-I don't want to take y-your food. I can make a plate."

He put his hand down. "Maybe I decided not to make you any. You have yet to sit here and have dinner with me."

Chloe stared at him. Something in her sensed he was hurt that she hadn't sat with him and eaten one of the meals he had prepared for ... *me?*

"I understand."

I want to spend the evenings with you. She did understand now. He had made dinner every night, and every night, she hadn't joined him. Drago had warned her; told her she was playing with fire, which was exactly what she had done.

Lucca raised his hand once more, bringing the juicy steak close to her lips, demanding she take it.

When I ask you to do something, you will do it.

Slowly parting her lips, she wished she could shut her eyes, but his gaze held hers prisoner. She took the steak into her mouth and slid her lips away from the fork. It wasn't until then that he let her eyes fall to her lap as she began chewing.

He smiled. "I told you, Chloe, that I wouldn't ask anything of you I didn't think you could handle."

She didn't expect him to set the fork back down then get up, going to the kitchen. When he returned to the table, he set a full plate down in front of her.

Somehow, in some way, he always seemed to surprise her.

"T-Thank you."

"You're welcome, darlin'."

It was easy for Lucca to eat after he sat back down, but for her, it wasn't. She had just sold her soul to the boogieman.

They ate their dinner in silence and, when he took their plates to the kitchen, she hoped he would release her. However, he had other plans.

She watched him go into the living room, taking a seat on the big leather chair before motioning her over.

She reluctantly stood, walking toward him with her hands desperately clutched together.

"I want you to sit"—removing the pillow at his side, he placed it on the ground at his feet—"right here."

The hand clutching turned into wringing as she grew extremely nervous.

Looking over at the big sectional, she tried to get out, "W-Why c-can't I-I s-s-s—"

"Because I want you to sit at my feet." Lucca smiled.

Chloe began shaking her head. "I-I don't think I-I can."

"Yes, you can, darlin'."

Seeing him lazily sit back in the chair, she figured any other woman would think he looked incredibly sexy and wouldn't have to be told twice. All she could think about, though, was how widespread his legs were, knowing his left leg might touch her.

When she didn't make a move to do as he asked, his voice took a commanding tone. "We made a deal, remember?"

I want to help you overcome your fear of touch.

She was sure she would never be able to explain why she followed his commands when his voice deepened. Yet, there she was, swallowing her nerves as she slowly placed herself on the pillow at his feet. She kept her back against the arm of the chair, sitting stiffly, careful not to even graze his dark jeans.

Now that she was down here, Chloe was too scared to even move, too afraid to be this close to him. He frightened her to the core, making her wonder what other games he had in store for tonight.

Lucca turned on the big screen TV. Scrolling through the channels, he settled on an old football game.

Staring at the screen, she didn't move an inch, waiting for him to move or make her do something else. Thankfully, he never did, seeming to be into the game, never even acknowledging her.

When she finally relaxed into the chair, the warmth from his leg less distracting, he turned the TV off, bringing her attention back to him.

Please let me go, she started pleading in her head.

"You may go——"

Chloe quickly jumped up before the last word was said. She didn't even look back as she went straight up to her room, afraid he might change his mind.

Now in the safety of her room, she rubbed her hand over her arm that was still warm from his close body. She did this unconsciously for several minutes, rubbing it over and over, before she dropped her hand, realizing she was trying to keep the warmth in. His warmth.

Chloe didn't know it yet, but the part of her that craved human touch was coming back to life. And soon, she was going to meet the part of her she had buried long ago.

ALWAYS

L ucca moved from his laid-back position to leaning forward, putting his elbows on his knees. He ran his hands roughly through his hair, thinking about how he hadn't even finished his sentence before she had disappeared.

Where Chloe couldn't run fast enough from him, he had wanted the opposite.

The whole time she had sat beside him on the floor, it hadn't been a test only for her, but for him as well. Lucca had told her he was going to help her overcome her fear of touch, but what he hadn't told her was that he was also going to fight the darkness of claiming her too soon. He wanted to make sure he could handle her closeness. To be close to his grasp, yet not claim her was one of the hardest things he had ever done. The twisted part of his brain had kept whispering, *Touch her, kiss her, take her …* But he hadn't. He had fought his dark urges … for her.

He planned to get closer to her every night. He imagined it was only going to get harder, painful even, to fight the darkness when his fingers finally moved over her scars.

Raising his head at the sound of footsteps, he saw Drago had come into the room. He put his head back down to run his hands through his hair.

"I don't see her handling this … you. She's too fucked up," Drago said, crossing his arms as he leaned against the far wall.

There was only one option. "She will learn."

Another question from Drago circled the air around him, "Is this girl really worth all this?"

Lucca closed his eyes for just a moment …

Chloe rejected the hand that came toward her. "S-Sorry. I'm germophobic."

"No, I'm sorry," Lake told her, holding up her hands. "If you ever need someone to talk to, I'll listen. I know what it's like to be alone."

Lucca watched the exchange from a distance. He had followed Chloe outside, but Lake, one of his soldier's daughter, had followed her out as well. She must have sensed Chloe's distress, just as he had, as he had watched her during the graduation party.

Before the girl turned, she left Chloe with some final words.

"You shouldn't hide your face. It's beautiful."

He didn't know what to expect from Lake when she had approached Chloe, especially after he had heard the horrors Chloe and Elle had gone through in high school, but he honestly hadn't expected that.

Staring at Chloe now under the lighted gazebo, surrounded by the flowers in bloom, it took his breath away. He had been waiting for this day for months now.

Keeping his distance from her and only watching her from afar was making him crazy. Not once had he been able to talk to her since that last time, but now the time had arrived.

Caging her in like last time, he blocked the entrance with his frame. "Hey, darlin'."

She looked up at him, startled.

Pulling out a cigarette, he placed it between his lips, making the stick bounce as he said, "I hear you're still saying you're a germaphobe. Have you ever thought of telling the truth just once?" He lit the end with his Zippo.

Averting her gaze to the pressure she made in her hands, her soft, unsure voice settled something inside of him. "I-It's not a lie."

Prove it then.

Taking a few steps forward, he stood over her, holding out his hand. "Come on, darlin'; just try it once."

If he still prayed, he would have in this moment. Watching her stare at the hand in front of her, he needed her desperately to just reach out and touch it.

Being too focused on her face, Lucca almost missed it——the slightest movement of her hand moving toward his before she stopped.

"I c-can't."

What she had just done was a sign. She feels it, too. Even if she was ignoring it, there was no denying there was an electrifying pull between them.

His voice took a commanding tone, not wanting any more lies, as he asked, "Why can't you?"

Her eyes met his, looking up through her dark lashes as she whispered her secret, "Because I'm afraid to."

She feared touch. That was something he knew from the beginning, but getting *her to admit it to him was something he needed if they were ever going to get her to overcome it one day. He needed her to begin to trust him with her secrets.*

He took a seat on the chair in front of her. "That wasn't so bad, darlin'." Taking a hit off his cigarette, he wanted more. "It's summer now, and you're still wearing long sleeves."

She gave no answer, but watching her check their length and pull down the sleeves of her black dress was all he needed to know he had been right again. Not once had he seen her in short sleeves, no matter the weather, which told him she was hiding something beneath the material.

Catching her eyes moving over him showed him some part of her was still intrigued by him.

Wanting to intrigue her even more, he pulled out his Zippo, flipping it open. It didn't take long to charm her with the glow weaving through his fingers.

"Are you going to college?"

"Yes, of course."

He began to weave faster. The importance of this question was something she wasn't going to be able to understand yet. "Where?"

"Stanford ... in California." She talked so easy when she was entranced by him, no stuttering.

He shut the lighter off with a flick, having got what he needed. "That's awfully far, darlin'. I guess you do get to keep running." Standing, he looked down at her again, taking in everything he could about her until the next time. It made the wait less painful.

Holding her breath, she didn't move.

The marks on her face had him thinking about what Lake had just told her.

"She is right, you know. Those scars are beautiful."

He had dreamed of touching them every day, and he was envisioning doing it right now. Touch her scar ... *the darkness whispered.*

Walking away from her before he did something he would regret was him walking away from his dreams. For a moment, he had almost felt what it would be like to touch her. For a moment, he had almost felt what it would be like to be with her. It was the most blissful thing he had ever felt in his existence...

Opening his eyes, there was no inkling of a doubt in his mind that, "She will always be."

THE FREAK AND
THE BOOGIEMAN

It was now a week since her and Lucca's arrangement had been made, and she had already grown used to the schedule of living there. Her days were spent keeping herself busy with schoolwork, which was surprisingly nice as she spent them alone. Well, as alone as she could be with Drago watching her.

Her fear of being there ceased, and she couldn't even admit it to herself, yet a part of her was learning to be happy. Since her scars, she had feared for her life, not only at school, but her home, too. To be in fear almost every moment of your life for years was something she'd had to grow used to, to keep her sanity. She had almost forgotten what it was like not to feel that way.

Chloe had hoped to achieve that at Stanford, but she still feared being all alone there, surrounded by new people who would stare at her like she was a freak. That didn't happen at Lucca's. She was never stared at nor treated like a freak because ... *here, with Lucca, I'm just like him. We're both monsters.*

The freak and the boogieman.

She didn't mind dinners with him anymore, either. They were quite peaceful in each other's company, and Lucca was a surprisingly good cook. If she didn't have to sit next to him every night, he wouldn't even bother her.

There was only one thing she truly missed, and that was Elle. Yes, she missed Amo, Nero, and even Vincent, too; but she had never been this long without talking to her best friend, and it was starting to get to her.

If Elle were here, it might not be ...

Pushing away the thought, she went back to the now finished assignment she had struggled with for hours. She went to submit it when a chat box appeared on her screen.

They are all wrong except for #8. Try again.

What the ...?

Chloe blinked at the screen, seeing if she was just exhausted from working on it all morning. However, the chat box was still there, proving her wrong.

Lucca's friend. The third person who knew she was here.

Ignoring the warning, she went to submit it again when another message came through.

You'll fail the assignment.

Biting her lip, she hovered over the submit button, contemplating. Her answers seemed right to her, but she had struggled a lot through them. She wasn't used to math being taught over the computer, let alone calculus.

She held off submitting just yet, and typed into the chat box, **Can you tell me how #1 is wrong?**

The problem immediately began to work out in front of her, making her mouth drop open at how fast it was completed. Needless to say, she was wrong.

Typing into the box once more, she quickly responded, **Thanks. I'll try again later**, before she slammed her laptop closed.

Dang it. Calculus was killing her, and it was becoming too hard for her to understand from over the computer.

Accepting defeat for now, she headed downstairs for some lunch. Once there, she noticed a motion in the backyard that made her curious to look out the back door for a better view.

Chloe peeked out to see Lucca down in the dirt. He seemed to be ... *gardening?*

"I see you finally decided to come down," Drago said in a gruff voice from behind her.

She quickly turned around, nervous that she had been caught staring at Lucca. "I-I came down to g-get something to eat."

"I'm sure you did. You don't come down for anything else." His sour tone told her he was not being sarcastic.

She looked out at the backyard again, at Lucca, knowing what Drago meant. The times she had spent with him weren't of her own accord; they were just when she had to, to honor the deal.

"He's not at work today?" The words seemed to slip out of her mouth as she watched Lucca wipe sweat from his forehead onto his black shirt.

"No, it's Saturday. You would know that if you quit acting like such a prisoner."

Turning around, she looked at him in confusion. "I *am* a prisoner."

Drago's appearance went dark as he took a step toward her. "We both know what being a real prisoner feels like, Chloe. Tell me, how is this compared to the last time?" He took another step toward her. "When you dream, who is it that haunts you? Lucca? Or the man who gave you those scars?"

She could only stare back at the huge man, knowing all too well he spoke the truth.

Leaving Chloe to her truth, he said one last thing, "I'm sure Lucca is hungry, too."

Turning back, she observed her captor for a few minutes alone.

We both know what being a real prisoner feels like, Chloe.

The way Drago had talked to her was like he had hinted . . . she was here for a reason. But . . . *I* am *a prisoner, aren't I?*

Shaking her head, she went to the fridge, deciding to make herself a sandwich. She made just one then put all the stuff back. Now staring at her lone sandwich, her eyes drifted to the back door. *Should I?* She shook her head harder, trying to get the thought out of her mind.

Grabbing her plate, she sat at the kitchen island and quickly ate her food, glancing out the window to watch him every now and then. To say the least, Chloe found it interesting that the boogieman knew how to garden of all things.

She cleaned up after herself then started back upstairs, but her feet stopped her when she went to look at Lucca through the window one last time.

A small voice she hadn't heard before whispered, *Do it.*

Chloe listened to the voice, making another plate. She decided he would probably be able to easily eat two, filling the bread with a bunch of meat, lettuce, and tomatoes. If he didn't like something on it, he could simply pull it off.

She took the sandwiches, along with a bottle of water, to the back door. By the time she opened it, though, she realized the mistake of listening to the unknown voice. But with Lucca turning to look at her, it was too late.

Biting her lip nervously, she went toward him, wishing she could turn back. Then, when she reached him, she paused a moment, looking down at him.

His long, unkempt black-brown hair that he kept slicked back lay messily around his handsome features. The dark jeans and black shirt he always wore were dirty, giving him an even rougher look than he usually had. She wasn't used to men who looked like him. She was used to well-dressed, well-groomed men who wore expensive clothes. He was the complete opposite.

Lucca waited for her to say something before giving her a smile when he realized she was taking in his appearance.

"Is that for me, darlin'?"

"Y-Yes. D-Drago said you might be hungry," she stammered, quickly moving her eyes to the plate.

"I'm guessing he made it, too." His voice seemed to lose pitch, like he was disappointed.

Chloe shook her head, looking at him again. "No, I did."

The smile was brought back to his lips as he pulled off his dirty work gloves and stood. Coming over to her, he took the plate and water from her. "Thank you, darlin'."

"Y-You're welcome."

She finally released the breath she held when he turned.

She found herself wishing he could be less good-looking. His combination of terrifying yet beautiful was too much for one man to have.

He took a seat on the grass, patting the spot next to him. "Come sit down with me." He didn't say it like a command, which was strange. It was more like he was asking.

Taking a deep breath, she found herself doing the opposite of what she thought she should, sitting on the grass a little over an arm's length from him and staring out at the stunning garden while he began to eat.

It was different being down here with the grass and flowers, like it was even more peaceful than it usually was in the gazebo.

From the moment she first stepped out here, the garden had taken her breath away, and it only continued to do so. It seemed to only grow more and more beautiful to her.

"I didn't know you gardened." The thought that was meant to stay in her head came out in a whisper.

"I don't really. I mean, I used to with my mom, here and there, when I was young, but it's more of a recent thing."

Chloe really looked around now, seeing that the garden looked better taken care of since she had first seen it months ago. That was why she thought it had only grown more beautiful.

Looking over at Lucca, an eerie feeling settled inside of her, something that sunk to her soul, and she asked, "Why did you start gardening?"

Asking him a question was a dangerous thing since the answer would be nothing less than the truth. You just had to be prepared for the answer.

His eyes turned the most beautiful shade of green she had ever seen as the sunlight played off them. It almost hurt to stare back at him, but to look away from them would be impossible.

"I did it for you," he revealed the answer she already knew. "When I saw you under that gazebo for the first time, surrounded by the snow, I wondered what you would look like surrounded by flowers instead. Then I wondered how much more you'd love it out here."

Swallowing hard, she finally managed to look away from him, taking in that piece of information and trying her best to understand it. To understand him.

I'll never understand him . . .

Lucca stood. "Stay here."

She watched him take his now empty plate and water bottle into the house. Then he returned a minute later, putting on his gloves and moving to the same spot where she had found him when she had come out here.

"Come help me, darlin'."

Huh? "What?"

"There's an extra pair of gloves in that bucket." He pointed to the bucket as he slipped on the last glove. "You wanna help me? Or do you wanna stay in the house all day again?"

She thought about the calculus she really didn't want to do before she stood and went over to the bucket, pulling out the spare gloves. She put them on before she came over to Lucca and got on her knees on the ground beside him.

"Do you know anything about gardening?" he asked.

Shaking her head, she figured she was in way over her head right now.

He laughed, sensing her thoughts. "That's okay. I'll teach you."

She swallowed. "Okay."

"I'm just cleaning up the garden, getting rid of weeds and any dead flowers." He showed her how to do so by explaining what the weeds looked like and how to spot which part of the flower was dead. "Now you try."

Going to the next patch of flowers, she carefully removed the weeds surrounding it and clipped off a now dead bulb. "H-How was that?"

Lucca grinned. "Perfect."

For the first time since being here, she smiled. "You were right."

Confusion marked his handsome face. "How?"

"I do love it more."

His features went back to his usual haunting appearance, knowing she was talking about her loving it more surrounded by flowers. "Good."

GOOD NIGHT

s his leg getting closer?

Chloe focused on the television screen, trying her best to ignore the heat coming from Lucca's leg next to her. She had thought it was getting easier, but tonight, she felt like there wasn't enough space between them.

Strands of hair moved off her neck, causing her to look back, and when she did, her breath caught in her throat. Lucca was twirling a piece of her black hair.

"Did you enjoy today, darlin'?" His voice was as dark as the strand he expertly twirled around his finger.

"Y-Yes," she quietly spoke.

"Would you like to help me finish up the rest of the gardening tomorrow?"

Her nerves over watching him continuously twirl her hair made her blurt out, "No!"

The stand he held fluttered to his lap, falling along with his face. "Okay."

"No, I-I mean …" She turned to better face him. She hadn't meant the word to come out as harsh. "I would like to, but I can't."

"Why can't you?"

"I haven't finished my calculus assignment, because"—looking down at her hands, she began wringing them—"I don't really understand it, and I have a test coming up."

"Oh." He once again picked up the strand of hair, beginning the twirling motion again. "If I can get someone to help you with your calculus tomorrow, would you want to help me garden on Monday instead?"

She looked up from her hands, stunned. "You would do that?"

"Yes, darlin'." He grinned down at her. "Even if you didn't want to help me."

Chloe found herself strangely smiling back. "If you're sure you can call in Monday to get off work, then I would like to."

He seemed to be amused by what she said. "I'm sure."

Unsure of what she had said, something told her she didn't want to ask.

"Okay."

After he gave her hair a final twirl, she sensed a longing in him as the silk left his fingertips.

"You may go to bed now."

Standing felt different than it had the other times. She felt the same release she usually did, but she didn't feel the need to run. *What's wrong with me?*

She slowly began walking away, trying to figure out this other feeling that seemed to be scratching to get out.

"Good night, Chloe."

Turning back to him, her heart stuttered. "Good night, Lucca."

"Where the fuck is she!" He slammed his fist down on the desk.

The two other men in the room looked down at their feet before one finally spoke up.

"We still haven't found her ye—"

"How fucking hard is it to find an eighteen-year-old girl?" When he slammed his fists down on the table again, he shot up.

"It's … It's like she disappeared. Like she fell off the earth."

Going over to them, he pulled a knife out of his pocket and put it to the man's throat. "Do you remember what we did to her?"

The man began shaking as he nodded.

"Your daughter is her age, right?" He lightly slid the blade over the man's now crying face. "You either find her, or I'll show you how a girl fucking falls off the face of the earth."

When the man nodded again, he let him go, and the two flew out of the room.

Sitting back at his desk, he leaned far back in his chair, closing his black, ominous eyes. The image of a fourteen-year-old her came to his mind as he started dreaming of the past...

The girl was starting to lose consciousness, and her now traumatized, gray eyes began to drift away. There was something he enjoyed about seeing the eyes change from the person they once were to the person they were after he was done with them. It was his mark; how he claimed them.

He had taken away the young girl she once was and made her into his beautiful creation. Her body, her mind, her soul belonged to him and always would ... until he took away her last dying breath.

Her eyes rolled to the back of her head before her eyelids closed.

"Good night, my little girl."

NOT EVEN GOD CAN SAVE A MAN WHO LAYS A HAND ON YOU

Coming *down the steps the* next day, she heard a voice talking to Lucca that she didn't recognize. *Has someone found me?* Their voices drew nearer, and then she could see a man in a suit with light brown hair. Lucca noticed her then.

"Chloe, I want you to meet Sal."

Chloe knew of Sal, had seen him around the Carusos when she had been with Elle, but she had never seen him so up close, never took a look into his deep black to deep blue eyes. Something about him made every hair on her body stand up and every alarm go off in her head.

"Hello, Chloe." He gave a wicked smile. "It's nice to finally meet you."

Frozen in place, she could only stare at the well-groomed man.

"Sal came to watch you and help you with your calculus while Drago and I take care of some business matters."

"H-He d-did?" Her shaky hands clasped together and squeezed.

Lucca stared at her for a moment before his voice turned dark. "Come with me, darlin'."

The command made her follow him through the house and down a hall. He opened a door, and then waited for her to go in first.

Stepping into what seemed to be his office, her heart began to pound then beat out of her chest as he shut the door behind him, closing them in.

Now alone, lines of worry marked his face. "Tell me what's wrong."

Still trying to shake Sal's eyes out of her mind, she tried her best to speak. "I-I just d-don't know him."

He took a step closer to her. "Drago is much scarier to look at than Sal, and you didn't know him, either, so don't lie to me, darlin'."

Biting hard on her lip, she thought she was going to draw blood soon. *I don't know why he scares me.*

Lucca took another step toward her when she didn't answer.

"I don't know …" she whispered. "I feel like I know him, but I don't."

Taking a final step, he pinned her against the big desk behind her when she tried to put space between them. They were barely inches apart when he picked up a strand of her hair and twirled it in the same motion he always did.

"Do you think I would leave you with just anyone, Chloe?"

Her chest fell as hard as she raised it. It was strange, and she didn't understand how, but somewhere deep down she knew he wouldn't. "N-No."

"Do you think I'd ever let someone get close enough to possibly touch you"—he pulled her hair ever so slightly around his finger, his eyes travelling down her pale face to her neck—"when I have yet to touch you first?"

She slowly shook her head, biting harder into her bottom lip. She was sure this was it, when he was finally going to touch her, though she wasn't ready. *Please, not yet.*

He looked at the dark silk he spun. "I keep twirling your hair around my finger, because this is as close as I can get to touching you for now. I promise you, no one else will ever touch you in this house or outside of it. Not even God could save a man who lays his hands on you."

The pressure in her lip lessened, and she breathed easier. She believed every word he said, but what scared her was that it also put her at ease. She was almost grateful about the fact she wouldn't have to worry about anyone ever harming her, let alone touching her again.

What is happening to me?

Lucca gave her a few inches of breathing room. "I consider Sal my only friend, but he's also more than that. I'm closer to him than I am to Nero, who's my own brother." This was one of those times he allowed any emotion to show. "My father took Sal in when we were young, and we were raised together. Sal may not be my blood, but he's my brother. I trust him with my life, and I trust him with yours.

He won't hurt you, darlin'."

Lucca wasn't the type of man to put trust in anyone but himself, so she would trust him at his word that Sal wouldn't hurt her, regardless that Sal made the hair stand up on the back of her neck.

"Okay."

He gave her a smile before letting the strand slip from his grasp. "Drago and I will be back as soon as we can."

Nodding, she put on her best brave face as she followed Lucca out of his office and back to where Sal was waiting. She sat down at the kitchen island with her laptop, while the men talked quietly amongst themselves. She couldn't help wringing her hands to the point her nails dug into her palms. Never did she think she would ever wish Lucca wasn't leaving her, not until now.

Chloe was left with two thoughts. The first, she wondered why Drago had been the one to watch her every move when it was Sal who was his real friend.

The front door closed, and she heard footsteps get closer. Turning her head, she swallowed hard, trying to keep down the unknown fear of the man Lucca called his brother.

Her other thought … *Why does he remind me of* him?

THE MONSTROUS NAME
THE BOOGIEMAN

Staring out the window at the emptiness surrounding them, Lucca focused on the dirt path, waiting for the cars to come into view. The Caruso family had arrived two hours earlier to scope out the place, something the possible enemy should have done. Their black Cadillacs were lined up in front of the empty warehouse, and each soldier was packing in case this was the year the Lucianos decided to end the peace.

Once a year, the two mafia families of Kansas City had a meeting on equal ground outside the city. It was a way to keep the peace between them; to keep another war from happening, as the last war had almost wiped out the Luciano name.

Lucca began flipping his lighter open and closed, not removing his eyes from the road. Since joining the family every year to the date, he had come here feeling nothing. This year, however, he couldn't help feeling an uneasiness in the air.

He was starting to lose his patience. He didn't like leaving Chloe at home while he was this far away with only Sal there to protect her.

If I didn't want to see him . . . I would leave.

Finally, the cars started appearing. Lucca watched them pull up and the men get out. He observed each man until he finally saw the one he was waiting for.

Lucca slid his lighter back into his pocket, hearing it hit the other metal object. Pulling out a big, heavy gold ring, he stared at the design of a rectangle with a stamped horseshoe in the middle, surrounded by small diamonds.

The warehouse door opened, prompting him to slide it back into his pocket. Turning around, he looked at the two long tables facing each other. Dante sat in the middle of one table with his consigliere, Vinny, to his right. There was an empty seat to Dante's left for him. However, he was waiting for the Lucianos to fill up the other table before he headed toward his seat.

Before he sat down, he placed his pack of cigarettes and lighter on the table. Then Lucca listened to the two bosses commence the meeting, not once speaking. Instead, he took in the men.

The Lucianos looked like the polar opposites of the Carusos. Just as much as the Carusos looked immaculate, the Lucianos looked rugged. The men who did wear suits were far from the expensive Italian ones the mafia was often known for. Grooming wasn't much of a requirement for them, either. Some men were also covered in tattoos from their hands to their necks. They were a rough-looking family, matching their surroundings of the rough area of Kansas City they owned. Here in this warehouse, the Carusos looked out of place, while the Lucianos looked at home.

A pair of dark-haired twins mostly covered in tattoos sat to one side, while on the other side was a hawkish man with brown hair who seemed to be doing the same thing Lucca was—taking in the enemy.

It was Lucca's job to know each and every one of them. The three were brothers, sharing the same father, but only the twins had the same mother. Angel and Matthias were younger than their older brother, Dominic. He and Lucca were both the underboss of the family, under their father. However, even though Dominic was slightly older than him, he hadn't been the underboss for as long as Lucca had. It was only a year ago that Dominic had taken the title.

Pulling out a cigarette, Lucca held it between his lips while he flicked his wrist, bringing the flame from his Zippo to light the end. He inhaled deeply as his eyes travelled to the man sitting in the middle of the table.

The Carusos called him by his last name, Luciano, but to his men, he was known by another name. A name his men gave him out of respect, a name to be feared. Dante told Lucca long ago not to call him by the monstrous name, because he was anything but, and he wasn't to be feared.

Luciano adjusted his suit jacket. "Before we end this meeting, you know I have to ask you, Dante, for a bigger territory over Kansas City."

"You should know the answer to that by now, Luciano, and my answer has yet to change after all these years."

A snide smile came to Luciano's thin lips. "I was hoping this would be the year we could forget that part of the contract."

"Maybe we should forget about the whole contract, then." Lucca knocked his cigarette ashes onto the floor. "I think time is making you forget how close to extinction the Luciano name is. It was the Carusos who wanted to end the war and decided to give the option of the contract so the Luciano name wouldn't die out. Tell me, how many of you are there now?"

Two of Luciano's men moved to stand behind him, while the only one to move behind the Carusos was Drago. The empowering man was bigger than the two Lucianos combined.

Luciano slightly flexed his jaw. "Me and my three sons will continue the Luciano name."

Lucca smiled as he inhaled deeply from his cigarette. "Yes, and thanks to the generosity of the Caruso family, you can continue to do so on the agreed-upon territory."

The air in the spacious warehouse seemed to be sucked away. Not until Luciano nodded his head did the air return.

Dante then nodded, standing up as he buttoned his suit jacket and bringing the meeting to a close. Luciano also stood, and the two men came out from behind their tables to shake each other's hand.

"Glad we could have another successful meeting. I'll see you next year, Luciano."

"Till next year, Dante."

The two men dropped each other's hand, and then Dante led the Caruso family out first. However, Lucca continued to sit there, watching his men and the Lucianos leave the warehouse one by one until only himself and one other remained.

Finally, he stood up, stepping on the little bud that was still smoking from where he had dropped it. Picking up his cigarettes and lighter, he put them back in his pocket while grabbing the heavy ring that weighed on him.

The cold man looked him up and down. "Next to your father, you looked like you were sitting at the wrong table. You could almost pass for a Luciano."

"Almost." He rolled the ring between his fingers, walking toward the only other man in the warehouse.

"Yes, well, we both know what you look like when you clean yourself up."

As Luciano's voice turned dark, Lucca's turned darker. "Yes, we do." Holding the ring out for him to view, Lucca continued, "Have you seen this ring before?"

Picking up the ring, Luciano's face began to match his voice. "No, I haven't. Why do you ask?"

Lucca flashed a cryptic smile. "I'm trying to find the owner of my new dog."

Understanding his innuendo, he gave the ring back. "I'm surprised you didn't put the dog down."

"I like dogs." He put the ring back in his pocket.

Luciano seemed amused by his choice of words. "Good-bye, Lucca."

Lucca stared into the soulless black eyes of the man before him. "I'll be seeing you, Lucifer."

He had wanted—*needed*—to call him by the name to show there wasn't one man Lucca was afraid of, not even the Devil himself.

Soon.

FROM THE BEST TO THE WORST KIND OF PEOPLE

Even though *Sal was Lucca's* friend, she expected him to hurt her at any second. She couldn't help it; it had become ingrained in her.

Sal raised an eyebrow. "I take it you decided not to turn in the assignment."

Huh? "Y-You're the o-one through the c-computer, r-right?"

Laughing, he took a seat next to her after pushing the chair far enough away from her to give her plenty of room. "Yes. Do I not look like a guy who could program your computer?"

"N-no. Yes. I m-mean … I don't know. I just thought you worked with Lucca, Drago, Nero, and the rest of them. They don't r-really seem to be the c-computer type."

"I do work with them." He looked at her in confusion. "Lucca hasn't told you what line of work we're in yet?"

Now she was the one who stared at him confusion. "Elle told me everyone worked for Lucca and Nero's father at the casino. Do you all not?"

An amused look came across his face. "Well, yes, I run the security there. I make sure everything runs properly, and I set up any new equipment."

"So, the rest of them work in security, too?"

"Uh, yes, in a way."

Chloe could tell by the look on his face that she seemed to be missing something. *Don't ask. You probably don't want to know.*

"W-What does Lucca do, exactly?"

"I think this is a question you should ask Lucca."

Looking down at her hands in her lap, she squeezed them. "I've been kinda afraid to ask him. I know he will tell me the truth, but I'm not sure if I want the full truth. I just wanted a gist of what he does to see if I should ask."

"Okay, well …" Scratching his head, he seemed to be thinking of the best way to put it. "His father is the president of the casino, and Lucca is the vice president."

Really? "I had no idea he was that high up. He doesn't wear suits like the rest of you."

Sal snickered. "Oh, yes, he is about as high as you could fucking go in the fam—I mean, at the casino."

She found herself smiling at the thought that Lucca wasn't as bad as she thought he was. "Well, that's not bad at all. I thought he might be into something illegal."

"Well, I wouldn—"

"What about Drago? He looks scary enough, like he's in security."

Another silence of thinking. "Yes, he's Dante's personal bodyguard."

She looked back down at her hands. "What about Amo?"

"He definitely works security." Sal's snickering had begun again, seeming to find Amo's job the most amusing.

"He is?" It was starting to make sense to her. *He does look like a younger version of Drago.*

"Yep, he works on the lowest level of the casino with Nero and Vincent." Continuing, he wore an even bigger smile on his face, "Amo specifically loves his job. Nero and Vincent have actually requested a position change from the basement."

Biting her lip, she felt confused. The three were almost inseparable, so she couldn't imagine why Nero and Vincent would want to leave when Amo didn't.

"How come Nero and Vincent don't like their jobs?"

Again, the wheels seemed to turn in Sal's head as he tried to figure out the best way to place his words. "Nero and Vincent don't like the view from the basement, but Amo doesn't seem to mind."

Hmm ... must be too gloomy for them. "I can see that. Amo isn't picky and is much easier to please over Nero and especially Vincent. Those two always have to get their way when we pick where to eat."

"Yeah ... Like I said, you should really ask Lucca about this stuff. I probably told you too much."

"I don't think Lucca would mind." Or, she didn't see why he would. She knew he would tell her if she was brave enough to ask.

"Well, if you tell him what we talked about, be sure to tell him that I told you Amo loves his job." He winked. "Lucca's the one who placed them there and would like to know at least one of them likes it."

"I-I will." By the way Sal was acting, something told her she might want to hold off asking Lucca about his job anytime soon.

"So, are you ready to start your calculus assignment, or is there something else you're too afraid to ask Lucca?"

Chloe couldn't believe it. Her fear of him had dissipated almost immediately when they had started talking. Sal seemed like the complete opposite of Lucca—so warm and inviting, and unlike what his deep black to blue eyes had told her.

Shaking off any remaining fear of him, she couldn't believe she had thought Sal reminded her of …

Chloe opened her laptop, unable to even put Sal's name in the same thought as a complete monster.

"Is something wrong, darlin'?" Lucca set his spoon down, watching her twirl hers in the homemade vegetable soup. "I can make you something else if you don't like it."

Chloe looked up from her soup, realizing she had traveled deep in her thoughts. "No, s-sorry. It's really good. I was just thinking, is all."

He watched her take a bite of her food with a fallen look on her face. "Did being with Sal still bother you after I left?"

"No, I liked him. He was nice."

She liked how Lucca only questioned her misplaced feelings of Sal in the beginning and not the fact that Sal might have upset her or done something to her. It showed her how much Lucca trusted him and that she could trust Sal, too. The strong bond between the two was obvious. *Just like Elle and I...* Seeing Lucca and Sal together made her want to be with her best friend.

"Then tell me what's wrong, darlin'. Is there something I can do for you?"

"I just miss Elle. We used to talk every day, and I feel like I haven't talked to her in forever. I don't even have a girl to talk to here, and I think it's just making me miss her more and more."

A deep, thoughtful breath came from his chest. "I'll see what I can do."

Really? "Really?"

"I can't promise you anything, but I'll see what I can do to make you more comfortable."

It was strange to think he would do that, considering he was holding her captive. She was slowly starting to learn that he wanted her happy for some reason. She was grateful for whatever reason it was.

Smiling, she told him, "Thank you."

After that, Chloe was able to fully enjoy the delicious meal. *Dang, he's really a good cook.* She hadn't had one bad meal since being here, and already she could see herself weirdly missing the food when she was finally set free.

"So, you liked Sal, huh?" he asked, grinning.

"Yes, he was really nice to me and patient while teaching me how to solve the problems."

"Good."

Looking over at him, she saw that Lucca didn't seem surprised by her answer.

"You knew I would like him, didn't you?"

"Yes, everyone likes Sal. I haven't met a person who doesn't like him, from the worst to the best types of people."

Chloe didn't doubt it. "He's like a genius, isn't he?"

Looking up from his food, he stared directly at her. "He's not *like* a genius, darlin'; he *is* one."

By the serious expression on his face, it was clear that Sal was even smarter than she believed to be possible. She just couldn't believe the polar opposites took to one another.

She wasn't sure if he would answer, but she was too curious not to ask, "Why did your father take him in?"

The question didn't seem to bother him in the least. "Sal had lived on and off the streets with his mother since he was a baby, but by the time he was ten, his mother had OD'd. She had been dead a while before my father picked Sal up, and after that, he became family."

"That was nice of your father."

He nodded. "Yes, my father took to Sal. He liked him better than he ever liked me. Sal is definitely the son he always wanted."

Sadness washed over her at his statement. She felt bad for the young boy who thought he wasn't the son his father wanted.

"I'm sorry you felt that way."

"Don't be sorry, darlin'. It never bothered me. I was never much for feeling anything, especially toward my father. I was glad Sal was able to have a relationship with a father figure, even if it was mine. He deserved it more than me."

She bit her lip as she stared down at her food, feeling every word he had said and knowing there was no jealousy of the relationship Sal had with his father. *Dang it,* she really wished he would stop surprising her with how little she understood him.

"I'm glad you two found each other then."

His eyes turned that beautiful shade of green. "And I'm glad you like him. It means a lot to me that you feel comfortable around him."

The crazy thing was, she had. She even felt comfortable with scary Drago. The question was: *how?* She wasn't comfortable with anyone, especially men. However, not once had she feared they would even touch her.

Chloe remembered then that, when Sal had sat down, he had pulled his chair far enough away from her and was very careful not to touch her during their tutoring session. It was the same with Drago. He was always careful of the distance between them and to not come close to touching her.

Looking into the green eyes before her, she now knew why, and it had been in front of her the whole time.

"You told Sal and Drago to be careful around me, didn't you?"

Smiling, he answered, "Yes."

"W-What did you tell them?"

Lucca leaned in, caressing a strand of her hair. "That they are only allowed to get so close to you." He twisted the strand around his finger once. "And that they are to never touch you unless it is life or death." Another twist made the strand wrap around the length of his finger. "Or I'll fucking kill them."

A cold tingle trickled down her body. She saw it in his eyes then, that he would even kill a man he considered a brother if he touched her. There was no question about it; she was sure he wouldn't even second-guess it.

"W-Why?"

He caressed the strand wrapped around his finger with his thumb. "For you."

It turned out that she not only never understood him, but *I don't know him at all.*

IS TODAY THE DAY
YOU WANT TO DIE?

Lucca parked his car in the parking garage, right in front of the door he expected the person he was waiting for to come out. Getting out, he leaned against the hood of his classic black Cadillac. Then, pulling out a cigarette, he lit the end. It was his first cigarette of the day, still being early in the morning.

He sucked the contents faster than usual as he waited. Then he pulled out another one, wanting to savor it.

It was rare for Lucca to need help, but he was going to ask for it. He needed to ask it from probably the only person who understood him; the only person who knew how his mind worked, because their mind was like his.

We both hear the whispers.

Finally, the door opened, and he heard the clicking of heels. The man to come out the door first held his hand up, stopping the person behind him. When he realized it was just Lucca, he exited, waving for the one he held up to come out.

The clicking of the heels moved closer until the stilettos stopped right in front of him.

"Why does it look like my big brother wants something from me?"

Lucca motioned to the two men standing behind her. "Leave us. I'm taking Maria to school today."

"No. No, you will not! I'm pissed at you. Don't leave me with this psychopath!" she yelled after her bodyguards. But despite her effort, the two men made their exit.

Removing the cigarette from his mouth, he looked at his sister incredulously. *"I'm* the psychopath?"

Maria crossed her arms. "Yes, you are an unstable and aggressive person who lacks empathy and remorse." She was obviously spending too much time in her psychology books.

"First of all, I'm the stable one; you're not. But I think you are forgetting a major part of that diagnosis. A real psychopath appears normal and charming, hiding the fact they are aggressive, and lack empathy and remorse." Taking one long and final hit, he tossed the bud to the ground. "Now, who does that sound like to you? Because it sure as fuck isn't me."

Uncrossing her arms, she flipped her long, golden hair behind her shoulder. "You were never good at hiding your true colors. Unlike you, I like the surprise when they find out I'm crazy."

"Because you are a true fucking psychopath."

Maria went silent for a moment, becoming serious. "Yes, but if I'm a psychopath, what does that make you?"

The question wasn't meant to be answered, because the question was an impossible one to answer. They both knew Lucca was too fucked up for a definitive diagnosis.

Folding his arms across his chest, he was done talking about who was more fucked up. "So, why are you mad at me?"

Stomping her expensive heel on the pavement, she huffed, "Because you kicked us out of the house!"

"I thought you liked it here? You're able to get into more trouble."

"I was *before* they amped up security. I practically have someone going into the bathroom with me now."

"Aw, the poor, poor mafia princess." He pretended to care.

"You know I don't like it when you call me that, Lucca."

"We both know that you do. Otherwise, you wouldn't act like one."

It was her turn to change the subject as she went toward the passenger door. "Are you taking me to school or not?"

Lucca moved swiftly, not letting her open the door. "No, I need your help with something."

She tapped her heel again. "That depends on what it is."

He gave her a warning look. "You'll have to keep it a secret." *Or I'll have to kill you.*

A wicked smile touched her lightly pink lipstick lips. "I've been waiting for this day for a long time, Lucca. I hope you've saved up enough money for the blackmailing I'm going to put you through."

Opening the door for her, he laughed mockingly at her. "No one's been able to blackmail me so far, princess."

She patted him on the chest. "Oh, poor, poor mafia overlord. I know your secret already. I've just been waiting for the upper hand."

Mafia overlord? "Have you been watching movies with Elle aga— Never mind. Just get in the fucking car. You don't know shit."

A perfect eyebrow rose. "Tell me, Lucca; is having her all to yourself everything you ever dreamed of?"

His voice went dark. "Get in the fucking car."

"I guess Amo doesn't stand a chance now with Chl—"

Placing a cold hand over her mouth, he shushed her. "Tell me, Maria; is today the day you want to die?"

SURE TO MAKE ANY GIRL
SUCCUMB TO HIM THEN AND THERE

Chloe was sitting at the kitchen island, eating her toast with orange juice and wondering why Lucca wasn't already up. He had always been well past awake by this time, and he had told her they were going to finish the gardening today.

When Drago entered the room, she expected Lucca to follow behind, but he didn't.

"He's not here. He left early this morning," Drago told her as he made himself a cup of coffee.

She looked at him, wondering why he had said that. "I-I didn't say anything."

"Maybe not, but you were looking for him."

Trying her best to swallow her dry toast, she clasped her hands together. "N-No, I wasn't."

Taking a drink of the dark liquid, he stared her down for a long, hard minute. "Are you sure about that?"

No.

The front door opening saved her from having to answer the embarrassing question.

Drago smiled, keeping his voice low for only her ears. "Looks like he's back just in time for you."

Turning, she saw Lucca come in with what appeared to be a blonde wo—

"Maria!"

Drago practically slammed down his coffee cup. "Oh, fuck no."

Maria came in, smiling from ear-to-ear like the beautiful goddess she was. "Hi, Chloe. Hi, Drago!"

"No, no, no. I can see where this is going, and I'm not having any part of it. I signed up to watch the one too scared of her own shadow, not the spawn of Satan."

Spawn of Satan? Looking over at Maria, who was dressed in a light rose-colored dress with nude pumps, she looked like a beautiful angel. Chloe always thought of her as one, too. She was the sweetest person in the world.

Maria looked like she was about to cry. "That hurt my feelings."

He laughed. "What feelin—"

"You are being rude," Chloe spoke without thinking, becoming angered by the man. "Maybe you need to go back to sleep, because you're not being very nice this morning."

Maria had to put her hand over her mouth to keep from laughing as Drago's face fell.

Grinning, Lucca stepped forward to stand beside Chloe. "Was he being mean to you, darlin'?"

She thought about it for a long moment as she stared at a now pissed off Drago. He had been trying to push her buttons about Lucca just a few minutes ago, and she had half a mind to say yes. *Or I'll fucking kill them.* But . . . she figured she would spare his life. *This time.*

"No." She smiled at Drago, brave only because Lucca was a step away.

Taking his coffee, Drago started to leave the room. "I'll watch them from the security room, but if they burn the house down, don't expect me to save them."

Now that he was gone, Chloe's focus went to Maria. "I can't believe it; you're here." She had sometimes felt as if she no longer existed, but now that someone was here who was actually her friend, she felt alive again.

"Yep." Maria smiled happily down at her. "Give me a second; I'll be right back."

She watched Maria head toward the stairs then looked back at Lucca, not understanding. "But why?"

He gave her a smile unlike one she had seen before. It was like a smile Vincent would give her, except it was more deadly and sure to make any girl succumb to him then and there.

"I told you I would see what I could do for you."

She had to pull her eyes from his, afraid the smile would work on her. "Oh."

Like always, he picked up a strand of her hair. "I know we were supposed to take care of the garden today, but I thought you would enjoy being with Maria more."

Watching him twirl her black hair around his finger was almost mesmerizing.

"Does tomorrow sound okay instead?"

"Y-Yes." Looking away from the twirling was hard, but she finally managed to look back up at him. "Thank you, Lucca."

Another deadly smile made her heart skip a beat. "You're welcome, darlin'." They heard Maria start back down the steps, and Lucca started to twirl the strand slower, like he was savoring it. "I'll be back later tonight."

When is later tonight? Where is he going?

The thoughts that popped into her head scared her to her bones. *Why did it matter?* It shouldn't matter. *It doesn't matter.*

The footsteps were now closer, and right before they were too close, the black lock fell from his fingertips with a final twirl.

Maria walked in, now wearing pink shorts and a tank top, carrying movies. "Okay, now we're ready for a girls' day!"

Chloe's cheeks started to feel warm. If Maria had walked in a second earlier, she would have thought something was going on between Chloe and Lucca.

Maria started pushing Lucca out of the way while she sat the movies down. "Okay, bye now, Lucca. You can go."

His dark voice came out as a threat as he walked away.

"Remember what I said, princess."

Her voice seemed to carry her own threat. "Don't worry; I'll play nice, overl—"

"Good-bye, darlin'. Have fun, because I won't be bringing her ass back."

"He's joking." Maria giggled as he slammed the front door behind him.

It didn't sound like he was joking.

Maria spread the chick flicks across the counter. "So, what do you want to watc—"

"How's Elle?" Chloe was unconcerned about the movies.

"She's good. Now, we have *Dirty Dancing, Greas*—"

"Just good? What about Amo?"

"Yep, both good. How about *Twilight?*"

She was crazily staring at her friend now. "Maria, you're going to tell them where I am, right? You're going to tell someone?"

Taking a long breath, she whispered, "I can't."

"W-Why? Lucca's forcing me here. I don't want to be here."

Maria was supposed to be her friend. She didn't understand.

"I ... I just can't, Chloe. I'm sorry." Maria hadn't looked in her eyes until now. "Listen, is he hurting you?"

Chloe could tell by the look on Maria's face that she already knew the answer. Still, she solemnly shook her head.

"Are you being mistreated in any way?"

Again, Maria knew the answer before Chloe even shook her head.

Her voice sounded sure when she said, "It won't be forever. I promise you, Chloe. He will let you go."

Chloe wasn't so sure. *I fear he won't ever let me go.*

Maria took a seat beside her. "Elle misses you. A lot. They both do."

She wanted so badly to cry. She missed Elle so much . . . and Amo.

"Elle says college just isn't the same without you, but she likes it so much better than high school. She doesn't get picked on anymore, and even though she wants you there with her, she still enjoys it."

It was bittersweet to hear. She was so happy Elle was finally able to like school, but she was sad she couldn't experience it with her.

"Amo misses you, too, but he's doing good." She went silent for a second, then continued with a smile on her face, "He works *a lot.* He really loves his job!"

She laughed, wondering why everyone kept saying that.

"That's good. I'm glad." Turning serious again, she looked over at Maria, wanting her to know how much it meant to her that she could hear about how her friends were doing. "Thank you."

"You're welcome, Chloe. Now"—she stood, smiling as she picked up a movie—"*The Little Mermaid?*"

Knowing that was Elle's favorite Disney movie, she smiled. "Sounds good."

THE WORD SHE WOULD
SOON FORGET

C *hloe felt like a girl* again as she spent the day with Maria. She was happier than she had ever been here and was so grateful that she had been granted the day with her. The only way her day would have been better was if Elle were here, too.

They were stuffing their faces with popcorn and watching too many chick flicks to count. By the time they moved on to *Bring It On*, it was getting pretty late.

Looking out the window at the pitch black, and then to the clock, she couldn't believe the time. *He's usually off work by now. What is he doing?*

She shook her head from the thought, wondering why she had even wondered it in the first place. *You miss him...*

Freezing in place, she didn't know where that thought had come from. It was like her voice, but it wasn't.

"What color do you like?" Maria asked, setting down her nail kit. When Chloe didn't answer, Maria gave her a worried glance. "Chloe?"

Trying her best to put her thoughts aside, she looked at the wide range of colors and saw the one she wanted hiding in the middle. "Black."

Maria gave her a scrutinizing look. "Do you wear any other color besides black?"

Looking down at her black leggings and oversized dark gray sweater, she gave her own scrutinizing look. "This is dark gray."

Maria rolled her eyes. "That is one shade away from black, and you know it."

"No, it's not." *It's more like a shade and a half.*

"What about this?" She held up a different polish. "I always wanted to see purple on you. It'll make your black hair and gray eyes pop."

Hell no. "Um, no. I'll take the black."

"Ugh, come on, Chloe! Why do you always wear black, anyway?"

"I don't know." She had to think deeply a second about it. "I guess I wear black because it doesn't draw more attention to me. I feel like, if I wear a color, it will make people look at me more."

"You two are perfect for each other," Maria mumbled under her breath, too low for Chloe to hear properly.

"What did you say?"

"Nothing." She smiled before grabbing two other small bottles of polish. "Will you at least meet me halfway?"

Chloe stared at the two colors she picked. One was a very dark purple, and the other a dark navy blue. Both were close to black.

"Fine," she grumbled. "Pick the one you like best." *Not like it matters, anyway. I'm not going anywhere.*

"Yay! I like this one." Unsurprisingly, she handed her the dark purple one.

Opening the polish, Chloe started to regret her decision when it didn't come out as close to black as she thought. She almost decided to grab the black instead, but she didn't want to get into an argument with Maria again, knowing Maria would win, like she always did when she wanted something bad enough.

Beginning to paint her nails a pink nude, Maria asked a question Chloe didn't think she would. "So, do you really hate it here?"

Stunned, Chloe looked at her questioningly. "Are you going to tell Lucca?"

"No." Her face held a definite possible lie.

Chloe pointed at the ceiling where possible cameras were. "Can Drago hear us?"

"No." It was another possible lie.

Chloe looked at her, trying to decipher if it was the truth or not before she gave up. "If Lucca weren't holding me against my will and would let me talk to Elle, then I . . . might not hate it. But it's a strong might."

"Do you like him?"

She did not just say that! "What!"

Blowing on her nails, Maria had no problem elaborating. "Do you, you know, *like* Lucca?"

"Are you seriously asking me if I like the crazy—and frightening, I might add—man holding me hostage?" *Am I in la-la land? What the hell is going on?*

Maria held up her hands. "Jeez, okay. I was just asking. Every girl falls in love with Lucca immediately, so I was just wondering if he got to you as well."

Every girl falls in love with—Nope, don't care.

Maria's voice changed, turning almost ominous when she asked, "Are you sure you're being held hostage?"

Is she crazy like him, too?

"What are you talking about, Maria? He won't let me leave. Drago watches every move I make. What does that seem like to you?"

"Sorry, I just—Never mind. I'm sorry. You're right."

A weird feeling started coming over her, not understanding why Maria wasn't the least bit concerned. It was like she was used to Lucca doing this, like it was normal behavior, like it was his job or something.

"Is Lucca the vice president of the casino hotel?" The words seemed to spill from her mouth.

Maria busted up with laughter. "That's a funny way of putting it. Who told you that?"

Putting the brush into the bottle of nail polish, a cold chill began moving up her back. "Sal did."

When Maria looked over at Chloe, she saw the serious look on her face. "Crap. He hasn't told you yet."

The chill spanned her whole body now. "T-Told me what?"

"You really need to ask Lucca about that."

"That's exactly what Sal told me," she whispered.

Closing her bottle of nail polish, Maria put it back in the kit.

"Uh, yeah, for a reason."

Chloe shook her head. "No, I-I want *you* to tell me."

Maria shook her head. "No way."

"Please, you're my friend, Maria."

Staring at her, Maria seemed to be contemplating something before she stood up. "Come with me."

What the . . . ?

"Hurry up," she told her, quickly going to the stairs and making her follow.

Running up the stairs after her, they went into the huge upstairs bathroom.

Closing the door behind her, Maria locked the bathroom door, making Chloe more chilled than she already was.

"You'll want to sit for this."

Taking a seat on the lip of the tub, Chloe felt like she was going to pass out.

"Why did we come in here?"

"The bathrooms don't have any video or audio surveillance," she said like it was no big deal.

"You said he couldn't hear us!"

"Yeah, well, I lied." Maria put her hands on her hips. "Now, do you want to know or not?"

No. She was now sure she didn't by the way Maria was acting, but that was the exact reason she probably should know.

Holding her breath, she uttered the word she would soon regret . . . "Y-Yes."

THE CALM BEFORE
THE STROM

Closing *the door behind him*, Lucca pulled out his keys to lock his penthouse at the casino hotel when he heard the door opening behind him on the other side of the hall. He turned to see Nero, Elle, Vincent, Lake, Adalyn, and Amo leaving Nero's penthouse.

Turning back toward the door and realizing he was a minute too early or late leaving, he slid the key into the lock, locking it.

"Hi, Lucca!" Adalyn slid out from behind the boys with a huge smile on her face.

Dammit. He was too tired for this and just wanted to get home.

Putting the next key into the top lock, he didn't turn around as he said, "Hello."

Lake was the next one to slide out from behind Vincent and

Nero. "You're making sure your house is awfully locked up for this to be a now guarded area."

To keep out nosey, little shits li—

"How come I've never seen the inside of your place? Have you been in there, Nero?" Elle came out from behind the boys as well.

Finally, Lucca turned around, leaning up against his door and crossing his arms. He looked at Nero, hoping he would lie.

Elle, Lake, and Adalyn turned their heads eagerly toward Nero.

Vincent looked at him in speculation as well.

Then Amo turned, too.

Nero looked at Lucca in pity. "No."

I'm gonna fucking kill you. His younger brother did not, in fact, lie for him.

"That's pretty weir—"

Vincent grabbed Lake to shush her.

"Yea—"

Nero did the same to his girlfriend.

"Kinda fucked up you haven't even let your own brother inside your place," Amo stated.

Lucca flexed his jaw, staring at Amo. A flash of him gouging out Amo's eyes appeared before him. Taking a single blink made the satisfyingly gruesome vision go away before he calmly looked at Elle.

"It looks just like yours and Nero's, but flipped. There's no reason to see it."

"I'm sure it's decorated differently, though. Has no one really seen it?" Lake asked, burning a hole through the door with her stare, like she was hoping to suddenly have X-ray vision.

"I've seen Sal come out of there before, but he's the only one, and it was just one time," Elle told her.

"Maybe he has a second entrance somehow?" Lake replied like he wasn't even there.

Lucca gave Nero and Vincent a look of death.

"Clearly, Lucca likes his privacy, and we should respect it," Adalyn stated.

He gave her a slight smile in return. "Thank you, Adalyn." Hearing maybe a swoon or two, he began walking toward the elevator.

The girls all followed behind him as he got into the elevator, passing one of his men who was laughing as he watched the floor.

"We're going to the diner to get something to eat if you're hungry," Adalyn offered.

"No thanks. I'll fix something when I get home."

Hurry the fuck up. He couldn't punch in the code fast enough to take them to the first floor when Amo finally got his ass into the elevator.

"Hmm … That's strange," Lake whispered loud enough for everyone to hear.

Fucking hell, what now? It seemed like the doors would never come to a close.

"What?" Elle was curious, along with Adalyn.

"Probably that I make my own fucking food," he mouthed off to the nosy girls. Chloe had practically been shocked he knew how to boil water.

"No." Lake smiled a bit too evilly before she continued, "Your hair

113

is wet. Who takes a shower at one of their houses only to leave for the other one? Must have gotten pretty dirty ..." she trailed off, giggling.

"Hmm ... What were you doing in there?" Elle giggled with her.

I'm gonna snap their little fucking nec—

"He probably does have that second entrance for his women," Amo said in a low tone, but not low enough for them all not to hear.

Cutting a blind Amo's throat with his pocket knife flashed before him, only to unfortunately disappear after he blinked it away.

"You should get one, Amo, so I don't have to see the fucking trash you take to your place every night."

The elevator went deadly silent at his words.

Amo didn't open his mouth, clearly too pissed and shocked that Lucca had known about the girls he brought home in the middle of the night.

Lucca wasn't done with him just yet.

Watching the numbers blink lower and lower, he knew the doors were about to open any second now. He waited until the very end before he looked at Amo one last time and asked, "How has Chloe been?"

You could practically see Amo killing him in his mind, just the way he had been. It was a question he wasn't able to answer, considering Chloe's phone had been with Lucca since he had taken her. Amo's countless texts and phone calls had all gone unanswered.

Now Lucca was happy he hadn't killed him. This was much better.

"S-She's doing good." Elle nervously tried to break the tension between the two.

At last, the doors began to open, and he gave his response to

Amo as he continued to stare him down. "That's good to hear."

Lucca let the girls off first, and when Amo passed, a sinister grin came over Lucca.

When another vision appeared before him, it wasn't of a horrific way to kill Amo. This one was altogether different. A vision that would soon come true, when Amo finally learned that, *Chloe is mine.*

After giving his order to the waitress, Amo's appetite seemed to disappear. It had actually disappeared in the elevator with Lucca.

Sitting at the end of the table, he didn't engage in the laughing from his group. He didn't even particularly want to be here, but he had cancelled on them so many times since Chloe had left for California that he didn't want them to think he had become broken. Even though he had.

It was like a piece of him had left with her, never to return until she did.

Amo replayed the night that went to shit over and over in his head. The night that only made her leave for California sooner…

Amo watched Chloe from the other side of the mall while she bought her suitcase. She was leaving tomorrow, and he hadn't even told her how he felt about her yet. He was a dumbass for waiting this long, but he was terrified of scaring her away. It had to be at the right time.

Seeing Chloe begin to exit the store, he couldn't believe he had spent three and a half years at high school with her and not once looked past her scars. He would regret those three and half years until the day he died.

He felt a moment of peace as he stared at her from afar. She took his breath away, but it was only for a moment.

Bang. Bang.

The calm before the storm had passed, and the beauty he had felt washed away. Now, all that was left was dread and terror. . .

He stood up abruptly, and the table went quiet.

"I'll be right back."

Amo headed out of the diner, needing fresh air on his face. As soon as it was, he felt like he could breathe again. . .

He opened his arms wide, watching Chloe run toward him. He was so close . . . so close to saving her. It wasn't until her body collided with his that he realized he had been holding his breath.

Wrapping his arms around her was the first time he was blessed with being able to touch the girl who had stolen his heart. The storm had passed, and in its place was true beauty, the kind you never thought to exist.

He held on to her, planning to never let go.

"I've got you."

This was the sign he had needed to tell her his feelings. She had chosen him. . .

The door opening beside him had him turning to see Elle coming outside.

"The food should be done any minute."

"You go on in; I'll be there in a minute," he told her.

She didn't make a move to go inside. Instead, she looked down at her feet. "I'm sorry she won't talk to you."

"It's not your fault, Elle. It's mine." There was a minute of silence between the two before he spoke again, "Is she really doing okay?" It was killing him not knowing if she really was or not.

Her voice became pained. "I think so. I text her every day, but I can't get her to talk on the phone with me yet."

"You haven't talked to her on the phone at all?"

Elle shook her head.

A small alarm went off in his head.

"Get her to talk to you on the phone. Make sure she's okay."

"Okay," she whispered.

"Go on in; it's cold out here. I'll be right in."

Going for the door, Elle then stopped with tears brimming her eyes. "I thought you were going to get her to stay. I thought you were actually going to do it when I failed. Turns out, neither of us were capable of saving her."

He had to turn away, his own vision becoming blurry …

"Wait," he stopped her from leaving his car so suddenly. "Stay and go to college here … with Elle and Lake. I can take some classes. Who is going to walk you to class when Elle or I aren't there?"

Chloe wasn't even able to look at him. "I'll have to get used to being on my own."

He tried again, "But if you stayed here, you won't have to."

"Elle won't have to watch out for me anymore. She can finally enjoy school without me getting in her way. I want that for her."

With each word she spoke, he was slowly starting to realize that whatever had happened back there, when she had run into his arms, it wasn't turning out like he had thought.

"What about you? What about me?"

Still, she couldn't bring herself to look at him. "I'll adjust. It will be good for me. You have Nero and Vincent and your job at the casino to keep you so busy you won't even remember me."

"I'll remember you …" He was barely able to speak.

The change in her started then. "That you walked me to class for a few months? That my best friend is your friend's girlfriend?"

Slamming his hand on the steering wheel, it all started coming out. "You're not like any other girl I know, Chloe." He took a breath to calm himself before whispering why she needed … why she had to stay here with him, "I love you."

Chloe jumped out of the car, running toward her front door.

"Fucking wait!" Amo ran after her. She had to listen. She had to stay!

"We're friends, Amo. If I stay … I can't. I will never be what you want. You need a girl like Elle or Lake. Even a girl like Cassandra would be better than me. You love being with your friends, and I like being alone. That's why I'm leaving."

It was an obvious lie. He knew it the moment it slipped from her lips. She was leaving because she was afraid. Afraid of this city. Afraid of whatever had happened to her four years ago. Afraid of him. Afraid that, for the first time in her life, she could be loved.

His voice went soft. "No one likes to be alone."

"I'm not normal; I'm a freak."

He could see it then. He had done the thing he had been afraid to do. He had scared her off.

"You said so yourself."

Amo's heart sunk to his stomach, thinking back to freshman year when she had come into the cafeteria with her fresh scars.

"Fucking freak!" he had yelled, making the lunchroom burst into laughter with the echoes of the word "freak."

Now it was him who couldn't look at her, too ashamed of the actions of his younger self. He hadn't even realized she remembered it, or that it had been him who had yelled it out. She had trusted him; forgiven him for the sick comment when he had yet to forgive himself.

"Why didn't you say anything?"

"What was I supposed to say?" Chloe began opening the door, ready to close him out. "Bye, Amo."

He felt her slipping away.

With tears welling, he told her, "I didn't mean it."

"It's okay, Amo. We're even. I called you a beast." Her voice came out calm as she went inside, even though he could see the tears beginning to touch her own eyes.

When she started closing the door, he knew deep down that it was going to be the last time he would see her. However, what he didn't know was that it would also be the last time he would hear her sweet voice.

"I can't be fixed. Not by you. Not by anyone. I'm just broken."

Shutting the door on him was her shutting him out forever.

As the tears fell down his cheeks, he didn't know who he was crying for more: himself or her because he hadn't been able to save her...

Amo refused to let the tears fall from his eyes like they had that night. *She's gone, but she's not gone forever. I will save her.*

HER BODY HAD BEEN
CLAIMED BY THE BOOGIEMAN

C *hloe sat there, frozen in* place, as her world slowly came crashing down around her. She knew she had been missing something over the past seven months, and now it all made sense. It was like a puzzle she hadn't been able to solve because she had been missing the final piece, and Maria had just given it to her.

She knew everything. How it all started with Elle, colliding them into the mafia world.

"This whole time, everyone knew but me?" she whispered, betrayal smacking her across the face. "Amo knew …? Elle knew, and she didn't tell me?"

"She was protecting you. We were all trying to protect you, Chloe. We weren't sure if you would be able to handle it," Maria told her.

Hearing a door slam from downstairs, Chloe jumped.

Maria stood from the edge of the tub. "Lucca knows I told you, and by the sound of that door slamming, he's not happy."

The underboss . . .

Her body was now shaking as she tried to stand. "Don't leave me alone with him."

"I told you, he won't hurt you, Chloe. I don't think you understand what you mean to him."

They could hear him coming up the steps now, only making the fear course through her faster.

"You have to tell Elle he's keeping me." But hell, after hearing what Lucca was, Elle wasn't going to be able to save her. "Amo, tell Amo. He will save me. Please, Maria!"

Shaking her head, Maria didn't give in to her pleading eyes. "I can't."

Yes, you can! She wanted to shake her. This was supposed to be her friend, but the girl before her wasn't.

"W-What do you mean, you can't? He's keeping me hostage."

The door handle began to jiggle.

"It's not what you think. You're here for a reason, Chloe," Maria whispered.

"Open the door, Maria," Lucca's dark voice came from the other side of the door.

"What does that mean?" she whispered back.

His voice turned dangerously darker. "Open this door *now*, Maria."

"I'm sorry," was all Maria said as she went toward the door.

Please, no.

Maria's hand twisted the lock, and the door began to slowly open.

His eyes landed on Chloe, his voice coming out in a commandingly low growl as he said, "Go downstairs and wait in my office."

"She deserved to know. She wanted to hear it from a friend. You should have told her by no—"

He shushed his sister and growled, "Now, Chloe," a bit harsher.

It was impossible not to obey him, and she hated that her feet began to take her out of the room.

Holding her breath as she passed him, she stared at his cold, blue eyes that made ice run through her veins. *How did I not see it?* The mafia practically oozed off him. The underboss screamed from him. *The boogieman* ... Now she knew why they had given him that name.

When he finally moved his eyes from hers to Maria, she was able to pick up her feet faster.

Running down the steps, she was prepared to run out the front door, when an unhappy Drago blocked her way.

"Office," he snapped at her like he knew exactly what she was thinking.

With nothing left but to accept her fate, she headed toward Lucca's office, hoping he wouldn't hurt his own sister and would let her go. Then maybe, just maybe, Maria would take pity on her and tell Amo about her kidnapping.

In his office, she sat down and began to wring her hands. Her hands were almost raw by the time the office door opened a while later. She didn't have to turn around to know who it was. You didn't need to see him to feel his presence.

Lucca took a seat behind his desk, silently staring at her.

Looking at the hands, she squeezed them with all her might. "D-Did you h-hurt her?"

"I thought about it," he revealed. "But no. Drago is taking her home."

Relief flooded her that Maria was okay. At the same time, she was terrified to hear him be so honest that the thought had occurred to him. She now only had one last hope, and it depended upon Maria. *Please tell Amo. He must save me.*

He leaned back in his chair. "Tell me, darlin', why are you more scared of me now than you were before?"

"B-Because now I know the real you," she whispered.

He raised his eyebrows. "Have I not shown you the real me from the moment I met you?"

Her eyes drifted up to look at him. His eyes had returned to the blue-green shade that had captivated her since their first meeting in the gazebo, just like his rough appearance had. He was unlike the others; darker than the others, and yes, she always knew that.

"But now I-I know the truth no one would tell me because they thought they were protecting me."

No one is who they seem. She hadn't felt this alone since she had first gotten her scars.

"All you had to do was ask. I would have told you everything and anything you wanted to know about me, about the family. I told you I would never lie to you, and I meant it. You were just too scared to ask, because then it would have been real. That's why I was waiting for you to ask me. I wanted you to be ready for the truth."

Her eyes drifted back to her lap, knowing he was right. That was why she hadn't asked him.

"And yes, they thought they were protecting you, but I didn't agree with it. They lied to you; pretended to be something they weren't. I never have. I've made it obvious who I am since the beginning. I've only ever wanted you to see me for who I am, Chloe."

She remembered back to the night he had repeatedly slammed the bat down on the lifeless body, and how he had looked right into her eyes, showing his true self ...

The thought that was meant only for her passed her lips, "You're a killer."

"Yes, I am. I have killed many and tortured more." The dark voice filled the space between them.

Chloe kept wringing her now tortured hands at how visible the monster in him was. She needed to get away from him. Far, far away.

Trying to calm herself, she began repeating the words, "Amo will come for me."

Lucca's voice turned deadly. "He's a killer, too, darlin'."

She started shaking her head, not wanting to hear it.

"He's killed, and so have Nero and Vincent."

Shaking her head harder, she refused to believe it. "No, Elle wouldn't be with—"

"She learned to accept it, just like you will." He said it like it was a promise.

"Amo's not like you."

"No, he isn't," he agreed. "Amo pretends to be something he's not with you."

Again, she shook her head, not believing.

She repeated the words of her last hope, "He's going to save me."

Standing, he went to the other side of the desk, towering over her. "You think Amo will save you from me?" He took a strand of her hair, wrapping it tightly around his finger.

Her breath caught in her throat, her words no longer able to come out.

"Look at me," he commanded.

When she didn't, he tugged the dark silk he held captive.

Chloe raised her gray depths slowly, meeting his blue-green ones through her lashes.

"No one is taking you from me, darlin'." Tugging her hair once more, he brought her closer to him. "You're mine, Chloe Masters. You have been since the moment I saw your scarred face. You just didn't know it."

For four long years, her body had been claimed by the one she had believed to be the most heinous of beings, but now she could feel the old bonds the devil had placed on her breaking, and new chains were taking its place. These chains were heavier, tighter, showing her that she had been claimed by a more evil being. Her body had been claimed by the boogieman.

Unraveling the strand around his finger, he was so close, almost brushing his fingertips upon her neck.

Slamming her eyes shut, she waited for it, for the moment when he would finally touch her. But seconds passed, and it never came.

She opened her eyes to find that he had already disappeared. However, the chains were still there, just as heavy, just as tight.

THE WAS IT;
THE TIME HAD COME

Chloe *had fought off the* nightmares every night since the last time, but not tonight. Her body now belonged to one monster, while her mind and soul still belonged to another. Letting her demons come for her, there was no use in fighting them anymore …

Her one final hope of being saved from the devil had disappeared. No one was coming to save her, and if someone did, it was far past too late. To save her now would mean that someone worse would have to take her soul from the devil and claim it as their own. However, a man like that shouldn't—wouldn't exist, and if he did, that wouldn't be saving her at all …

"Chloe … Chloe, wake up and everything will be okay." The repeated words brought her out of the nightmare.

Opening her eyes, she saw Lucca sitting on the edge of the bed, playing with the ends of her hair that rested on the pillow.

Afraid, she quickly sat up, scooting away from him, the nightmares and her tiredness not helping.

"You really think I would hurt you, darlin'? After seeing you like that?"

I don't think you understand what you mean to him, Maria's words echoed in her mind.

Balling up her fists, her nails touched her palms and a wince of pain reached her face.

"What's wrong?" Lucca began studying her.

"N-Nothing."

Turning on the bedside lamp, he looked back at her, seeing that her balled-up fists were tainted pink. "Let me see them."

"I-I'm fin—"

"Either hold them out, or I'll do it myself," he cut her off.

Swallowing the lump in her throat, her hands shook as she uncurled them, revealing her inflamed and bloody palms.

Without a word, he got up and left the room.

Minutes seemed to pass before he came back with a box. Returning to the edge of the bed, he opened it, revealing a first-aid kit.

"Come closer to me," he instructed in a melodic voice.

She found herself obeying him, scooting slightly closer. It was either that or he would move her himself.

"You are going to let me touch you now, darlin'." He didn't ask for permission; he was telling her.

"N-No." She tried to scoot back, but he leaned into her, placing both hands on either side of her and giving her no space and nowhere to run.

The voice that was once melodic turned dark and commanding. "You *will* let me touch you now."

She closed her eyes, holding her breath. This was it; the time had come.

Holding as still as possible, she felt cold fingertips lightly touch her fire-hot hands. His cold ones turned hers over and began to soothe over her palms.

She opened her eyes then to see Lucca's full attention on her skin. It almost seemed like he was memorizing her hands as his cold fingertips smoothed over the inflamed areas, carefully dancing around her cuts.

His hands left hers, going into the kit and pouring alcohol onto a pad. When the cold touch returned, she slightly jumped back, making him look into her eyes.

Staring into his, she saw they now appeared fully green, without a trace of any blue.

"This will hurt."

She nodded slowly, unable to look away from his green depths.

Now when he touched her, she didn't move away from his touch. She found herself unable to look away from him. It was like she was glimpsing a different side of him.

He pulled his eyes away from hers, bringing his attention back to her hands. Bits of his dark hair that was usually slicked back had fallen in front of his face. He uncaringly left them there while he tended to her hands. It looked like … *he cared,* if that was even possible.

It did sting when he swiped the pad along her cuts, but physical pain no longer bothered her. It could never compare to the pain of mental torture she'd had and still continued to endure.

Lucca took his time cleaning each cut, making sure not to miss any open wounds. Going into the box again, he then pulled out an ointment and started applying it to the entirety of her palms.

The ointment felt good on her raw skin, along with his light, icy touch. She was still mesmerized by the man before her.

He then took his time wrapping each hand with white gauze. After it was secured, he brushed his finger over one of her polished nails.

"I like this color."

Feeling the need to explain the dark purple shade, she said, "M-Maria picked it."

"It looks nice against your light skin," he murmured.

Chloe seemed to snap out of it when his fingers lingered on hers for a moment longer. She quickly pulled her hands away from his, unable to stand the closeness of him any longer.

Did I just let him …? She swallowed hard, not understanding how she had let him touch her for so long.

When he packed up his case, his green eyes disappeared, along with his softer demeanor. "I want you to trim your nails tomorrow when you wake up." He got up, turning the bedside light off. "Go back to sleep."

Breathing heavily, she lay back down, scooting to the middle of the bed and securing herself under the covers like it would protect her from him.

She watched his dark figure move through her room and into the attached bathroom where he closed the door behind him.

Trying to slow down her breathing, she took long, deep breaths. *You will let me touch you now . . .*

She could still feel the icy touch that smoothed over her pained palms, like they had been imprinted by his motions. She should have revolted against his touch, but instead, it was like he had put a spell on her.

She could hear the water running in the bathroom, the sound bringing her calmness.

Go back to sleep . . .

Another long, deep breath and she closed her eyes, drifting off. It was obvious his spell still had a hold on her.

Lucca washed his hands then splashed the cold water onto his face, trying to get himself under control. Touching her while she watched had been better than anything he had ever experienced in his life. He had touched many women, but not one who felt like her.

If he had to go the rest of his life only able to simply touch her, he would. Even if that meant his dark side would never be appeased by the twisted things it wanted to do to her, he could live with that.

It was everything he could do not to go back out there and do it all over again.

Do it, his darkness whispered.

Pushing back his hair with his damp hands, he tried to push out the image of running his fingers over her scars.

You know you want to . . .

"Shut up," he whispered harshly at himself in the mirror.

As much as he wanted to, now wasn't the time. She was more frightened of him than ever, thanks to Maria. He had wanted to be the one who told her when she was ready to accept him for who he was. Now everything he had worked for to get her to be comfortable with him, to trust him, had flown out the window, and he was starting back from square one.

Going to the bathroom door, he switched off the light then opened the door, staring out into the room and seeing Chloe already fast asleep.

He quietly took a seat on the chair in the corner. Leaning back, he got comfortable for the night ahead, not wanting to leave her to the nightmares again.

She had practically destroyed her hands, and he had a feeling he was to blame after making her face the frightening truth in his office.

Knowing he had pushed her too far, he had left her alone, letting her retreat to the safety of her room. Instead, she had only made it her hell by self-mutilating herself. *Never again.*

Lucca couldn't help thinking back to what Chloe had repeated. *Amo will come for me . . . He will save me.*

For a man who wasn't supposed to feel anything, those words had cut him deeply. She couldn't see it yet, didn't even know that was the exact thing he was trying to do.

WE ONLY SEE WHAT
WE WANT TO SEE

When *Chloe woke up the* next morning, she felt like death. Her hands were sore, and her mind was foggy from pure exhaustion. If she hadn't gotten the deep sleep she had after Lucca had come in, she wasn't sure what kind of state her mind would be in.

Raising up in bed, she saw that it was ten past eleven, much later than she was used to waking up.

Her eyes drifted to the unbroken music box that Lucca had given her. Then they drifted to the silver nail clippers she hadn't seen before right next to it.

She remembered the request he had asked of her last night, realizing he must have set them there to make sure she clipped her nails. She usually kept a bit of length on them; that's how she liked them. It was a bad nervous habit she had adapted—wringing her hands that turned into digging her nails into her skin when she was scared. She couldn't explain why she did it.

Not wanting to part ways with her nails, nor wanting to do everything Lucca asked, she ignored his request, going into the bathroom to wash away the horrors of yesterday.

She quickly used the bathroom, brushed her teeth, and then hopped into the shower. When she got out, she noticed the ointment Lucca had used last night, along with a new bandage on the bathroom counter.

Why? She would never understand him and why he did the things he did. Even though it might have been a thoughtful gesture, it still came from a deranged man.

Staring at her sore and swollen hands, she saw that she hadn't done this amount of damage to herself in a long time. She figured it was best to use the supplies he had set out.

Finally dressed, she then headed downstairs, figuring it was safe since Lucca would have been at work for hours by now. However, she learned that assumption was a mistake when she made it downstairs to see Lucca was in the kitchen, cooking.

Just when she was about to turn around, he looked up and saw her.

"Good morning."

"M-Morning." Not wanting to blatantly run away from him, she spotted her laptop on the kitchen island where she had left it last and decided she would run back upstairs with it.

Once she retrieved it, she turned around, but his voice stopped her.

"Lunch is almost done."

"I'm not very hu—"

"I didn't ask if you were hungry, darlin'. Now, sit."

She didn't know why she had thought she could actually escape him. Turning back around, her body followed his order.

Lucca looked away from the stove to her. "Did you cut your nails?"

She brought her hands close to her body, trying to hide them. "I-I don't like my nails short."

Coming over to her, he reached into his pocket and pulled out a small pair of nail clippers, setting them down in front of her. "I'm not going to let you do that to yourself again, Chloe. I want you to keep them short. Do you understand?"

She nodded, defeated yet again.

His voice seemed to turn softer. "When you get over the habit, you can grow them out again."

Biting her lip, she nodded again. "O-Okay."

He looked at her for a second longer before going back to the stove to finish cooking lunch.

Chloe picked up the clippers and began to trim her nails as short as they could go. She understood why Lucca was making her do so. It was something she should have made herself do forever ago. She just hated how her body felt the need to please him no matter how much her mind wanted to fight it. Something about Lucca had always called her body to his, but her mind knew better, always realizing how dangerous he was.

Every now and then, she would glance out of the corner of

her eyes to watch him cook. Then she would snap her eyes back to what she was doing when she found them lingering. Each time she glanced, she told herself that was the last time, but that was never the case.

His face held the same thoughtfulness and care when he cooked as it had last night while caring for her hands. She found it too hard not to watch him when he was like that. It was rare and unexpected from a man like him.

Finishing her nails, she cleaned off the counter and threw the clippings away before sitting back down to find a cheeseburger and fries waiting in her spot.

She dressed her burger with some of the condiments he had laid out as he took a seat beside her with his own plate. She had eaten countless cheeseburgers but, taking a bite, she had to admit this one was pretty freaking good. *Of course, it is.*

He was really starting to get on her nerves at this point.

Chloe finished her food in record time, not knowing if it was because it was so good or because she wanted to escape upstairs.

"T-Thank you. It was delicious."

"I'm glad you liked it, darlin'." He smiled, picking up their empty plates.

She reached for the laptop, more than ready to go upstairs.

"I took the day off to finish gardening," he told her, setting the dishes in the sink.

She froze, having forgotten about that. *No wonder he is here.*

"Do you still want to join me?" He wasn't commanding her; he was simply asking.

Clutching the laptop, she tried her best to lie. "I-I have a lot of schoolwork I n-need to do."

"Okay, darlin'. I just thought you might enjoy some fresh air. But if being in the house every day doesn't bother you, then I understand."

"I j-just have a lot of work to do," she tried to lie again, though she knew it was bullshit. Not on the account of what had happened last night, but because he specifically brought Sal in to help her with her schoolwork so she could. *Dang it . . .* She was starting to feel bad!

He smiled, leaning against the kitchen counter. "I said I understand, darlin'. Go and get your schoolwork done. It's more important."

Is he being sarcastic, or just really freaking nice?

Biting her lip again, she tried to decide. *What is he trying to do to me?*

She shook her head, hoping it would shake the thoughts away while she headed for the stairs, not wanting to give in to feeling bad about not wanting to spend the day gardening with a freaking murderer.

"Okay, bye."

Laughing at her abrupt departure, he raised his voice so she could hear him as she ran. "All right, I hope you get lots of work done, darlin'."

Running into her room, she shut the door behind her before setting her laptop on the small desk in her room. *Ugh! I hope you get lots of work done, darlin'. Like, what does that even mean?*

Whatever Lucca was trying to do to her, she wasn't buying it. He was a lunatic, and that was it.

Taking a seat, she opened the laptop to see what schoolwork

she had. Nothing she had to do was immediate, so she sat there, twiddling her thumbs, trying not to think about him. Finally, she decided to try to work out some math problems for the test that was coming up to see if she still understood what Sal had taught her.

She hadn't even been working on the problems for ten minutes when a chat box opened up.

How's the calculus coming along?

Rolling her eyes, she thought that was awfully convenient. **Did Lucca ask you to check on me to see if I was doing schoolwork?** Thinking better of it, she then asked, **Is this Lucca?**

What? No? Did something happen? Ha-ha.

Before she answered, she got up to look out the window. Lucca was already in the garden, dirty and hard at work. *Well . . . Dang.* That just killed her theory.

Going back to the computer, she reread his reply, not liking the laugh he added to the message, knowing he was most likely smiling on the other end of the computer.

Typing into the keyboard, she wanted him to know she no longer bought the innocent way he had explained the mafia. **VP, huh?**

Well, I tried to warn you a little, but you weren't hearing it.

That isn't true. **That's not true!**

I gave you the version you wanted to hear, didn't I?

Staring at the keyboard, she immediately typed in the letter "N," but she couldn't finish the word, knowing deep down he was right.

We only hear what we want to hear, and we only see what we want to see, Chloe.

Her eyes wandered to the window, her thoughts on Lucca, before she snapped her eyes back to the computer and typed, **You still lied to me, along with everyone else.**

Did Lucca lie to you?

She bit her lip, unable to lie. **No.** If anything, he was too honest.

Then what's the problem?

Um, the fact that he is crazy. The underboss. Keeping me hostage. That was just a short list, but she wasn't going to tell his best friend that. **Nothing.**

Are you sure about that? Ha-ha.

Yes!

Okay then, if you're sure.

Ugh, she must not understand guys in general, because she didn't know if that was sarcasm or not.

Tapping her fingers, she thought there was something she had been wondering since finding out about the mafia. Sal's genius intrigued her, and she wanted to know what he really did for them since she didn't think he only handled security.

What do you really do? Like, *really do?*

Patiently waiting for a response, she didn't get one until minutes later, and it wasn't what she had expected, yet should have.

I'm his right hand.

She knew exactly who he was referring to.

So, you help him get into trouble, then?

Or I help him get out of it.

There was one last question she wanted to know the answer to. She just didn't know how to ask it. After last night, the way Lucca had talked about Amo, like he was no different than him, and that Nero and Vincent weren't, either, she had to ask, **Is it possible to still be good, but also be in the mafia?**

I guess you'll have to find out.

Chloe left the computer then, going to the window and looking down at Lucca in the garden. He had that look on his face, like he cared about what he was doing, concentrating carefully on the task before him like it was the most important thing in the world. Even though she didn't want to admit it, she liked that look on him. It suited him. And every time she watched him when he had that look, she felt fully transfixed.

The more she looked at him outside, out of these walls, the more they began to bug her. *I just thought you might enjoy some fresh air. But if being in the house every day doesn't bother you, then I understand.*

She hurriedly went back to her desk. *No, no, no, no, no.*

She peeked toward the window, seeing the sun shining. *Don't do it. Don't listen to him.*

Birds started chirping while they passed her window...

Looking down, she felt nothing but defeat. *Dang it!*

THE MOST
BEAUTIFUL PRISON

The second she opened the door, Lucca's eyes met hers and the most beautiful smile touched his lips. He had stopped what he was doing, resting back on his heels and waiting for her.

With each step into the garden, the sun and wind began to pick her up, making her defeat feel less painful.

She stopped, standing a foot away from him. You would think she would have to look down on him considering he was on the ground, but she really didn't. The top of his head came to her chest. Her short stature only made her feel more inferior to him.

A helpless breath came out. "I-I changed my mind."

He just simply continued to smile. "Okay, darlin'."

The response he gave her was one she hadn't expected. She

waited for the part where he was going to say "I told you so," but it never came.

Removing his gloves, he left them in the dirt before standing up and closing the distance between them. He stood before her and held out his hands. "May I see your hands?" This wasn't a command. He was politely asking for permission.

She should have said no, turned around, and left, but that wasn't what her body did.

Raising her bandaged hands, she held out her palms to him.

Taking a final small step toward her, he slowly placed one of his hands under hers. Her hand only gave a small jump when his fingertips touched her. She found them to be very warm from wearing gloves.

She held her hand stiffly on top of his, while he used his other hand to pull back the bandage to carefully look at her palm.

Why am I letting hi—

Just like that, he put the bandage back in place before he held her other hand, repeating the process. Again, he only held her hand for a few seconds, looking it over and putting the bandage back in place before pulling his hands away from hers. He didn't linger, let alone touch her long enough for her to freak out.

Lucca went to the bucket, picking out a pair of soft gardening gloves. Then he came back over to her, stretching out the opening in the glove for her to slide her hand through easily.

She held her right hand out again, and he began slipping it on carefully over her bandage.

"I don't want you using your hands too much, so take it easy."

Nodding, she then held out her left hand.

"If they start to hurt, or even get sore, I want you to stop for me, darlin'."

"O-Okay."

"Then you can just stay out here, keeping me company, and enjoy not being in the house." Grinning down at her, he made sure the second glove was secured.

When he dropped his hand from hers, she couldn't help slightly smiling back at him. She liked how she allowed him to touch her, and how he didn't abuse it.

Lucca went back to the dirt, putting on his gloves and getting back to work.

Confusion was all she knew anymore. Never had she understood Lucca, and now she no longer understood herself. The longer she continued to be here, the more confused she got.

Working on the garden with him, she did as she was asked, being careful with her hands and not overworking them as the day went on. Sometimes she found herself just sitting there, taking in the beauty of it all. Something about the garden just fit so well around her. It brought a feeling in her that was indescribable, one she hadn't truly felt before. It was like she felt at ... *home.* She shouldn't, though. It should feel like a prison, but it didn't. And if it was, then it was the most beautiful prison she had ever seen.

In her world, places like this didn't exist, but here, for some reason it did. *I did it for you.*

Chloe's eyes drifted over to a sweaty Lucca, who was now putting the tools away. *What do you want from me?* Nothing. She had nothing to offer him. What he wanted or expected from her, she didn't know, but she did know that he was going to be let down when he found out she had nothing to offer. Chloe just hoped he would let her go in one piece when he found out.

After Lucca put all the supplies away, he sat down beside her to see his hard work come to fruition.

"What do you think, darlin'?"

"It's beautiful," she whispered.

"It'll be prettier in the spring when the flowers come back."

It didn't matter to her. She loved the way it looked in all stages. She only wished she could have seen it before his mother had died.

"C-Can I ask you a question?"

He turned toward her. "I told you, you can ask me anything, Chloe."

"What did it look like when your . . .?" She trailed off, unable to get the question out, afraid it might upset him.

"When my mother took care of it?"

She nodded.

Lucca's eyes scanned over the expanse of the huge yard. "It just looked fuller, healthier, and even seemed brighter. The majority of the flowers died off with her. I've gotten some of them to grow back, but others, I'm still trying."

She didn't doubt that one day he would get it to return to what it once was, if not better. The changes she had noticed since the first time she had seen it were drastic.

She loved hearing about his mother. It made him seem more … *human*. Looking over at him, she only wanted to hear more, hoping it would help her understand why he was the way he was.

"Will you tell me what she was like?"

"Her name was Melissa, and she had blond hair like Maria, and the greenest eyes like Nero. She was the sweetest, kindest person you could ever meet, and everyone loved her. Being home with her children and the garden was all she ever wanted or needed." His eyes turned darker and his voice became somber. "None of us deserved her, not my father, and especially not me. For her being so sweet, I can't imagine how it felt for her first child to come out a monster." He briefly paused before continuing, "But not once did she love me any less, not even when she saw me at my worst."

Chloe quietly sat there next to him, not knowing what to say to a man who thought of himself as a monster. And there weren't words to say, nor comfort she could give to help with the loss of his mother. She could tell that he had loved her, but she wasn't even sure if he knew it deep down, because he only thought of himself as without feelings.

They sat there peacefully for a while, neither one wanting to ruin what was there before them or between them. She wasn't sure how much time had passed before he spoke.

"I'm going to get cleaned up then start us some dinner. Take your time."

He was leaving her now, but she needed to tell him something before he did.

"Lucca …?"

He stopped, looking down at her to where she sat in the grass.

It was hard to look away from the ocean of flowers that swayed in the wind, reminding her of waves, to Lucca, but she wanted him to see that she meant every word.

"If she were still here, I think she would be happy with what you've done. She would love it out here, just as much as I do."

It was obvious how much he wanted to reach out and touch her in that moment, but he didn't, content enough with the words she had given him.

"I think so, too, darlin'."

Chloe continued to sit there, watching him walk away. With each step he took away from her, she couldn't help feeling the less beautiful the garden became now.

EVERYTHING CAME
AT A PRICE

When *the plate of meatballs* and spaghetti were set down in front of her, she couldn't help smiling.

Lucca noticed as he sat down beside her with his own plate. "Is this okay?"

"Yes." That was the thing. Every day he would make her dinner, and every time it was a meal she liked. However, not once had he asked her what she liked or didn't. He always strangely knew. "Spaghetti and meatballs is actually one of my favorites."

He looked pleased. "Well, good. I hope you like it."

Picking up her utensils, she took a bite of the spaghetti, knowing it was going to be good, but not as good as it tasted the second it was in her mouth. She should have known based on the sole fact that he was Italian.

"It's the best I've ever had."

"Thank you, darlin'." Cutting into a meatball, he asked, "What's your favorite meal?"

Hmm. She had to think about it for a moment. It was a hard question when you had delicious food in front of you and you weren't a picky eater to begin with. "That's hard, but I think my favorite meal would have to be chili."

He didn't seem to believe it as he made a dubious face. "Chili?"

She made her own incredulous face back at him. "What's wrong with chili?"

"I've just never heard of anyone saying their favorite food is chili. I don't think I've ever even had a good enough chili for me to like it."

Thinking about it, she never heard of anyone liking it that much, either. It seemed to be one of those things you could live without, unlike pizza or fries.

"Well, when it's the right chili, it's one of the best meals you can have."

"What do you like about it?" he asked curiously.

"I don't know really." She went deep in thought, trying to figure it out before it hit her. "It just makes me feel warm and at home, I guess ... And happy. I feel happy when I eat it. Is that weird?"

Looking at her with green eyes, he shook his head. "No, darlin'."

"I think I just like it so much because it was the only thing my mom was good at cooking." Her mother had stolen the recipe from her sister, which was the only reason it tasted good in the first place.

"I've never made it before, but I'll see if I can make it for you."

"That's okay. I don't wa—"

"No, I want to. I can't promise that it will be any good, but I want to try for you."

"Okay. T-Thank you." She smiled, going back to her food.

The rest of the meal was enjoyed in silence. It was too good to continue talking. It really was the best spaghetti she had ever eaten, even up until the last bite.

Not until the last bite was taken and Lucca got up did she realize what was next.

She nervously got up, picking up her plate. "I-I can take these to the sink and d-do the dishes for you."

"That's okay, darlin'. I don't want you to get your clean bandages dirty."

When the plate slipped away into his grasp, she felt her hope of not having to sit beside him go along with it. She had gotten used to sitting so close to him on the floor every evening, but this was going to be the first time since finding out what he did for a living. She could also feel this time was going to be different because he was starting to touch her now.

Lucca placed the dishes in the sink and went into the living room, taking his seat in the big leather chair and placing the pillow down for her beside his feet.

She hadn't moved an inch.

"Come here, Chloe," he commanded, sensing her nerves.

Her body moved like it always did at his demands, not stopping until it fulfilled what he wanted by sitting down on the pillow beside him. She sat stiffly with his widespread leg closer than usual.

"You've been fine around me all day, darlin'; why are you so nervous now?"

He's right, she told herself in shock. She had been nervous around him when she had first come downstairs, but when she had gone outside to the garden with him, she had been fine. Maybe it was the calmness of being outside, or even the calmness of him today. However, the moment it was time to sit here with him, it had all changed.

Holding her hands together, she wished she could squeeze them. "B-Because I know you've been waiting all day for this."

As Lucca reached down and picked up a strand of her hair, she felt his cold fingertips ever so lightly brush her neck, making her question if it really happened or not.

"How did you know?" he asked darkly, beginning to twirl her hair.

"I can just feel it." *In my bones.*

"Do you know why I like sitting here with you like this every night?"

She shook her head, unsure if she really wanted to hear the answer.

"It relaxes me. Calms me …" He paused, wrapping the hair tighter around his finger. "And it stills the darkness."

"The darkness …?" she whispered, feeling breathless.

"The part in me that whispers for me to do very dark things."

Turning, she looked back at the chilling man. "The part that makes you the underboss?"

Lucca nodded.

Turning away from him, not wanting to look at him when he answered, she asked, "H-How did you become the underboss?"

"My last name and my father. Only men with the Caruso name can hold the position of the boss or underboss. Me being my father's firstborn son is what solidified my position, as my father was once the underboss before he took his father's place. It's been that way for many generations."

She looked back at him, shocked by the information he had given her. "So, you will take your father's place one day?"

He ran his thumb over the dark silk, feeling its soft texture. "Yes."

She should have expected that he would, but a part of her seemed to have blocked it out, not wanting him to continue the dangerous lifestyle.

"Who will take your place as the underboss, then?" Each question she asked and each answer he gave only made more questions arise.

"It depends on when I take his place. Most likely, it will be Nero, if he wants it."

"Oh." *I wonder if Elle knows that.* "How old were you when you became the underboss?"

"My father had appointed Enzo his underboss until I was ready. He didn't carry the last name Caruso, so I took his place when I became twenty-one."

"They made you the underboss so young?"

He smiled at her obvious concern. "Well, I became a made man when I was seventeen."

"You did? You weren't even an adult." She didn't think it was possible to become even more shocked.

"Yes, you are to be of age when you become made, but I was the exception."

Chloe swallowed. "W-Why?"

"I did something that would only scare you away from me if I told you." He unraveled her hair, only to wind it around his finger again. "Maybe one day I will tell you, darlin', but not today."

Taking her eyes off him, she was more than thankful that he hadn't told her, knowing that whatever it was had to be horrific for him to be made that young.

"What do you do as the underboss?"

"I make sure the family runs smoothly, and that my men are in order, along with many other things."

She remembered then about Sal telling her he had given Nero, Amo, and Vincent their jobs.

"What job did you give Amo?" she asked.

A smile started to appear on his face. "What makes you ask that?"

"Sal told me he worked in the basement of the casino."

"Really?" he asked, still smiling. "Sal talked to you about the family?"

"Yes. Well, sort of." She looked down at her hands. "He told me you were the vice president."

Lucca threw his head back, laughing, which she didn't appreciate very much since it was at the cost of her naïveté.

"It's not that funny," she said when he didn't stop laughing.

"I'm sorry, darlin'. You're right." He got out one last small laugh before continuing, "What did Sal tell you about Amo's job?"

"Nothing really." She shrugged. "He just said that you gave Amo, Nero, and Vincent a job in the basement, but said that Nero and Vincent wanted to be transferred out for some reason. Sal did specifically tell me to tell you that Amo loves his job, and even Maria said he loves it."

The smile on his face had yet to disappear while he kept spinning her hair. "They did, huh?"

"Yes." *What is going on?* Something told her she might not want to hear exactly what Amo did.

"Well, the basement is actually an underground casino. They are kind of like bouncers."

She looked at him strangely. "An underground casino below a casino?"

Lucca winked. "Exactly."

An illegal casino covered by a legit one? The more she thought about it, the more it made sense, yet also only confused her more.

She gave up trying to understand it. She still felt like she was missing something, though.

"What do the bouncers do exactly?"

"They watch the floor, looking out for any customers who may not be following the rules and also making sure that the customers, along with the workers, are safe at all times."

"Oh, that sounds kinda nice." *They make sure everyone's safe.* "Why do Nero and Vincent hate it then?"

"You would have to ask them. I put a lot of thought into giving them that position, and I thought they would all love it, not just

Amo." He thought about it for a second. "Well, Vincent did love it there for a while … Maybe one day, I'll show you down there and you can find out for yourself."

Chloe stared at him for a second, thinking he looked awfully innocent, but she didn't know why.

"You won't give Nero and Vincent a new job?"

His innocent act quickly changed to a sinister one. "I can, but that doesn't mean I want to, or that I will. They need to work up from the bottom like everyone else."

She could understand that they were new to the family and shouldn't get special treatment. *At least Amo's happy.*

Her mind instantly drifted to sad thoughts of being locked up here without her friends.

Sitting back up against the couch, she sat stiffly again without realizing she had loosened up or the fact his dark jeans had been touching her arm, which she suddenly moved.

A scent of strong, clean mint touched her nose. It was so fresh and cool, almost tingly. Taking a deeper breath made her recognize the scent was him.

Never before had she noticed his smell until now. She should still smell her own floral scent since they both had taken a shower after gardening, but it had faded and now the only scent that kept surrounding her was Lucca.

Lucca rubbed the hair he held. "What's wrong, darlin'?"

Clasping her hands together, she wished she could wring them, but she was unable to with the bandages. Not wanting to tell him she liked the way he smelled and that it made her feel uncomfortable, she nervously gave him half the truth.

"I-I miss them."

He went silent but continued to twirl her hair. Then his voice finally reached her ears. "Do you want to talk to her?"

Turning, she looked at him, more surprised by this than by anything else he had said all night.

"Elle? You'll let me talk to her?"

She knew before the next few words were passed his lips that it was too good to be true. *Everything* came at a price.

"Yes, darlin' . . . But you will have to give me something in return."

HOVERING HIS FINGERTIPS OVER THE TOP OF THE SCAR

"W-*What do you want?" she* whispered, wishing she hadn't asked. "You will have to let me touch you …" Letting go of the strand he held, he leaned over. Then he raised his hand to the scar on her face, tracing it as he hovered his fingers from inches away. "Here."

Her racing heart thumped through her ears. "If I-I say yes, y-you'll let me talk to Elle?"

Leaning back in the chair, he removed the hand that was dangerously close to her face. "Yes, but only for a few minutes, darlin'."

"W-Why are you letting me?" It was too hard to believe, even if he was getting something out of it. Lucca had proved up until this point that *whatever he wants, he takes.*

"I have pushed her off long enough by texting, and she's now demanding a phone call. It's to the point she will know something is wrong if I don't let you talk to her."

"I-I'll do it." *Maybe I'll be able to warn her.*

It was like he could sense exactly what she thought as his eyes went dark. "I'll be right here listening, so you won't be able to try anything, Chloe. You *have* to make her believe you're in California. Do you understand?"

You have to make her believe you're in California. She understood exactly what that meant, knowing Lucca wouldn't be above hurting Elle. "Y-Yes."

His eyes changed back, softening now. "If you can do that, I'll let you talk to her every once in a while."

"Really?" She couldn't help feeling an ounce of hope.

"If it will make you happy"—he ran his fingers down a strand of her silky hair—"then yes, darlin'."

Giving him a smile, she couldn't believe how she was getting used to him touching her hair in the little time she had been here. Chloe was trusting him, even when he got extremely close to her skin.

Pulling out her phone from his pocket, he pulled up Elle's contact. "Ready?"

No!

She somehow managed to nod, silently hoping she could pull this off.

Lucca handed over the phone to her after dialing.

Holding her cell phone that she hadn't touched in weeks up to her ear felt almost foreign. She listened to the ringing, waiting for Elle to pick up while taking deep breaths, trying to calm herself. Finally, the phone was answered on one of the last possible rings with a sweet and happy voice she hadn't heard in far too long.

"Hello!"

She felt ghost tears wanting to fall from her eyes. It was indescribable how happy she was.

"Chloe …?" The excitement in Elle's voice started to fade.

Chloe was too afraid to speak; afraid her voice would betray her and alarm Elle.

She felt her hair move and looked over to see Lucca twirling a strand. Staring and feeling the repetitive motion begin to soothe her, she calmed enough to speak.

"Hey, Elle."

"I'm so happy you called me, Chloe. I've missed you so much." Elle was now getting emotional on the other end.

Focusing on his hand twirling her hair, she kept it together. "I know. I've missed you, too. I still do."

Elle sniffled before laughing it off. "How are you? How's school? Tell me everything!"

"It's going okay," she told her, not wanting to oversell it. "It's just different, I guess, and you're not here with me, but I'm doing good. School is keeping me pretty busy."

"Is everyone treating you nicely?" Elle asked. It was what she was obviously worried about the most.

Chloe pulled her eyes up to Lucca's face. "Yes, no one is picking on me or calling me a freak here."

"Oh, thank God." A weight seemed to lift off her friend. "I was so worried about that."

"Now it's your turn to tell me everything. How's college?"

Chloe listened to Elle tell her everything she had missed and what college life was like for her. She expected Lucca to take the phone away, as he had said only a few minutes, but he didn't, seeming content with listening to her voice and playing with her hair. Strangely, she found it kind of nice.

"How's California? Is the weather as nice as it seems?" Elle asked after she caught her up on all her life events.

"Yeah, it's … um … sunny. The weather is great." *I hope.* Not wanting to push her luck for much longer, she decided it was time to wrap it up. "Well, I have an early morning tomorrow—"

"Aren't you three hours behind? It's not that late there, I don't think." Elle sounded like she was checking the clock on her phone to see what time it was.

Quickly, she tried to think. "Uh … yeah, but I have an assignment to still finish."

"Oh. Okay. I understand."

"I've really missed you, Elle. It was good to hear your voice again."

"Me, too. Thank you for calling me. I've worried about you so much." The emotions seemed to come back to her friend.

Chloe bit her lip. "Don't worry about me. I'm doing good."

"Promise?"

Pausing, she found it again hard to answer, until Lucca lightly tugged on her strand of hair. "Promise."

"Okay, I'll let you get your work done now. Bye, Chloe." It was obvious how hard it was for her best friend to say good-bye, and she found it equally as hard.

"Bye, Elle."

She pulled the phone away from her ear and ended the call. It really sucked having to give it back to Lucca, but she was grateful for the time he had given her.

Blue-green eyes slowly started to travel down her scar, making her remember that a debt was to be paid.

"Come closer, darlin'," Lucca's voice was dark and melodic.

Her breath caught in her throat as she watched him widen his legs, giving her room to move between them.

Following the voice, she did as he commanded, knowing exactly how he wanted her positioned by instinct alone. Chloe was on her knees now, in front of him, as close to his legs as she could get without touching them. Closing her eyes, her lashes fell to her cheeks, waiting . . .

Lucca moved his hand, hovering his fingertips over the top of the scar that graced the right side of her face. When the cold, light fingertips touched the top of her scar, she went deathly still.

No one had ever touched her scars. Never had she let anyone touch something that was so personal to her. Now, here she was, letting the most dangerous and frightening man she had ever met touch something that had been given to her by a man just like him.

He ran his fingers ever so gently down her scar that ran from just above her eyebrow until it disappeared right below it. Then he ran it even gentler over her closed eyelid, making it feel as if it was just the wind touching her. When he reached the continuation of her scar right under her lower lashes, he paused.

"Look at me, Chloe."

Opening her eyes, she looked into his blue-green ones that were gradually beginning to look more green, transfixing her, along with his voice, his presence, his icy yet soft touch.

"I've waited for this very moment." Moving his fingertips, he began again slowly smoothing down her scar. "Dreamed about this moment for the longest eight months of my life. Ever since I first saw you in that shop, looking at the music box."

"W-We first met in the gazebo …" Her voice trailed off.

"I had been watching you for a week before that, darlin'." He continued gliding his fingertips up and down her scar. "I was watching Elle's house when a black BMW dropped her off from school. I had this strong, instinctual feeling to follow, and even though I didn't understand it at the time, I listened to my gut. I still hadn't seen your face before I followed you into the shop, but then, when you turned around and I saw your beautiful face, it was like the world stood still. That was when I knew"—Lucca cupped her face, using his thumb to smooth over her scar—"that you were mine."

Chloe's mind raced with her heart, trying to comprehend everything he had just told her.

"It was everything I could do not to take you then and there," he confessed.

But you didn't, not until several months later … That only made her mind and heart race more.

"Y-You said y-you took me to save me."

"I did."

She could feel it then. Something she had been missing fell into place as Drago's words flew through her mind, *We both know what being a real prisoner feels like, Chloe.* Then Maria's, *Are you sure you're being held hostage?* And, *It's not what you think. You're here for a reason, Chloe.*

"Why am I here?" she whispered. "Tell me why I'm really here."

Still caressing her scar, he shook his head. "I can't tell you, darlin', not yet."

"You told me I can ask you anything. I need to know why I'm her—"

"You can, and I will answer anything and everything you want to know, but not this. Not until the time is right." He pressed his hand deeper into her skin. "I need you to trust me, Chloe. Will you do that for me?"

A sudden feeling came over her as she stared into his intense eyes. She couldn't understand it. She only knew she believed in it, trusted in it. It was … *instinctual.*

"Y-Yes."

"You feel it, too, don't you?" He didn't need the answer, because the feeling was shared between them, like a bond.

The feeling had been there since meeting Lucca, just how it had been for him when he had first seen her. She had subconsciously pushed away the intense feeling because it frightened her, yet it only grew stronger the more she was around him.

He smiled. "It took me a week to understand it, darlin'. Let's see how long it takes you."

"I-I met you in the gazebo a week later … You bought the music box a week later."

Lucca nodded.

She was unsure if she ever wanted to know what the feeling meant, more frightened of it now that she knew he felt it, too.

Taking one final swipe across her scar, he released her.

The loss was evident, not only on his face, but in his voice. "You may go to bed now, darlin'."

Chloe stood from her knees, still in shock of what had taken place. "G-Good night, Lucca."

"Good night, Chloe."

The shock never left her body as she left him behind and went upstairs.

In her room, she opened the music box and listened to the beautiful tune, feeling her heart grow heavier, heavier, heavier, while the chains he placed on her body grew lighter, lighter, lighter.

She reached up, touching her scar. The loss wasn't only felt by Lucca, but by her, too.

HIS DREAMS OF FULFILLING HIS DARKEST NEED WOULD HAVE TO SUFFICE

laying back everything that had just occurred in his mind, he recalled her voice, her face, her scar. It was like he could still feel her on his fingertips. They had just left her face, and already he couldn't wait until the next time he could touch her.

It was the most erotic thing he had ever experienced, and he had only touched her face.

Lucca only hoped he would be able to control his darkness when he finally allowed himself to take more from her. Some time would have to pass before he did, though. Not only was Chloe not ready, but neither was he. He couldn't trust the darkness with her yet.

Until then, his dreams of fulfilling his darkest need would have to suffice.

Lucca felt like he had made up for yesterday, and then some. When he had started the day, he had felt like he had only gone backward. Now he felt like he had taken ten steps forward.

She had to face the feeling she was running from. And even though she still didn't understand it, it was only a matter of time before she would. It would click, *just how it did for me . . .*

Taking one last look at the scar on her face, he couldn't wait for the day he could run his fingers across it. Beautiful.

Watching her car pull away from the shop then disappear, he went back to the music box she had been looking at. It had been obvious that it meant a great deal to her.

He carefully opened it, allowing the lullaby to play once more.

The older woman came to stand beside him. "I just had a girl in here looking at——"

"I would like to purchase it." The words came out of their own accord, knowing he had to be the one to have it.

"I'm sorry, but I have to decline. The girl who was just looking at it seems to really want it, so I'm reserving it for her."

He closed the music box, silencing the room. "You're going to turn down money today, even though she may not come back?"

"For her, yes. Try back in a couple of weeks, and if she hasn't taken it, I'll see if I'm ready to part with it."

Lucca nodded understandingly. He respected the woman for doing that. He would have demanded it otherwise, if he hadn't seen how much the girl had fallen in love with it.

Deciding to leave, he figured if he was meant to have it, it would still be there when or if he came back . . .

The shop was five minutes from closing when he came back a week later.

Wasting no time, he went right to where the music box sat, finding it still there, like it had been untouched.

The woman noticed him immediately and began shaking her head. "I'm sorry, but it's only been a week."

Pulling out his wallet, he laid down three thousand dollars in cash.

She only shook her head again.

For the past week, he had only thought about the look on Chloe's face when she had been looking at the piece while it played the lullaby. That was exactly how he hoped she would look at him one day.

He had met her tonight, and even though she hadn't looked at him like that, he knew deep down that one day she would.

Lucca sat down another thousand. "This is as high as I'm willing to go."

She seemed to contemplate it for a second, but only a second. "I'm sorry, sir, but it's not about the money."

"I'm not leaving here without it," he told her with certainty, the strong feelings he felt finally making sense. "This means something very special to the girl . . . I love, and I have to be the one to give it to her."

ONLY TIME WILL TELL

Only time will tell,
    How a month spent with the boogieman,
    Locked away from the outside world,
Will go.

Only time will tell,
How a month spent with the broken girl he loves,
That he has all to himself,
Will go.

Only time will tell,
How unbearable it can get,
How blissful it can be,
Or anywhere in between.

Only time will tell,

When the month comes to an end,

If it's worth repeating for her,

And if it's everything he thought it

Would be.

I'M COMING, CHLOE

A month had passed in these walls, and what had felt like a prison now felt like a haven. For years, Chloe had woken up every morning afraid of what the day would bring at school and even at home. She had been tortured day in and day out by horrendous people who only ever made her feel like a freak. Yet, the monster who was keeping her here never harmed her and had only made her feel less like a freak every day.

Chloe continued spending her days doing her online classes, and her nights with Lucca. It was nice, calming, even safe here with him, and she trusted him since finding out she wasn't brought here just because he wanted it so.

There was a reason for her being here, something that had been made obvious by the select few who knew she was here, along with the feeling in her gut. Therefore, she would stay until she upheld her side of the deal with the boogieman. The problem was, when it came to an end, would she be able to walk away? Not even she knew.

She had grown used to many things, but the scariest one of all ...

Lucca grabbed her by the wrist, stopping her from leaving the kitchen. "I want you to try something."

Every day he touched her more and more, and she was getting used to it more and more. His goal of helping her overcome her fear of touch was working.

In the beginning, he had always asked permission or warned her of his incoming contact, but as the month progressed, every now and then he would touch her without warning. It scared her shitless at first, yet the more he did it, the better she recognized and committed his touch to memory. There was still a split second of terror, but then she would realize it was Lucca and her fear would subside.

The hand circling her wrist grew firm, reminding her it was only him.

"W-What is it?"

Leading her over to the stove, he then released her to open a pot. He dipped a spoon into the mixture then brought it to his lips, cooling the hot contents with a gentle blow.

"You made me chili?" she asked, surprised by the kind gesture.

"Don't get too excited. I found the recipe online, and I'm not sure how good it will turn out."

"It smells good." She was warmer already by the smell alone.

When Lucca moved the spoon to her lips, she let him feed her. The chili was warm, but ...

Reading her expression, he asked, "Bad, huh?"

Yep. "N-No, it's um … different."

Putting the spoon back into the pot, he dipped out some more chili then took a bite himself. Immediately, he made a face.

"That's fucking disgusting."

Chloe started giggling.

Smiling down at her, he laughed with her. "What did I tell you about lying to me, darlin'?"

"I'm sorry. I just didn't want to hurt your feelings. It's okay," she tried to console him. "You can't be a master chef all the time."

"Well, it's good I made this for backup then." Opening the oven, he showed her an incredible-looking homemade, chef-style pizza.

"Are you serious!"

Everything he ever cooked was beyond perfect and delicious. Well, besides the chili. That was made up for, though, by the pizza that looked worthy of a million-dollar chef.

Gardener, master chef, handsome … He's almost perfect. Almost.

"Sorry, darlin'." He winked. "It'll be done in just a bit."

Chloe playfully rolled her eyes before going to sit down at the kitchen island.

The phone in his pocket began ringing, and he pulled it out of his pocket. When he saw who it was, he handed it to her.

Smiling, she took the phone and answered, "Hey, Elle!"

"Hey, Chloe. How was your day?"

They continued to talk, telling each other about their day like they usually did.

Lucca had been letting her talk to Elle every night, putting just as much trust in her as she did him. It was a good trade off and helped make her feel more comfortable and less cut off from the outside world.

Her beautiful prison was beginning to feel more and more like … home.

Amo was at Nero and Elle's place to see if they had made any dinner. It was becoming a habit to come over when he got desperate for food, having nothing at his place since he hadn't been to the store in a while. He would play up just coming over to talk to Nero, and then, without fail, Elle would ask him if he wanted anything to eat. Amo was beginning to think that Nero was catching on, though.

When Nero had invited him in, Elle was talking on the phone. It didn't take him long to figure out who she was talking to and begin eavesdropping.

He never thought Chloe would ignore him for this long. Not once since leaving had she sent him a message, let alone called him.

It doesn't make any sense. Chloe wasn't the type of girl to hold a grudge. She had proven that when he found out she had known it was him who had called her a freak.

A strange feeling had settled over him after she left, and it only grew stronger the longer she went without contacting him. He didn't know what it was exactly—the answer just out of reach—but he would figure it out.

"It's getting pretty cold here," Elle was telling Chloe. Then her face started to change, a concerning look coming over her face as she listened to Chloe's reply. "It is?" She paused, listening to the other end, now looking confused. Then she hurriedly said, "Oh, okay then. Talk to you later. By—" When she pulled the phone away from her ear, she stared at it strangely. "That was weird."

Amo took a step toward Elle, uncaring if she knew he had been eavesdropping, every alarm in him going off. "What is it?"

"I thought California was flooding from all the rain?"

It had been all over the news that California was getting massive amounts of rain. He had even worried about Chloe being in it and had checked to see how much rain she was getting at Stanford.

"Yeah . . .?" Amo took another step toward her.

Elle's eyebrows came together, still staring at the phone in utter confusion. "She said it was sunny and pretty."

The wheels began to turn. "That doesn't make any sense."

"She probably just didn't want you to worry," Nero pointed out.

He looked over at Nero, who didn't seem worried, then back at Elle. "Did she say anything else?"

"No, she just said she needed to go because dinner was done."

Amo and Elle clearly had the same thought. *Chloe can't cook.* She had a housekeeper back home, Lana, who had made her every meal since her father had become mayor.

"I need to go." He could almost touch the answer now.

"Elle is about to make some dinner; you sure you don't want to stay?" Nero asked, stopping him.

Amo didn't even answer his friend as he flung the door open and left. Picking up his feet faster and faster, he started running, the pieces falling into place around him.

I'm coming, Chloe. I'm coming to save you.

He just hoped he wasn't too late.

THE DEATH OF AMO

Chloe *was sitting on the* floor next to Lucca like she did every night, with his dark jeaned leg touching her arm—another thing she had grown used to over the course of a month. The activity that had started out with watching TV was now their talking time. She enjoyed listening to him talk mostly about his mother and family. His work, they would only talk about every now and then. Admittedly, the mafia fascinated her. *A little.*

They were talking about future plans for the garden when Drago came rushing into the room with a frightened look on his face. "Get her upstairs. Someone's here."

Lucca quickly stood from the chair, but stunned, it wasn't until Lucca grabbed Chloe's hand that she was able to move and get up.

The air around her seemed to change then, like she could almost feel the person was here for her. *Who's here?*

Holding her hand, Lucca led her to the foyer and toward the stairs.

"W-Who is i-it?" she managed to get out.

"It doesn't matter. I need you to go to your room and lock the door," Lucca told her with urgency as Drago went to the front door and looked out the peephole.

"P-Please tell me who it is." She felt herself dragging her feet, trying to slow Lucca down.

"You got about thirty seconds to get her the fuck out of here," Drago announced.

Lucca swooped her up, cradling her to his chest as he easily scaled the steps two at a time.

She found herself wrapping her arms around his neck and slamming her eyes shut by how quickly he ran up the stairs with her, afraid he might drop her. He never even came to close to it, though. His build and strength effortlessly got him to the top of the stairs. It was the first time she realized how strong and fit he actually was, feeling it in the arms that held her.

Chloe thought he would set her down when he reached the second floor, but he didn't. He continued to hold her as he headed to her room. It all kind of seemed like a blur, until he kicked her door open ...

Drago opened the door the second Amo stepped up to it. He was surprised, not expecting Drago to be on the other side.

Amo tried his best to look past the only other man who was bigger than him in the family. Drago only beat him because of his age, spending years upon years at the gym, making his muscles have muscles.

"I need to speak with Lucca," he said when Drago didn't move to let him in.

"He's not he—"

A loud thud rang out that sounded like a door being thrown open.

"Yes, he is." Amo shouldered past the big man.

Inside, his eyes followed up the staircase to the hallway the noise had come from. Adrenaline started pumping throughout his body. He could practically smell the tension in the room, his fear of being right coming true.

"Go wait in his office," Drago said, closing the door.

"By all means, lead the way." Amo motioned for him to go first.

Looking at him for a split second, Drago looked him up and down before walking toward the living room to take him to the office.

Amo slowly stepped toward the stairs as he watched Drago's back progress farther and farther away from him. When he knew he could get enough of a head start, he dashed up the stairs with everything he had.

I'm here, Chloe!

"Lucca, please tell me who it is," she begged as he carried her into the room.

"Drago didn't say, and it doesn't matter." He placed her carefully on the bed then lightly grabbed her by the neck, forcing her to look directly into his eyes. "You're my only concern, Chloe. No one can know you're here."

The hand he had placed around her throat was an act of possession, an act that should have terrified her, yet it didn't. And his words had been said with such force that she knew her life depended on it.

That was the only thing that terrified her—the reason she had to be in hiding.

Understanding, she nervously nodded.

A look crossed his features when he released her, one she had never seen on him before. It was a look of ... *pain*, so raw and real that it took her breath away.

Suddenly, they heard a commotion coming up the stairs, followed by an even bigger one.

"Stay here," he whispered before shutting the door behind him.

"Where the fuck is she!" a familiar voice boomed through the walls.

Her hair stood up as she jumped off the bed. *Amo!*

"What the hell do you think you're doing?" Lucca hissed at him from the other side of the door.

"Chloe!" Amo yelled even louder. "I know she's here, you fucker."

She moved to the door, hearing Lucca's voice become deadly as he said, "What did you just fucking call me?"

She slowly reached out to the doorknob. *He'll kill him. Lucca will kill Amo if I don't do something.*

Amo's voice was now on the other side of the door, clearly standing in front of Lucca. "You heard m——"

Chloe threw open the door, knowing if she let him finish that sentence, she would be hearing the death of Amo next.

Amo, who had gone toe-to-toe with Lucca, had a moment of complete and utter shock upon seeing the girl he had confessed his love to before his eyes slowly moved back to Lucca, pure rage seeping through his features.

He took a step toward him. "You motherfu——"

Lucca placed a strong hand on his chest, stopping him from coming any closer. "You need to get yourself under control." His voice still carried the same deadly tone.

Drago, who had followed behind Amo and had been letting Lucca handle him, stepped forward, getting in arm's distance of Amo.

Amo looked between the two men closing in on him, then to Chloe, who was staring in horror, squeezing her fists. He could see that Drago and Lucca wanted him calm for Chloe's sake. If she hadn't been here, though, he knew he would most likely be knocked the hell out by now.

"Are you okay? Has he hurt you?" He spoke directly to her, looking past Lucca.

Lucca swiftly moved, having reached his limit, and slammed Amo up against the wall on the other side of the hall. He held him by his throat, digging his arm into Amo's neck. "You know more than anyone that I would never fucking hurt her," Lucca told him in a deadly tone.

Chloe's short nails tried their best to dig deeper than they already were into her palms, scared out of her mind that instead of hearing Amo's death, she would now witness it with her own eyes.

Do something! That new voice she had only heard a couple of times rang through her head, giving her enough strength to muster up some words.

"L-Lucca, p-please."

He didn't move his arm from Amo's throat, the darkness in him getting closer and closer to the surface.

She tried again in hopes to calm the darkness. "L-Let him go ... f-for me."

At that, Lucca lessened his hold, warning him, "You touch her, I'll rip your goddamn throat out."

Each word had been spoken with a lethalness she had never heard from Lucca before.

When Amo nodded, Lucca released him. Then, letting him walk past, he stood by as Amo slowly stepped toward her where she still stood inside her bedroom.

She started backing up when Amo reached the doorframe.

"Chloe ..." He paused. "I've ... I've missed you."

She couldn't help looking at Lucca, who stood behind him, waiting to hear what she had to say just as much as Amo. Then her eyes drifted to her wringing hands. "I-I've missed you, too," she confessed.

Amo closed the distance between them. "I've called you so many times, and you never call me back."

Chloe wasn't sure what she could or couldn't tell him, so she gave him a half-truth. "I wanted to, but I didn't know what to say."

It was obvious how much he wanted to touch her when he said, "I've been so worried about you. I knew something wasn't right, and I'm sorry I didn't figure it out sooner. I'm so sorry, Chloe."

Biting her lip, she wrung her hands even tighter. She had waited for him to save her in the beginning, but now . . . now he was too late.

He held out his hand to her. "Come with me, Chloe. I'll get you out of here."

She shook her head. *Please go. I don't want to break your heart again.* She wasn't sure she would be able to handle it a second time.

"Why?" He took another step toward her, making her back up because of his closeness.

"I-I just can't," she whispered.

"Yes, you can, Chloe." Amo continued looking down at the girl who was now hiding her face under her veil of hair. Her not agreeing to come with him was making him more furious, shaking with rage and the force it took to control it. "What is he doing to you? What has he done?"

She looked up at him, wanting him to know that Lucca wasn't hurting her. "Nothi—"

"I know he's done something!" Amo's anger was full-blown. Unable to face the truth that she would want to stay with Lucca, he grabbed her. "I'm getting you the fuck out of—"

She instantly tried to jerk away, his foreign touch feeling like a sting, unwanted.

He took his hand off her the second he realized what he had

done. "I'm sorr—"

Lucca didn't even let him finish before he had stepped in front of Chloe and pushed him halfway across the room. "I told you what would happen if you fucking touched her."

Somehow, Lucca was even more lethal than he was before. The darkness had fully reached the surface now as he stalked Amo. Chloe was sure he would kill him. He had promised he would, and Lucca kept his promises. She either had to watch her friend die, or she had to try to talk the darkness in him down. Both scared her just as equally, but only one would end in death.

She feared the other would seal her fate forever.

Chloe began begging, "P-Please, don't do it. Don't hurt him." Closing her eyes, she reached out, touching his arm. "Please, Lucca, don't hurt him."

Lucca stopped stalking him, but his heavy breathing, along with the heat that came from his body, showed her he hadn't been persuaded yet not to rip his throat out. Therefore, she wrapped her hand around his strong arm as she brought herself closer to him, touching her body to his. She held on to him as hard as she could, hoping he wouldn't move, afraid that the slightest movement would end in Amo's death.

Finally opening her eyes, she saw Amo's face from behind Lucca's arm and regretted ever opening them.

Chloe had done it again, except much worse. Now she had completely shattered his heart.

"Take him to my office," Lucca directed toward Drago. cutting his fierce eyes deeply into the man before him.

Stepping inside the room, Drago grabbed Amo roughly by the arm.

Chloe closed her eyes again, hiding behind Lucca, unable to look at how heartbroken Amo was any longer. She tried to melt into Lucca in hopes of disappearing.

She might have saved his life for now, but it sure felt like she had killed him, anyway.

I'm so sorry, Amo.

Amo had to look away from the girl he loved, unable to stand the fact she was touching another man. He had only touched her once before today, when she had run into his arms. Now she couldn't wait for him to let go of her; couldn't stand the feel of his touch. She had been completely repulsed, jerking away from him as if he had hurt her, as if he was a monster, *as if I was holding her captive.*

However, that didn't happen when she had touched Lucca.

He could feel her slipping through his fingers.

Amo had always thought himself one step ahead of Lucca by becoming friends with her, hiding the family and the things that made him a soldier, only ever showing her the good in him. He even had the one-up of being closer to her in age and protecting her at school. Now, he was sure Lucca had always been a step ahead of him.

Drago pushed him, making him walk faster down the stairs.

"This is fucked up what he's doing; what you're doing to her,"

Amo spat to the man behind him.

Drago pushed him again. "Shut the fuck up. You don't even know what you're talking about, kid."

"I know there is no fucking way she agreed to come here. She's afraid of him."

"Did she look afraid of him to you?" Drago questioned.

Silence was his answer.

"To me, she looked afraid of you ... when you touched her."

Amo stopped walking. His jaw flexing.

"Don't be a dumbass. I'll kick your ass, and that girl won't be able to stop me." He shoved Amo's shoulder to get him to start walking again.

"I'm going to kill him," Amo said under his breath.

Drago quickly pushed him into the office, closing the door behind him. "You are a fucking dumbass for even thinking those words, let alone having them come out of your fucking mouth," he told Amo with a look of warning.

"What, you going to tell him? Is Lucca your family no—"

Drago grabbed him by his jacket. "Get your shit together. Then maybe, by the time he gets down here, he'll spare you your fucking life."

Amo spat in his face. "He's a fucked-up piece of shit who should be nowhere near her. He took away the girl I love, and you're crazy if you think I'm leaving here without her."

Letting him go, Drago laughed in his face. "You better pray to God that girl is doing everything she can up there to save your ass."

Fucker! The thought of Chloe up there, touching Lucca, sent him in a rage.

Amo went to punch Drago, but he grabbed Amo's fist, squeezing it so tightly that Amo could feel his bones starting to bend.

"You fucked up by touching her. Touch her again, and he will kill you. Chloe is his. Get that through your fucking skull before you get yourself killed." When Drago heard something snap, he released him.

Amo held his broken hand to his chest. "I see how it is. The *family* over family. I guess Lucca is your blood now."

"You don't get it, do you? You think he's done all this just to steal away your high school crush?" Drago started to leave, opening the door, but then paused and looked back. "He's the underboss; you are a soldier. Learn your fucking place."

Amo wanted the last words before Drago could close the door. "Thanks for the advice, Uncle."

A NIGHTMARE THAT WILL HAVE YOU BEGGING ME NOT TO WAKE YOU UP

Even after *Drago closed the* door behind them, Chloe continued holding on to Lucca, not wanting him to change his mind and go after Amo. Her heart thumped out of her chest now that she was alone with him. She had no idea what to expect from him as he continued to remain still. All she knew was that he was still. *Too still.*

The heat from his body began to warm hers. It was like she could feel the darkness boiling inside. Like a bottle that had been shaken too many times and was about to burst. Somehow, in some way, she was going to have to try to contain it to keep her friend alive. Unfortunately, she knew that was going to come at a price.

Lucca suddenly moved, turning around and grabbing her, then pushing her up against the wall of her room. It made Chloe gasp at how quickly he had turned the tables. Now all that heat and darkness were directed at her.

He pinned her with his body, keeping her caged in. Both hands firmly gripped her hips as he leaned forward, resting his head in the crook of her neck and taking deep breaths.

She stood there stiffly, too afraid to move. She wasn't afraid for herself, though, knowing by now Lucca would never hurt her. Not even the darkness would.

"W-What are y-you going to do with him?" she managed to get out.

"He touched you. I told you what I would do if anyone ever laid a hand on you," Lucca spoke with finality.

"H-He won't do it again. I-I won't let him get close enough to, if that's what it takes."

"Baby, I'm not ever letting anyone get that close to you again." He removed a hand from her hip and gently grabbed the wrist that had been touched by another man, lifting it up to eye level. "Did he hurt you?"

She knew her reaction to Amo touching her made it seem like he had, and in a way, he did, but it hadn't physically hurt her. It was only mentally. "N-No, it just felt … strange."

"How so?"

She stared at his thumb as he rubbed it back and forth over her wrist. *Why doesn't it feel this way with him?* "Like it felt wrong."

He brought the inside of her wrist up to his lips, his cool breath hitting a sensitive area. "Good."

Chloe bit her lip hard, knowing exactly what he was about to do, and when his lips touched her skin with a kiss, her heart stuttered from his tenderness. It was like he was trying to replace the touch that wasn't his, washing away any trace of another man. She had expected it, prepared for it to sting, never before having a man's lips touch her, but that wasn't what happened.

Her mind had repelled Amo's touch, only to accept Lucca's. It shouldn't have accepted either's, since her mind had belonged to the devil for years.

However, when he placed another kiss on her wrist, she could feel that the old chains that had ahold of her mind were actually weak and broken. It was only a matter of time before her mind would finally be freed from the devil.

With the hand that was inches from his lips, she reached out, lightly touching his hauntingly beautiful face, caressing. "W-Will you let him go for me?"

Letting go of her wrist, he returned it to her hip. "He saw you, darlin'. He knows you're here now. If I let him go, it'll put your life at risk, more than he already has by coming here."

Continuing to touch him in hopes it would help Amo escape death, she trailed her fingers down to his beard, the rough texture tingling her fingertips. "Maria came here; you let her know I was here."

"That was strategic. Maria also knows I'd kill her if anyone found out you are here because of her." He moved his head to press deeper into her touch.

"Amo won't tell anyone if it could get me hurt. You know he

won't. Please, just let him go."

"Why should I?" Lucca's eyes and voice became dark, letting her know she wasn't going to like what was going to be said next. "What do I get out of it?"

Chloe's hand fell from his face, her heavy chest becoming heavier, making it even harder to breathe. "W-What do you want?"

Lucca leaned down, bringing his lips to her ear and sending shivers down her spine. Then he whispered, "The things I want from you, darlin', will give you nightmares, ones like you've never had before. A nightmare that will have you begging me not to wake you up."

Even though his breath was cold and she shivered with each word he spoke, her body betrayed her as it began to burn, making it feel as if she had frostbite. *If I say it, there's no turning back.*

"I … I'll do anything you want."

His cold breath whipped at her skin again. "Prove it."

"H-How?"

Raising up to his full height, he stared down at her, moving one hand up the back of her body to her hair where he grabbed a fistful, forcing her to look up at him. "Let me kiss you."

The little part in her mind that was still chained by the devil screamed at her not to do it, knowing that if she agreed, her mind would be free of him. She also knew that new chains would take their place, claiming her once again. Her mind would belong to the boogieman.

Chloe nervously licked her lips before she nodded, succumbing to him.

Both the hand on her hip and in her hair tightened as he positioned her just the way he wanted her before he leaned down, claiming her luscious bottom lip between his.

Her eyes slammed shut the second his lips touched hers. She kept perfectly still. The only thing moving was her heart as it attempted to beat out of her chest.

"Kiss me back," he growled hungrily.

Chloe gasped. He seemed like he had been starved of any affection for years.

When he took her bottom lip between his teeth and bit down, a noise escaped her throat. It wasn't a sound of pain, but pleasure, scaring her to her core.

She moved her hand to his chest to try to put some distance between them, but when her palm landed over his heart, she could feel it beating fast and strong. The rhythm matched hers, as if their hearts beat as one.

Instead of pushing him away, she found herself moving her mouth with his, lightly kissing him back, wanting to satiate the part in him that clearly needed her; the darkest parts in him that had been starved. It ignited a small fire deep down inside of her that had been hidden.

The devil's chains keeping her mind captive began to melt away by the small fire Lucca had ignited, and Chloe's mind found freedom for the smallest fraction of time, before brand-new chains claimed her mind as his.

The boogieman had successfully claimed her body and mind.

Now her soul was the only thing left to steal from the devil. Her soul, however, wasn't going to be taken as easily.

Swiping his tongue over her lip, he suddenly pulled away. His heavy breathing was just as harsh as hers, revealing it had been hard for him to pull away, and his voice was strained when he told her, "If I don't stop now, I'll take you right here."

She froze, knowing exactly what he meant, as his hardness that was pushed against her belly was now evident. "I-I c-can't."

He calmed himself, taking deep breaths. "I know, baby. That's why I stopped."

Trusting that he wouldn't, she relaxed into him again.

She could feel the darkness seeping deeper and deeper, going back to its home inside Lucca. The darkness had been calmed *for now.*

Looking up into his intense blue-green eyes, she hoped what she had given up had been worth it. "Promise me you won't hurt Amo, and that you will let him go."

Lucca moved the hand that was in her hair to her throat, lightly gripping her fragile neck. "Say that you're mine, darlin'. I want to hear you say the words and mean it."

It wasn't the dark voice that commanded her. He wanted her to say the words herself.

"I am yours," Chloe whispered, giving herself fully over to him ... *forever.*

He leaned down one final time, again taking her bottom lip between his teeth and biting down before pulling back and releasing it. "I hope you know what you just did," he whispered sinfully before he released her, removing his hand from her throat.

The chains that now captured her mind tightened. *I know.*

Walking away from her, he had another request. "Pack up all your things."

"W-Why?" she asked in confusion.

"You'll see." The way he said it made her think she didn't want to find out, but she was more worried about someone else.

"S-So you won't hurt him?"

He smiled. "Pack up your things, darlin'."

When the door closed and he was gone, all she could do was hope he wouldn't hurt Amo.

Alone, she touched her swollen lips. Lucca was right; *what did I just do?*

She couldn't believe she had been the one to reach out and touch him, when she was only just learning to accept Lucca's touch. There hadn't even been a sting, no wrongness in it. Scariest of all ... Chloe had just gotten her first kiss, with the promise it wouldn't be her last.

She wasn't the type of girl to dream about her first kiss. How could she when she only ever wanted to never be touched again in her life? Therefore, never had she thought she would get a first kiss, let alone have her first be with Lucca, the boogieman.

Everything that had just happened scared her shitless. She kept repeating the same words in her head, trying to keep her sanity. *You had to. You had no choice. You did it to save Amo.*

After a while of repeating the words, the lines began to blur. She didn't know if that was what she truly believed, or if it was what she had led herself to believe.

You had to . . . You had no choice . . . You did it to save Amo . . .

Did she?

HOW BEUTIFUL IT IS.
HOW PAINFIL IT CAN BE

Flicking his lighter open, *Lucca* lit the end of his cigarette while staring across his desk at Amo. Neither of them spoke, both simply silently killing the other in their minds as Lucca continued filling the room up with smoke.

"How'd you do it?" Amo was the one to speak first, unable to stand the silence any longer.

Understanding what he was asking, Lucca told him, "I grabbed her before she could get on the plane. Then Sal handled everything else, making it appear like she got on and has been in California." Taking a long hit, he finished with a smile, "Then she woke up here, where she's been well taken care of."

"So, you fucking kidnapped her," Amo stated matter-of-factly.

Exactly. He hit his ashes into the ashtray. "Yes, for her own good."

Amo stared at him like he was deranged. "I thought you were fucked-up, Lucca, but I didn't know you were this fucking psychotic."

"There are reasons for what I did, Amo."

"Oh, I'm sure your fucked-up self has come up with a whole list of reasons to justify what you did." He laughed mockingly. "Let's be honest, though; we both know that you're delusional, a stalker, and now a kidnapper."

"I am well aware of what I am," Lucca told him darkly, taking a final hit before he crushed the butt out in the ashtray. "But do you know why I would go to those lengths? To have Drago stay here just to watch her? You know what he's capable of; the things he provides to the family."

You could see it start to turn in Amo's head; the things he had been missing from the second he had walked in the door. However, he quickly made them disappear, unable to face the facts.

"No!" His booming voice rose. "You wanted her all to yourself, to fill that sick obsession you have with her."

"I would have taken her the moment she turned eighteen if that was it, and you know it." He decided to reveal how fucked-up he really was, letting Amo begin to understand how important she was to him. "I thought about taking her before she was eighteen. Then, when she turned eighteen, it was the hardest thing I ever had to do not to take her then and there. I almost did it, too, but I had to wait. I waited seven fucking months for her."

Amo knew his words were true. And even though she might

have been there for a reason, he couldn't take it.

"You know I'm not leaving here without her, and if you let me walk out that door, I won't stop till she is free."

"Did she look like she wanted to leave?" Lucca reminded him.

Standing up abruptly from the chair, Amo clearly wasn't able to handle what Lucca was telling him.

A part of Lucca enjoyed it, reveled in it. He'd had to watch him from afar with Chloe almost every fucking day for far too long, wishing he had been in Amo's shoes many nights. The other part of him felt pity for Amo for losing her, knowing she was the most beautiful creature on this earth, *but she's mine.*

"She has been freer here with me than she ever was outside these walls."

"What are you trying to say?"

Lucca stared him down. "You know exactly what I am saying."

The rage and adrenaline that came from Amo had him squeezing his broken hand into a fist. "Those seven months you stalked her, just watching her, I actually spent with her, talked with her, got to know her. I was her protector and her friend. She was free with me. Then you fucking stole her from me before I had the chance to make her more than that." Amo's face twisted evilly, a snarl coming into his voice. "You couldn't handle it, could you? Couldn't handle that I was with her and you weren't. How does it feel to know you had to kidnap her to get her to spend time with you?"

Lucca slowly stood, having reached his limit. He had been generous enough to speak to Amo man-to-man instead of underboss to soldier. That time, however, was over.

Coming out from behind his desk, he got face-to-face with Amo. "You need to remember who you are talking to." His voice was dark, forceful, and commanding. "Leave, and if anyone asks why you came here, you came to talk to me about your position at work. Someone finding out she's here will only put her life at risk."

Amo didn't make a move to leave.

"The only reason I'm still giving you the option to walk out of here alive is because I know you care about her enough not to risk her safety. I would have killed you the second you got here, but I need Chloe to want to look at me for the rest of her life," he threatened.

"You think you're going to get her to fall in love with you?" Amo went to the door, agreeing to leave, but clearly not giving up on her. Then, deciding to part with final words, he delivered his final blow. "You are a psychopath who's incapable of love or ever being loved. She belongs with me, and you know it; that's why you took her. You will never love her the way I do. You just want to fuck her."

Before Amo could even open the door, Lucca struck out, shoving him against the door swiftly while pulling a blade from his pocket and holding it to Amo's throat. It was a blur for Amo, but a calculated move for Lucca, showcasing the difference in the positions they held in the family, and why he was the underboss, while Amo was only a soldier.

Seething with the rage he felt on Chloe's behalf, Lucca pressed the knife bitterly against Amo's throat, spewing, "You looked at her every goddamn day at school for three and a half years, and not once did you ever give her the fucking time of day. You claim to love her, but *where the fuck were you!*" he yelled, digging the edge of the blade in deeper, his harsh words lashing at Amo like a thousand whips. "When she and Elle were bullied, when Elle was taking beatings to keep her from being touched, when she was called a freak, where were you, Amo? How could you pass her in the halls with those scars and not do something? Not protect her?"

Amo's face fell at each harsh question. His anger slowly dissolved into pain as everything Lucca said hit him like a ton of bricks, making him feel like the trash he was.

Taking the same cynical tone Amo had just given him, Lucca continued, "Let's be honest; she wasn't going to spread her legs for you, so there was no need to, was there? You were too busy calling her a freak with the rest of them."

A paling Amo quickly realized Lucca had found out his deepest, darkest secret.

He wanted to leave now, but he couldn't with Lucca pinning him, forcing him to listen to what he had to say, forcing him to face the truth and accusations of those words.

"You had to be told to look in her fucking direction and give her your precious time. I didn't," Lucca growled, never letting up on the knife. "It took me one look to fall in love with her. *One look* to want to know everything and anything about her. *One look* to feel protective of her, like my life depended on it. *One look* to want to kill whoever gave her those scars."

Blood now trickled down Amo's throat.

"If you're meant for her, then how have you slept without finding out who did those things to her, who made her the way she is now?" Lucca stared Amo down, his eyes boring into the weak soldier's. "I bet you didn't even know those scars were given to her; that she wasn't actually in a car crash. You didn't even know that she suffers from insomnia because she's too afraid to sleep in fear of the nightmares. Admit you didn't even know!" Lucca roared.

Ashamed, Amo shook his head. He was slowly beginning to break down. The strong Amo he had been moments ago had vanished before Lucca's eyes.

Resisting the darkness that wanted to slide the blade into Amo's neck was unimaginable, but Lucca was doing it. *Besides, this feels so much better.*

"There is so much you don't know about her because you were too focused on lying to her, pretending to be someone you're not, afraid of scaring her away. You have done *nothing* but hinder her because you think she's weak when, in reality, she's stronger than anyone I have ever seen."

Pain then entered Lucca's voice that also showed through his blue-green eyes, something he had never shown a man before, let alone one of his soldiers. "You will *never* know the love I feel for her. How beautiful it is. How painful it can be. What it felt like when I first looked at her. And what it felt like when I thought I might lose her before I could even save her. You will never know true love until you experience true fear. And you will never feel those toward her, as I am the *only* one for her. She. Is. Mine."

Amo was almost there. Almost a broken human being. Lucca could stop now and show mercy, but he wanted Amo's punishment to last a lifetime. A sentence he deserved for letting Chloe walk through hell even for one day.

"If Elle hadn't seen us that night, I don't want to think where Chloe would be now, or how she would have ended up, because you sure as fuck wouldn't have protected her. You, Nero, and even Vincent are pieces of shit for letting them go through that hell."

Lucca didn't hold back on him, and he didn't feel an ounce of guilt over it. His soldier deserved it after trying to do the same to him. The only difference was Amo was blinded by infatuation, mistaking it for love, whereas Lucca recognized the pureness of what he felt for Chloe.

She was his soulmate.

"You will *never* deserve Chloe. The same way Nero will never deserve Elle. Nero will spend the rest of his life trying to, but I won't let you try and deserve her.

"I wanted her so badly that I actually wanted to trade places with you for those seven months … But not anymore. Now, you have to look at yourself in the mirror every fucking day for the rest of your life and see what a disgusting piece of shit you are. That's why I'm not going to kill you." Lucca removed the blade from his throat, but he still made Amo stand there like a wounded animal, not releasing him just yet. "I want you to live every day knowing that I'm with her and you're not. Knowing that she belongs to me and me alone. To die little by little every time you see us together, just the way I did when I saw her with you."

Now, he's broken.

The hope Amo had, the same hope that had shown in his eyes, for being so close to being with Chloe was so small now compared to when he had first gotten here. Lucca didn't want it gone completely, though, or it wouldn't hurt him as much when he looked in the mirror every day, or at Chloe, or even at Lucca.

Turning away from the broken man who was now hunched over, only being held up by the wall at his back, the broken man who could no longer look at him from the shame he felt, Lucca went back to his desk, from where he watched Amo in pity.

He pulled out another cigarette and put it to his lips, lighting the end with the flick of his wrist. "Get the fuck out of my face and don't ever step foot in my home again. Come anywhere near Chloe without permission, you'll never see her again. Lay your hand on her, and I'll keep my promise to rip out your fucking throat." Taking a hit, he shooed him away. "You are dismissed."

Struggling, Amo pushed himself off the wall, holding his damaged hand to his body while he left. He didn't say a word; he didn't have to. His face said it all. Amo was losing the girl he loved to Lucca and was now feeling her slip from his fingers.

Running a hand through his hair, his own words hit him like a ton of bricks. *What it felt like when I thought I might lose her before I could even save her.*

He had felt that true fear twice. Each time she had survived, it was the most peaceful and heavenly feeling ... Only for it to kill him when he had to watch Amo be the one to console her.

You would think that the first time would have been the worst, but the second time had been just as excruciating, heartbreaking, and unbearable.

To die little by little every time you see us together, just the way I did when I saw her with you . . .

PRAYING TO THE GOD THAT HE DIDN'T BELIEVE EXISTED THAT SHE WAS STILL ALIVE

MONTHS EARLIER

Lucca was watching the casino floor, his mind elsewhere. Chloe was here at the casino hotel, in Nero's penthouse, hanging out with the girls. She was so close, yet so far away.

Every day that he waited for her, he knew it was another day closer. But to him, it always felt like an eternity.

The phone ringing in his pocket had him pulling it out to see it was Nero calling. He answered it immediately, putting it to his ear.

Before he could even speak, Nero asked hurriedly, "Lucca, where are you?"

A sinking feeling hit his heart. His instincts knew something very wrong was happening, and somehow, he felt Chloe was involved.

He was already moving toward the elevator. "First floor."

"The girls … Someone broke in. We're in the elevator …" Nero seemed to lose all hope as his voice trailed off.

The phone fell out of Lucca's hands as a sharp pain dug into him, right in the chest.

Changing directions, Lucca headed toward the emergency stairs since Nero was already using the elevator. He hit the door, causing it to fly open as he started running up the stairs, running as fast as his legs could take him. *Don't You fucking do this to me!* he began cursing God, a figure he had not believed in for years.

There were twenty-three floors.

I haven't touched her yet.

Twenty-three floors that separated them.

I haven't felt what it's like to kiss her.

Twenty-three floors he had to climb to save her.

I haven't told her I love her.

Each flight he climbed, a number passed, telling him how many more he had to scale.

Don't You dare fucking take her from me!

Not once did he stop, not once did his body slow. His mind and body were strong, willing him to reach the top, while his heart began to compress inside his chest. A heart that shouldn't beat, because he didn't have one. A heart that only beat for Chloe. A heart that was rapidly collapsing in fear of losing her.

Eleven …

He was halfway there now. It seemed to take forever. His only hope of Chloe living was in the hands of someone else reaching her soon. *Save her, Nero*. Someone else saving her who wasn't him, no matter how much it was killing him. *Save her, Arno.*

Fifteen …

The numbers seemed to blur by, along with images of the future they were supposed to have together.

Nineteen …

Chloe sat smiling in the middle of the garden, surrounded by beautiful flowers.

Twenty …

His hand running through her long, silky hair.

Twenty-one …

Her peacefully sleeping in the bed next to him.

Twenty-two …

Kissing her under the gazebo while she wore a white dress.

Twenty-three …

When he hit the door in front of him, it opened with a slam, presenting the long hallway. *I'm close, darlin'.*

The adrenaline that still coursed through his veins had him reaching the end of the hall, opening the broken door to Nero's place and running up the steps, praying to the God he didn't believe existed that she was still alive.

Reaching the top steps, he saw a glimpse of Chloe in the bathroom, and a wave of relief washed over his body. Lucca found complete and utter peace in that millisecond. Knowing that her heart was still beating made his beat stronger.

The fear of losing her was now replaced by retribution when he saw Vincent on top of a man whom he was beating to death.

Grabbing Vincent's shirt, he pulled him off the man he was about to murder. "Don't you dare kill that fucker."

Taking in the man on the floor, he studied him, trying to figure out who he was and what he was doing here. His gut had an eerie feeling that he already knew.

Sal came up the steps then, carrying a bat, having been notified from the security cameras.

"Fuck, man. He got Al. They should be cleaning him up, no—" He quickly shut his mouth once he saw the girls.

Taking the bat from him, Lucca gripped it, finding himself thankful he had a friend like him. "Thanks, Sal."

Raising the bat above his head, he swung it down on the man's leg.

The beautiful sound of bones shattering filled the space.

Vincent shouted, "Enough!" over the sound as the girls held their hands over their ears.

Lucca wasn't close to done, though, letting the darkness have what it wanted, crashing the bat on the other leg.

Beginning to raise the bat for a final strike, Amo yelled, "Fuck! That's enough!" which made him pause with the bat reared back.

Following his voice to the bathroom, his eyes landed on Chloe, who was sitting in the bathtub. She was motionless, nearly catatonic, staring him dead in the eyes. Fear of him was evident in her gray depths.

Chloe had yet to see him this way. She hadn't seen what he was capable of, seen that there was true darkness in him.

Gripping the bat tighter, his knuckles grew white.

This was his moment, when he could either hide his true nature from her or present it to her; show her what was to come and the type of man she was really going to be with.

His decision was made in a split second as he slammed the bat down on the broken body one last time, watching her eyes and expression while he did it, never taking his eyes off hers.

She hadn't flinched, moved, or changed her expression, telling him she had witnessed a brutality of that nature before.

Letting go of the bat, he took a deep breath, the smell of blood calming him.

He slicked back his hair that had fallen around his face, a smile touching his lips. The darkness was satiated.

"Now, that's fucking enough."

It all came crashing down, however, when Amo wrapped his jacket around Chloe's shoulders and said, "Let's get you home."

The darkness that had settled came roaring back when she held Amo's jacket to her tightly.

Watching her be comforted by another man ate away at him. Seeing a jacket that wasn't his wrapped around her as she clung to it crushed him. The girl he loved so deeply being scared to even pass him was heart-wrenching.

She hadn't the slightest idea the pain he was going through, the true fear he felt of losing her, or the love he had for her.

Watching the beautiful, broken girl pass him by without knowing any of those things as she walked with Amo slowly but surely started to kill him inside.

ALLOWING MONSTERS LIKE HIM TO ROAM THE EARTH

PRESENT TIME

hloe sat nervously on her bed with her stuff packed, like how it had been when she had first gotten here. *Where is he taking me?*

A quick knock on the door before it opened had Drago coming in. "You all packed up?"

She nodded nervously. "Where am I going?"

"You're moving into Lucca's room." Not an ounce of sympathy was in his voice.

"I-I a-am?" That was the last thing she had expected, and it scared her more than anything she could think of.

"Yep. Let's go," he told her, picking up her bags.

More nervous than ever before, she shakily got up from the bed, following behind him as he headed out into the hall. Stopping, she grew confused when he didn't go to the room across from hers and instead started heading down the hall toward the stairs.

"W-Where are you going?"

Drago stopped, turning to see she was standing in front of the door opposite of hers. "I told you. Lucca's room."

She didn't understand as she continued to stare at the door she had seen Lucca go in and out of every morning and night over the past month.

"I thought this was his room."

Drago set her bags down before walking to the door and opening it. Turning the light on, he let her see inside the bedroom.

Her eyebrows slowly came together in confusion as she walked into the room. It was nice, but felt a little young, and nothing at all like Lucca. *This isn't …*

"This isn't his room, is it?"

"No, it's Leo's. Lucca started sleeping in here a little bit after you got here."

Chloe bit her lip. "He did?"

"Yes." He turned the light off, a not so subtle sign that it was time to leave.

She clasped her hands together, beginning to wring them, as she let that piece of information set in. Then she followed Drago again, this time to Lucca's real bedroom, passing the steps and going toward the other wing of the house.

Finally, Drago opened the door at the very end of the hall,

allowing her to go in first.

This room definitely seemed more like Lucca. It was huge and darkly lit, with dark wood and dark colors. It seemed and smelled almost earthy, manly, and Chloe found it pleasing.

"Lucca will be in later." Setting her things down in the middle of the room, Drago turned to leave.

"D-Drago …?"

"Yes?" He stopped, turning back around.

"Thank you for telling me." She knew it probably wasn't his place to tell her about Lucca sleeping in Leo's room, as Lucca seemed like a very private man where it concerned his men, but she appreciated it all the same.

He gave a brief nod before leaving, closing the door behind him.

Taking a shaky breath while she looked around the dark room, she held herself tightly at the mere fact of being in the boogieman's most intimate space. She couldn't help wondering at what moment her path had led her here, or if this wasn't her rightful path and she had been stolen off hers to walk down another.

The chains that held her body and mind gripped even tighter.

Lucca waited until he had calmed himself down before leaving his office. He had to let the darkness simmer enough before he could be near Chloe again. Though, he wasn't entirely sure what he had to calm down from the most: finally kissing her, or Amo finally seeing he wasn't the man for her. Both had brought the darkness out equally.

Heading toward his bedroom, he passed Drago along the way.

"I took her things to your room. Chloe's waiting for you there."

"Thank you." He nodded his head and then stopped. "There's something I wanted to ask you."

Drago paused, turning around to face him.

"Did you break Amo's hand in hopes that I would think that was punishment enough?" Lucca studied his face, seeing a slight change in his stoic demeanor, which told him he had been right to think that. Drago had known Lucca wasn't going to let him leave without physical pain.

"It will not happen again," Drago told him firmly.

"Thanks for doing it for me," Lucca said from over his shoulder as he continued toward his room, satisfied with Drago's answer.

"Why?" Drago asked in confusion.

Lucca smiled. "Because now I get to tell Chloe you were the one who hurt him."

"Fucking asshole," Drago mumbled under his breath.

Chloe sat alone on the edge of Lucca's bed, nervously waiting and not knowing what else to do. The door opening had her back straightening, hoping her wait was coming to an end.

When she saw that it was, in fact, Lucca coming in, her back somehow went even straighter.

"You didn't unpack?" he asked when he saw her bags on the floor, untouched.

Looking down at the hands in her lap, she started wringing them, wanting to scrape her skin off. "N-No. I didn't know where to put them."

His hands suddenly appeared on top of hers, stopping her from the damage she wanted to inflict. "You've been good about not doing this all month. Is it because of him, or because I moved you here?"

Biting her lip, she wanted to blame it on having to sleep in here with him, but truthfully, she had started wringing her hands when Amo had come for her.

"Did you hurt him?" she whispered.

"Drago broke his hand—"

"He did!" she exclaimed more than asked, her eyes shooting up to his.

He gave her hand a squeeze. "Yes. His hand will heal, though. It'll be fine."

"That wasn't very nice of him." Chloe relaxed a bit. She supposed she had hurt him way more than Drago had. *I broke his heart . . . again.*

A smile tugged at Lucca's lips. "You'll have to tell him that, darlin'."

"I'll think about it." Drago still scared her from time to time.

The hands that covered hers now moved in a light, soothing motion over her palms.

"Thank you for letting him go," she told him.

"You're welcome." Keeping one hand on her hands, he lifted the other to swipe her hair behind her ear so she couldn't hide her face from him. "You know, if he does anything like he did again, there will be no saving him," he warned her, promising her she wouldn't be able to help him next time.

Swallowing, she could barely get the words "I know" out.

He was making it very obvious how possessive and protective he was of her. A part of her secretly appreciated it—needed it after all she had been through—never having to worry about being touched by anyone other than him.

Amo was the only one she was worried about Lucca's protectiveness hurting.

Reaching into his pocket, Lucca pulled out her cell phone, placing it in her open palm.

Looking up at him, she couldn't believe it. "Y-You're giving it back to me? Why?"

"Because I want you to know that I trust you just as much as you trust me, darlin'." Leaning down, he placed a kiss over the top of her scar. "And I'm tired of pretending to be you every time Elle texts."

Chloe giggled, trying to imagine him texting Elle as her. "I'm sure I'll have fun reading over the texts you sent her."

"Well, I just used a bunch of emojis, really." He laughed with her, twirling a piece of her hair around his finger. "Be sure to use the black heart one. I used that one a lot."

"Why the black heart?"

He tugged on her strand playfully. "Just seemed like one you'd like."

Smiling, she finally began to fully relax.

He let go of her hair, letting it fall to her chest. "Go get ready for bed, darlin'. You can unpack your things tomorrow."

Tensing right back up, she got off the bed and went to her bags, quickly pulling out the things she needed. She was thankful that her thickest fleece pajamas were clean. They also covered her whole body, which she was the most thankful for.

Her nerves were getting the best of her as she then went into his bathroom and started getting ready for bed. She liked her showers in the morning, so she found herself hoping that was okay with him, since she was sleeping in his bed.

Once she was ready and done with the bathroom, she found herself staring at the door, her nerves racking throughout her body, frightened to sleep beside the boogieman.

It's going to be okay. He won't hurt me. She kept repeating those words in her head, trying to muster up enough courage to open the door.

When she had pushed it off for long enough and an ounce of courage had been mustered, she opened the bathroom door.

When she walked out of the bathroom and into the dark room, relief washed over her, beyond grateful when she noticed Lucca was already fast asleep on his side of the bed. Then she found herself staring at the sleeping, haunting man for a few moments, seeing he wore his normal black T-shirt, the covers only coming up to his hips as he slept on his back, thinking how beautiful he looked, even in his sleep.

Lucca was a handsome man. She always thought that was what made him so deadly.

Quietly and carefully, she went to the other side of the bed and crawled in ever so slowly. She was so afraid of waking him as she gently pulled the covers over her. Then she positioned herself as far away from Lucca as she could possibly get, clinging to the edge of the bed.

It definitely felt awkward to be in his bed, with him only a foot away, and was even painful at first as she tried to get comfortable in a bed she hadn't slept in before. However, exhaling deeply, she was finally able to relax. And when she snuggled the blankets around her more tightly, the smell of the room soothing her, she found comfort … soothing to her soul …

When he was certain Chloe had fallen asleep, he turned on his side to face her back, seeing her long, black, silky hair fanned out across her pillow. He loved everything about her hair: the color, the feel, the smell. He loved the way it looked right now. And he loved the way she looked in his bed.

Reaching out, he started to pick up a lone curl at the end of her hair, when a whimper had him pausing. Then another whimper escaped her.

The nightmares were coming.

Right when the screams started, Lucca moved closer to her shaking body. He could only hope what he was about to do would make the nightmares disappear without waking her up.

He pulled her back into his body and into his arms, holding her tightly, unable to bear her pain any longer. And miraculously, the cries returned to whimpers and her shaking lessened, until they both disappeared ... along with her nightmare.

Lucca had left the Catholic faith after his mother's passing, knowing there was no way God could exist if He could take away a human being as pure as his mother while allowing monsters like him to roam this earth. Many nights, he would even question his own existence, wondering why it hadn't been him instead of her.

Holding Chloe to him, it was now hard for him to think God could not exist. There was no way Chloe could exist if God didn't. She was made special ... Made for him.

The question of why his mother had been taken and not him had finally been answered.

He was here on this earth for her. To save her.

ONLY BE TOUCHED
BY LUCCA

eaning back in his chair, he felt on the brink of insanity. He had grown used to always knowing where she was for when he wanted to see his creation. But now, it had been over a month since he had last seen her. Escaping him twice.

His obsession with her had grown over the years, becoming unhealthy. Even he knew that. It was to the point where his memories of her weren't enough, and he was ready for new ones.

He had been so close to making new memories with her, too, but he had been denied each time.

"Lucifer …" His two most competent men entered the room. "We think we may have found her."

The desolateness he had felt was immediately replaced by hopefulness.

Standing up, he was eager to retrieve the girl he had marked years ago. "Where?"

The bravest one cleared his throat. "You're not going to like it."

Hopefulness was replaced by fury. "Where!"

"We believe she is at the Caruso home."

His black eyes glowed, fire igniting in his blood. "You're sure of this?"

"There is no way to know for certain until we get inside the home, but we were led there tonight by her friend, the soldier Amo. We have been suspicious of her being there, and his arrival and departure were alarming, confirming our suspicions."

Sitting back down in his chair, Lucifer had his own suspicions of the Carusos, the ring Lucca had shown him almost validating it, but he trusted his man wouldn't have turned rat.

I'm trying to find the owner of my new dog.

An evil grin appeared on his face. "Get ready for war."

I'm coming for you, little girl . . .

Chloe shivered as she went down the steps the next morning. She felt like she had slept well . . . right up until the end when a nightmare she couldn't shake woke her up. It had been stronger than usual, creating a sinking feeling in her gut. Something just didn't feel right. *The devil seemed too real . . .*

Holding herself, the shaking only grew worse.

"Are you okay?" Drago asked with concern when she came into the living room.

She found herself looking around the room. "Y-Yeah, I-I—"

"He's in his office." Drago seemed more concerned now. "Why don't you go in there? He won't mind."

Her mind and body followed the path to Lucca's office, needing his presence.

Lightly knocking on the door, she heard a "Come in" a second later. Then she opened the door and saw Lucca sitting behind his desk, smoking a cigarette. That was when she snapped out of it a bit, wondering how she had gotten here.

Lucca seemed surprised to see her when he looked up from his work. He quickly put out his cigarette, then tried to clear the smoke with his hands, making it dissipate faster.

"Darlin'?"

"I-I'm sorry I-I bothered you." She turned abruptly to leave.

"Chloe." His voice was commanding, stopping her in her place. "Come to me."

Turning back around, she held herself tighter as she obeyed him, moving around the desk to stand beside him.

Studying her, he became worried. "What's wrong?"

"I-I-I don't know," she nervously confessed. It was impossible to explain. The nightmare hadn't been like her others.

"Darlin' …" His face softened. Taking her hand, he pulled her closer, telling her in his commanding tone, "Come here. Sit with me."

Her body fell into his lap, not knowing if it craved his touch or if it was because he had given her a command. It was all very strange to her—trying to deal with this new version of herself who could only be touched by Lucca.

Lucca turned her to the side on his lap so she could rest her head on his chest. He rested one hand at her back while he rested his other hand on her thigh.

It was the first time she had ever been held by a man. She felt stiff at first, but her body didn't let her for long, needing his embrace to soothe the nightmares. She could feel herself melting into him the longer she sat there.

"Was it a nightmare?" His voice was quiet, soft, yet strong. Just like his touch.

I'm coming for you, little girl . . .

She could only nod her head, remembering what the devil had said to her in her dream.

Lucca removed his hand from her thigh, touching his fingertips to her face, where he lightly traced her scar. "Was it about the man who gave you these?"

There was no more pretending that she had gotten them from a car crash, not from Lucca. He had known the second he saw her for the first time that they had been caused by a knife. "Y-Yes."

"The scars on your face aren't the only ones he gave you, are they?"

A cold chill coming over her body had her looking up at him, staring into his haunting blue-green eyes. She slowly shook her head.

He had hinted at their second meeting when she had been wearing long sleeves in the summer that he knew, but she had never confirmed it. *Or maybe I did.*

"Show me," he ordered.

Biting her lip, her hands shaking, she slowly pushed up her right and then her left sleeve as far as they could go, revealing several scars on each arm. Her marks spread out from right above her wrist to the top of her shoulders.

She hadn't shown anyone besides Elle. And no one had ever suspected her of having more scars than the ones that marked her face.

Taking his time, Lucca touched each revealed scar on her arms, tracing, studying how thick they were and how deep the bastard must have gone based upon how high they were raised. Each mark almost glowed against her pale skin.

"Is this all of them?" he asked with a hint of doubt in his voice, seeming to know it wasn't.

She swallowed hard. *Don't make me tell you.*

"Tell me where the rest of them are."

"A-Are you going to make me show you?"

"Not today, I won't," he assured her, still lightly touching each scar.

She whispered the place not even Elle knew about, "M-My s-stomach."

He didn't respond, continuing to look, touch, and memorize the scars on her arms before pulling the sleeves of her sweater down to cover her cold arms back up.

"T-They're hideous, aren't they?" she asked while confessing how she had felt about them ever since first looking at herself in the mirror.

Lucca grabbed her face, forcing her to look at him. "Don't you *ever* speak those words again. Do you understand?"

She tried nodding her head in his grip. "Y-Yes."

Loosening his hold, he moved a finger to her full lips, caressing over the scar he hadn't yet touched that went an inch above and below her lips. "You and your scars are the most beautiful things I have ever seen."

Her breathing hitched as he moved his face closer to hers while moving his finger from her lips to position her for the taking.

"Don't you ever think they're not," he whispered, his breath teasing her lips.

She closed her eyes as he pressed his lips against hers.

This kiss was slower than the first and not as demanding. Just him leisurely tasting her bottom lip.

The last time, he had tasted of cool mint. This time, she could still taste the cool mint, but it had a smokiness to it from his cigarette. The two opposite flavors mixed, tasting of fire and ice and making her lips and body tingle.

Lucca biting her bottom lip caused a noise of pleasure to escape her throat, like it had the last time. He smiled against her lips before he smoothed his tongue over the pressure he had caused, soothing it just for a moment before he pulled away.

"I think you like being bit, darlin'."

A flush appeared on her cheeks as she blushed at his words and her body's betrayal.

"It's not a bad thing." He smiled before placing a light kiss on her lips.

Her belly became warm at the quick kiss. It was sweet, something she wasn't very used to from the possessive man.

Unconsciously licking her lips, she noticed she still tasted of him— the mint with the hint of smoke. Tasting exactly how he smelled.

That made her ask, "Why did you put your cigarette out when I came in?" She realized then that she hadn't smelled smoke on him much lately, which surprised her.

"Because I don't like smoking around you if we're not outside."

"It doesn't bother me," she told him, not wanting him to not smoke on her account. The smell had strangely never bothered her.

"I know, darlin', but I don't want you inhaling it," he told her, revealing that it had to do with her health and not with the fact she might not like it.

Thinking deeper about it, this was the only room in the house where she could smell smoke.

She clasped her hands together when his hand moved higher up the outside of her thigh. "I-Is this the only room you smoke in?"

His eyes didn't waiver from her face as she looked down at her hands. "Now it is, yes. I have to be able to smoke while I'm working."

"Now it is?" she questioned.

"I quit smoking everywhere else in the house once I knew you were coming here."

"Oh." Chloe didn't really know what to think of that. It seemed like he had done a lot of things for her since he had first met her. *I don't think I'll ever know everything he has done.*

"What is it?" he asked, twirling a strand of her hair between his fingers.

"W-When did you start sleeping in Leo's room?" She had a feeling she knew why, and she also thought she knew when.

He twirled and then un-twirled her strand of hair before he answered with sadness in his voice, "The first time you had your nightmare, it took me too long to get to you. I started sleeping in Leo's room after that because, no matter how fast I ran, it still took too long to get to you."

A little piece of Chloe's heart broke at hearing him say those words. She could feel the pain behind them, like there was more to it than she knew or even could understand.

She wanted him to know something, something that had been hard for her to admit to herself at first.

"Y-You've helped ease the nightmares."

He stopped the motion of twirling her hair as he focused on her eyes. "Is that so?"

"Y-Yes. I've noticed that, when you're around, they seem to go away."

"I'm happy to hear that, darlin'." Beginning the motion of twirling her hair again, he asked, "Are you feeling better now?"

She nodded.

Even though a part of her still felt it strange to be held by him, her body and mind felt immensely better being around him. Something about Lucca called to her body. It needed it, craved it, which had only amplified after the horrible nightmare.

"Would you like me to take the day off? I could go make us

something to eat, and then we could watch a movie if you wanted." He paused for a moment. "Or I could call Maria and ask her to come over."

Smiling up at him, she felt appreciation that he would do that for her, although he was still unhappy with his sister. "That depends. What would you fix me to eat?"

He smiled back, pleased that she was choosing to spend the day with him. "Whatever you want, darlin'."

She didn't even have to think about it. "Chocolate pancakes."

"Then chocolate pancakes it is."

Getting up from his lap, she saw something gold flash out of the corner of her eye. It had her looking at his desk to see what it was. And when she did, her smiling face slowly changed into a look of fear as she reached out, wanting to see if it was real or if she was imagining it.

The second her fingertip touched the ring, she knew it wasn't just an illusion, and her mouth opened to scream, but nothing came out.

I'm coming for you, little girl . . .

Lucca touched her shoulder, the worry back in his voice. "Darlin'?"

I've missed you.

When she continued staring at the ring, he turned her to face him. Then, holding both of her shoulders, he lightly shook her. "Chloe. Chloe!"

Staring at Lucca now, the devil's voice disappeared and she began to unfreeze. Now she was trying desperately to get away from him, away from his touch. Trying her best to fight him.

"Stop it!" Lucca commanded. "Tell me what's wrong."

"Why do you have it!" she screamed. "Why do you have the ring?" Ghost tears tried to fall down her face as she struggled against him, not wanting to believe he could have had something to do with what had happened to her.

"I took it off the man who bro—"

"You're lying!" she cried out, still without the tears, though they desperately wanted to be there. It explained how he knew everything about her.

Pulling her to him, he held her body with one arm while grabbing ahold of her face with his free hand, making her look into her eyes.

"Look at me." His voice became melodic and strong. "No, I'm not. I would *never* lie to you."

Closing her eyes, she let him hold her to him fully now as she pressed her face into his chest.

She didn't have to see the truth; her heart could feel it, knowing he couldn't have been involved. It was the scared little girl who had been living in her for almost four years now who had needed the reassurance. The scared little girl who had screamed for someone like Lucca to save her that night ... only for no one to come. The scared little girl who now had her savior and was petrified to even think about losing him.

AS HE TOOK THE SIGHT OF THE OTHER

ucca dragged the body, taking him to the steel pipe that was in the back corner of the room.

"WWWhere a-am I?"

The fucker wasn't dead, but he was fucking close to it.

The sound of metal chains echoed throughout the dark, cold concrete room.

"W-What are yyou doing?" he cried, trying to lift his body unsuccessfully.

A loud snap followed by something locking in place silenced the room.

Staring down at the broken man who had passed out, Lucca gave a yank to the chain that locked his ankle to the pipe.

"OWWWW! Whhhat do you want from mee?" More tears fell from his eyes.

"Who were you looking for?"

"I ddon't know."

Another yank to the chain pulled at his shattered leg, making him wail in pain.

"Who were you looking for?"

"I ddon't know!"

Lucca squatted next to the man, noticing a gold ring on his finger. Pulling out his knife, he grabbed the man's hand then spread his fingers open before placing the blade right under his ring.

"Now—"

The man began repeating, "Please don't."

"—tell me who you were looking for in the penthouse."

"I ccan't tell yyou!"

Lucca sliced into his finger, cutting deeply.

"SSScars!" the man screamed, and Lucca immediately stopped, relieving the man from his pain. "The girl with the ssscars."

Lucca stared down at him. "That so?"

"Yes." He took a thankful breath.

"Unfortunately"—he sliced into his finger again—"you came after the one who's mine."

Now that he was sawing into the bone, the screams that filled the air only grew louder . . . until the man passed out cold.

Pulling the ring off the now chopped off finger, Lucca wiped at the blood, revealing the diamond's surrounding the horseshoe . . .

Staring down at the horseshoe ring, Lucca put it back in his pocket to look at the frail, malnourished Italian man who no longer resembled himself. His hair and beard were matted and long; burns, scars, and bruises now riddled his body; and most of his teeth had been removed, along with all of the nails on his toes and nine fingers.

Lucca stalked toward the man chained up in the corner. "You lied to me. You said you weren't there that night."

Shaking his head, the man tried to scoot into the corner as much as he could. "No, no, no, Mr. Caruso, sir."

"She remembered your ring," he warned.

His face morphed into pure terror, his hands coming together in prayer. "I cccann expllaiin, sir. Pleaseee, let me explain."

Pulling out a cigarette, Lucca held it between his lips as he took out his lighter and let the glow burn the end. "Go on."

"The ffffirst night you told me she was yourss, if I told you I wwwas there the night she got her scars, you would have killlled me. Thennn I would have been no good to you, sir. I did it for youuu, sir."

Lucca held the cigarette between his lips as he reached out and grabbed the chain, pulling it with all his strength and bringing his captive to him, flattening him like a pancake.

The man hit his head hard on the concrete, unable to move his fragile and tormented body.

Squatting down besides the man's head, Lucca then held open his right eye, not letting him blink, while he took the cigarette out of his mouth with his other hand and hovered the burning end over the eyeball.

"Did you lie to me about anything else?" he demanded.

The weak man tried to move but couldn't. "NOOO! I swear!"

"You're right"—Lucca brought the burning stick closer to the eye he held open so tightly it looked like it was about to pop out at any second—"I would have killed you."

Shoving the cigarette down, he smashed it into the man's pupil until it no longer burned, using his eye as an ashtray.

Only Lucca and the concrete walls laid witness to how a man's screams sounded when he went blind in one eye. And then again, a few moments later ... as he took the sight of the other.

THIS TIME FELT DIFFERENT. MORE . . . FINAL.

Chloe sat on Lucca's bed, holding her knees to her chest and rocking herself back and forth. The pit in her stomach had only grown since her nightmare this morning, making her sick. The air around her felt heavy, making her suffocate. She could feel something coming. Something very bad was about to happen, and she was afraid her fate would be fatal this time.

The horseshoe ring, along with the devil's ominous black eyes, wouldn't leave her mind.

He's coming for me . . . He promised.

Drago was alerted to a presence on the security monitors. A car was pulling into the long driveway. It had a sign on top of the vehicle, showing it was food delivery. He hadn't ordered anything, so he quickly called Lucca to see if he had. However, the call went straight to voicemail, his signal most likely blocked from where he was.

When the car stopped in front of the house and a man in uniform got out with a pizza bag, he figured Lucca had ordered it to feed Chloe since she hadn't eaten anything and he was most likely going to be gone for a while.

Getting up, he headed toward the door and got to it just as the delivery guy knocked.

He cracked open the door with his hand on his pistol at his lower back, seeing the uniformed man holding the pizza bag.

"Delivery for Lucca Caruso."

Drago nodded then pulled his hand from his pistol, opening the door wider.

The delivery man placed his hand inside the bag ...

POP.

When the shot fired through the bag, Drago realized his grave mistake.

Going for his gun, he took a step toward the man, when ...

POP.

Both shots had hit him in the chest before his gun was at his side.

Lifting up the gun, he saw now that other men had gotten out of the car, all holding guns.

POP.

He pulled the trigger, but his aim wasn't true as a bullet lodged itself deep in his own arm.

Knowing he wasn't going to make it, his only hope was to warn her.

"Chloe, hide!" his voice boomed.

POP.

Refusing to go down, he went to tackle the man.

POP.

Drago's body slumped to the floor as his mind began to fog. He had failed.

I'm sorry . . . Chlo—

When Chloe heard the loud noises, she held herself tighter.

"Chloe, hide!" she heard Drago's muffled yell.

She moved a millimeter before a familiar voice spoke to her, freezing her in place.

Stay still, little girl . . .

More shots rang out before there was only silence.

. . . Or it'll just hurt worse.

A tear fell from her eye. A real, single wet tear touched her cheek.

The door slowly creaked open, and the figure of a man stood in the doorway. He looked just how he had four years ago, like he had come out of her nightmare, his black eyes still glowing with evil.

She closed her eyes. *Chloe, wake up and everything will be okay.*

"I've missed you, little girl."

Lucca walked out of the place he held his captive prisoner, waiting for his sins to wash away once the fresh air hit him, like they always did. This time, however, they didn't, and his heart sunk deep as the feeling he and Chloe shared began to fissure, telling him something terrible was happening.

Grabbing his phone out of his pocket, he saw he had a missed call from Drago. Quickly, he called him back.

ANSWER!

There was no answer.

Now running to his car, he called Sal, who picked up on the first ring.

"House, now!" was all he said before he hung up, throwing himself into his Cadillac and starting up his car.

Sal would be able to see what was happening on his computer. He would be able to help and assess the situation since he was closer to the house.

Lucca drove at breakneck speeds. He was too far away from the house. Too far away from Chloe once again. This was now the third time this wretched, hopeless feeling had taken over his body.

However, this time felt different, more … final.

Stay with me, Chloe. Please don't leave me.

He'd had her now, tasted her, felt her. Living even this short amount of time with her, he knew one thing for certain.

I won't be able to live without you.

PRESSING PLAY

ucca's *heart shattered into a* billion and one fucking pieces the moment he stepped into his house and saw Sal's sullen face, along with the blood covering the entrance to his family home. The darkness instantly rose, demanding to go after her that second, but Sal calmed him, telling him he needed to find out first where they took her, along with devising a plan to get her out safely.

Lucca asked to see the security tapes of what exactly happened, wanting to see it himself instead of being told. Then he watched every part of it: Drago fighting as he went down, and how Chloe simply sat there, too fucking afraid to even move.

It was clear there was only one person at fault. *Me.*

He took responsibility for everything: not being there to protect her himself, needing retribution after the look on Chloe's face this morning and what she had told him. She had said that one of

Lucifer's men, who had held her down, had worn the ring while Lucifer had marked her body repeatedly.

Lucca had held her for a while until she had calmed, while the darkness had only grown inside of him. Then, afraid the darkness would blow at any second and not wanting to hurt her or force her into something she didn't want, he had left. He had needed to take it out on the same man who had held her down while she had been tormented.

Raking his fingers through his overgrown hair that had reached the nape of his neck, he couldn't understand it. He had been so careful . . .

Then it occurred to him. The only thing he hadn't planned. *Amo. . .*

Sal's voice cut through his thoughts. "They are still working on Drago, but they say it doesn't look like he will make it."

Fuck! Drago was one of their best. Lucca needed him more than ever right now, but instead, he lay there, dying on a fucking emergency room table because of Lucca's stupidity.

"There's something else . . ." The sorrow in Sal's voice became more evident. "Lucifer left this."

Lucca stared at the disk his friend held out to him. "What is it?"

"You'll want to watch it . . . alone."

The moment he took the disk from Sal's hands, the sinking feeling returned. He knew what the disk held would haunt him for the rest of his life.

Sal was no longer able to even look at Lucca as he headed out the door to give him some privacy, telling him, "I only watched a few minutes of it before I had to turn it off."

Staring down at the disk, Lucca shakily put it in the computer. A sick feeling coming to his stomach, his finger wavered over the play button.

If she lived it, I can watch it.

Pressing play meant changing his life forever ...

A LIVING, BREATHING NIGHTMARE

FOUR YEARS AGO

T*hump.*

What was that? Looking at the clock on her nightstand, Chloe saw that her parents wouldn't be home for another couple of hours. She was still shaken up from the beating Elle had taken at school, so she told herself it was messing with her mind.

Turning off the lamp, she snuggled back under the blankets, her brain still filled with the images of Elle lying on the pavement, until she fell back asleep.

Her sleep didn't last long before a hand covering her mouth woke her up to a living, breathing nightmare.

She struggled against the dark figure, but it didn't last long. A hard force knocked her out cold …

Her body being slammed down on a table had her jolting awake. A scream escaped her as she saw men surrounding her in an unfamiliar room.

A tall, slender, older man with black hair and matching black eyes seemed to be the one in charge as two of his men held each of her arms while a third one held her feet.

An evil twist to his lips appeared before he ordered, "Take off her shirt."

"NO!" Chloe struggled even harder against the men, her tears blurring her vision. She was shocked by how fast her tears had been created before they could even fall.

Despite her best efforts, the two men who were holding her arms ripped off her shirt, exposing her bra.

"Please, please!" she begged, praying they would release her as they removed her shirt completely.

A flash of gold on one of the man's fingers crossed her vision as he grabbed at her shirt. It was a huge horseshoe diamond ring that she was sure to never forget.

The man who was apparently the leader approached her with a blade, his eyes skimming over her. She felt so small in that moment. Disgusting … Worthless … Tainted as they all stared down at her exposed skin.

Why is this happening to me?

The cold metal table underneath her was a stark contrast to her burning face from what seemed like pointless crying.

"Please! Stop!" No amount of kicking and fighting was a match for what felt like millions of hands holding her down.

The laughter from the evil man who held the knife rang through her ears mockingly.

"Stay still, little girl"—he drew the knife closer to her face—"or it'll just hurt worse."

Looking at his abnormally large, black eyes, she was sure she was looking into the eyes of the devil.

The silver blade inched closer and closer to her right eye until it was mere centimeters from her pupil.

"Don't blink."

A tear welled up in her eye, making it even harder to keep her eyes open. Her body began to tremble. She was going to blink.

"Don't blink, little girl," he warned again.

The tear fell, and her eyes started to close ... *God help me!*

The second her quivering lids shut, she felt the cold knife pierce her skin above her right eyebrow. It sunk deep and true, causing a shrill sound unlike any she had ever released to fill the air around them.

The pain only grew worse as he dragged the blade down her skin slowly, painfully. He then released the pressure on her skin, only for him to dig it back in right under her eye and begin it all over again.

Her shrill screams filled the space once more. However, the struggle in her was dying as she became too weak.

Lifting up the knife, this time he held her face roughly, shushing her screams while he cut a line down the right side of her lips.

When he pulled away again, letting her come up for air, the adrenaline she had used to fight was now gone.

As her blood trickled down her face and burned into her skin, she knew she would never forget the feeling when her tears met the blood to scorch paths of bloody tears down her face.

"Please, just kill …" It was hard for her to whisper her plea through her hoarse voice, but she had to try, hoping for mercy.

The maniac began to laugh while he caressed the edge of the blade over her skin. "Little girl, this is only the beginning."

Closing her eyes, another tear fell, mixing with the hot blood. Mercy wasn't going to be given tonight, leaving her with one final hope. To be saved.

The knife pierced her skin over and over as he cut into one arm … then her other arm … then her stomach. The agony and torture only continued. With every single cut that was given, she could feel him lay claim to her.

Heavy, cumbersome chains were placed on her body with each mark, her mind with each evil laugh she heard, and her soul with each time she heard the words "little girl." They wound and wound around her, pulling tighter and tighter …

Eyes beginning to blink slowly, she could feel herself drifting off now, the pain becoming too much to bear.

Her one final hope of being saved from the devil had disappeared. No one was coming to save her. And if someone did, it was too far past late. To save her now would mean that someone worse would have to take her soul from the devil and claim it as their own. However, a man like that shouldn't—wouldn't exist. And if he did, that wouldn't be saving her at all ...

The girl was starting to lose consciousness, and her now traumatized, gray eyes began to drift away. There was something he enjoyed about seeing the eyes change from the person they once were to the person they were after he was done with them. It was his mark; how he claimed them.

He had taken away the young girl she once was and made her into his beautiful creation. Her body, her mind, and her soul belonged to him and always would ... until he took away her last dying breath.

Her eyes rolled to the back of her head before her eyelids closed.

"Good night, my little girl."

The door opening had him turning his head to see his man pushing another man into the warehouse.

"Oh God!" the man cried, trying to get to the little girl, but his men wouldn't let him. "What did you do to her!" he screamed.

Lucifer slid the knife over the unconscious girl's body. *I made her beautiful.* "I warned you that the longer you took, the longer I would have with her, Maxwell."

"My daughter ... How could you ...? Why did you do this ...?" The little girl's father fell to his knees.

"This city is in need of a change." Turning, Lucifer wanted to see his face as he said, "Dante Caruso may have gotten you elected, but he no longer controls you. I do. You will do anything and everything I ask. Don't"—he pointed with his knife to the camera that had been recording the whole time—"and I will happily remind you who you and your precious family belong to." Walking up to the man on his knees, Lucifer touched the blood-dripping blade to Maxwell's face. "Do we have an agreement?"

Tears ran down Maxwell's face as he nodded. "Yes."

Going back to the girl on the table, he picked her up, cradling her in his arms as she slightly started coming to.

Leaning down, he whispered into her ear, "I'll have you again, little girl. Next time, I won't be giving you back. I'll kill you, and then you'll be mine forever."

Before handing her back to Maxwell, he held his new daughter to him tightly. A daughter who no longer belonged to Maxwell, but to the devil himself.

Chloe's mind flickered back to life when she heard a loud crash. The pain she felt was unbearable to her soul.

Opening her eyes, she realized she was in her father's arms as he took her down a hill to the wreckage of his car. Placing her in the wrecked car, he then pulled out his cell phone, dialing three numbers.

Her eyes opened and closed, seeing the mangled car around her as she heard her father's distressed voice.

"My name is Maxwell Masters, and there's been a terrible accident …"

DEATH WOULD FOLLOW

When *the screen went black*, it took everything in Lucca's power to keep down the bile rising in his throat. He wasn't a man with a weak stomach. He had inflicted some of the sickest shit you could ever see. However, it was something altogether different when he had to watch a helpless, innocent young Chloe beg and plead while she was marked for the rest of her life.

The already shattered remains of his heart managed to shatter into even tinier pieces as he felt a pain unlike any before. It wanted to break even a man as strong as him, but he couldn't—wouldn't—let it. Chloe had lived it, and he had witnessed it. Now she could give some of her burden to him, and they could share it *together.*

Pulling out the disk, he crumbled it in his hands. No one would be able to see its contents again.

The phone ringing on his desk had him staring at the

unknown number.

Sal came in with his laptop then, having been notified of the call and telling Lucca exactly who was on the other end.

Lucca picked it up and waited for Sal to give him the thumbs up.

Sal nodded.

Calmly, Lucca hit the answer button and put it to his ear.

"Hello, Lucca. I have something of yours," Lucifer mocked.

A low growl escaped Lucca's throat. "If you hurt her, I'll fucking kill you and anyone else carrying the Luciano name."

"Hurt her? I need her. It was only a matter of time before you came for me, anyway. We both know that."

He did know.

"Don't worry; I'm not going to hurt her ..."—Lucifer paused, his voice becoming proud—"like I did your mother."

The darkness in Lucca rose, grinning for what was to come.

"That was all I was waiting for."

At Lucca's words, the line on the other end went eerily silent before it clicked, ending the call.

Lucifer had just sealed his own fate. The only reason Lucca had kept him alive this long was to prove the man had had a hand in his mother's death.

Getting up, he didn't have time to waste. "Go fetch my dog."

"Where are you going?" Sal asked as he stood.

His voice was grave and dark when he answered, "Suiting up."

Now he had grounds for war.

He opened the door on the top floor of the casino hotel, not waiting to be invited in.

Dante was in the process of bringing a full glass of dark liquid to his lips, but stopped the moment he saw his son entered his office. His cold, icy blue eyes became colder as he took in his son's appearance, immediately knowing nothing good was about to come out of his son's mouth.

Lucca pushed back his freshly cut hair that highlighted his trimmed and shortened beard. Then he adjusted his all black suit while he stood menacingly in front of his father. You could practically smell the rage and thirst for blood coming off of him in waves. It was a rare and frightening sight for anyone to see. The image even gave grown men nightmares.

It was never a good thing to see Lucca dressed in a suit and tie. When the boogieman did put on his black suit, it always meant one thing … Death would follow.

"Explain," Dante demanded.

"You wanted proof before you wanted war …" The door opened again, and Sal brought in a bound and blind man. "Here it is."

Taking in the deformed and tortured man was another sight many weren't ever privy to. Lucca's masterpieces were works of art, and he was a true artist.

Leaning back in his chair, Dante smiled. "This the man who

broke into Nero's, trying to get to Maria?"

"Yes, but he wasn't there for Maria."

An eyebrow raised. "Then who?"

Lucca looked down at his malnourished dog that was silent. "Chloe Masters."

"Nero's girlfriend's scared little friend?"

Lucca adjusted his suit again, those words pissing him off. "You will not speak about her in that way."

Dante saw it then. "You're not fucking serious," he scoffed.

"I am very fucking serious." The words were spoken in a low growl.

"She's still practically a child, Lucca." His father's face became furious, knowing the severity of how his son felt about her by the look in his eye alone. Dante was bewildered, which made him angry. Lucca didn't express feelings toward his own family, let alone a girl. "You expect her to stand by you and handle the life you lead? She's damaged and weak."

"I told you not to speak about her in that way. Next time, I will make sure those words are your last," he warned him one final time. "She is neither damaged nor weak, and she will learn to stand beside me."

The boss shook his head, making it apparent he would never give his blessing. "You are forgetting something ..."

"What, that she's not Italian?" Lucca smiled. "A rule that will end when I take your place."

"What did you just fucking say?" Dante's icy eyes steeled into him.

"You heard me. We're getting tired of choosing women based on blood."

"You think I'm fucking stupid?" Dante huffed. "I know this, but the higher-ranking members in this family must always be full-blooded Italian men. You, most of all."

"We do not have time for this right now," Lucca growled. He had wasted enough time getting to Chloe already.

Filling his father in quickly, he told him about Lucifer being the one to scar Chloe, him protecting her and keeping her at the house, Drago going down for her, and how Lucifer was now holding her captive.

Dante listened to the story, realizing how far down the rabbit hole his son had gone, and all for a girl.

"My men are not going to go to war for you right this second over some girl, not when we don't even know if Drago is still alive or not!" He had raised his voice, hitting the table, before he got his anger back under control. "Even if I told them to, we've been at peace for years. They will not risk that and their lives. They would retaliate against us."

Lucca kicked the blind man at his feet. "Tell him why he marked her."

"Heee wanted Maxwelllll in his pockket, to give him information on youu orrr anything that coullld take you down."

The fury Dante held was now turning from Lucca to Lucifer.

Lucca continued the explanation himself, "The only reason he hasn't gotten to you yet is because Sal has outsmarted him and Drago has blocked him for all these years. We just never knew it was Lucifer then. When we suspected him, we needed the evidence."

"Fuck." Dante took a swig of his drink, trying to simmer himself down. "We have to think carefully and plan even more carefully. I am not taking my men to war right this second, not for her. That's the price you will pay for putting her above Drago and the rest of the family."

I thought he would say that.

This was exactly why Lucca had needed the final piece, why he'd had to wait and plan carefully, just like his father had said. Otherwise, he would have made Lucifer's death more imminent.

His haunting voice gave the command, "Sal ..."

Sal pressed a button on his phone.

"Don't worry; I'm not going to hurt her... like I did your mother."

Dante leaned forward as he stood up, his ice-cold eyes promising retribution. "The Caruso family goes to war. *Now.*"

THE DARKNESS
IN ITS TRUE FORM

hloe was back where it all began four years ago, in the cold warehouse that sat in the middle of nowhere. The same men who had taken her before brought her here, except for one of Lucifer's three men, the one who had worn the horseshoe ring.

She'd had nightmares of this moment ever since he had first let her go. *I always knew this day would come.*

Her wrists and ankles were tied with tight ropes. Her hands constantly moved, wringing, which only caused the ropes to burn her skin.

The devil placed her freezing body on a chair that sat in the middle of the desolate building. As he stared down at her, she could see the victory in his sick, black eyes.

"They're here," one of his men told the devil as she heard several cars pull up in a distance.

"Lucca?" the little girl in her helplessly whispered for the only man capable of saving her.

"You really think he's going to save you?" Lucifer pulled a long piece of fabric out of his pocket before tying it around her head to cover her mouth as she struggled against him. "That didn't work for you the last time, did it?"

It was dangerous thing to have hope. For her to hope to be saved this time when no one had come for her the last. This time, however, she now knew a man like Lucca existed, and the feeling they shared kept telling her one word over and over. *Believe.*

Lucifer ran his fingers roughly down her face. "I have dreamed of getting you back ever since I let you go. I've waited a very long time for you. Too long. I made myself sick over wanting you."

Chloe breathed so heavily she thought the fabric that was tied around her mouth was going to suffocate her. Every time he touched her, it left a trail of scorching fire that continued to burn her skin, unable to burn out. Feeling every touch he left on her, the pain of it started to consume her. She wanted to wash it away, yet she feared that soap and water wouldn't ever fix it.

He brought his hands to her hair, grabbing it so hard he was practically ripping strands out. "At first, I wanted to kill you. But when Lucca took you away from me, I realized I wanted something very different."

She didn't think it was possible to see anything other than the nothingness in his huge, black eyes, yet she saw something different now—obsession.

Chloe's eyes teared when he brought his face closer to hers. When she closed her eyes, the pooling tears fell as she felt his disgusting, cold tongue lick the scar that rested along her cheek.

"How does it feel to have three men want you? Me … Lucca … Amo …" When he uttered the last name, he could see the shock on her face. "Yes, you'll have to remind me to thank Amo for leading me back to you. I might even let him live … if Lucca hasn't killed him already."

Another tear fell down her cheek. She tried to pull her hands apart, wanting the rope around her wrist to release her.

"Soon, I will have you, my little girl. I just have to take care of business first," he whispered the promise to her before he released her.

That was when the door to the warehouse opened.

Lucca?

Men started filing in. Men she had never seen before. She quickly realized it wasn't Lucca or any of the Caruso family. These men weren't dressed in fine Italian suits and shoes. Most of them were only wearing parts of a suit, like a jacket or slacks, but they weren't made of fine materials. These men looked rough, almost like Lucca, but with a different quality to them.

Three men approached the devil, two of them being twins. All three had tattoos and were wearing several rings on each of their hands. All of them had something to them that reminded her of him.

"What's going on, Lucifer?" the one who seemed to be older

than the twins asked.

Lucifer ... That name gave her chills.

"I've told you; the family is being threatened. That is all you or anyone else needs to know." His voice had risen as he addressed all of his men, not just the one who stood before him, making them all scatter across the building to prepare. "Every fucking one of you will protect me and this family. No matter what."

The three seemed skeptical of Lucifer before they finally noticed her. They stared intently at her for a moment, their eyes gazing down at her scarred face.

Chloe held her breath, unmoving, as the identical twins stalked toward her. The two then parted off at different times, walking around her slowly in a perfect circle, looking down at her like a hawk does before it strikes its prey.

"Who is this?" one of the twins asked as he passed in front of her to walk around her back.

Lucifer grinned evilly. "My prize."

The other twin passed her front while they continued to circle her. "We'll watch over her for you then. Won't we, Matthias?"

"Yes," Matthias agreed, smiling as his eyes swept over her body.

The two were mirror images of each other, even down to their tattoos. She had no clue how to tell them apart.

Chloe swallowed hard and deeply, her eyes travelling to the third guy who had first spoken to the devil. He hadn't taken his piercing gaze off her, sending her already shivering body into more violent ones.

He stalked close to her now, until he stood right in front of her, staring down, his eyes roving over her scarred face. This close to him, it was obvious to her exactly who he was. His beard had hidden his identity from far away, but up close, you couldn't miss the fact that he was Lucifer's son.

When he walked behind her, she prepared herself for what he was going to do to her. Then she felt something warm over her shoulders, and then her arms.

Looking down, she saw that he had placed his jacket over her. It was warm from being worn, and it heated her bone-chilled body, giving her some relief.

All she could see was his back when he walked away from her, now jacketless, until he resumed his spot of watching her from afar.

She looked down at her wringing hands and her wrists that were becoming sore. The many men that filled the room with their guns made her feel a strong shift within herself, a feeling that intensified the strange thing between her and Lucca. It made her lose all hope of wanting Lucca to even save her.

If Lucca were to come, it could cost him his life, something she wouldn't be able to live with. Not only because she would hate herself for it, but because she now knew what it was like to be safe with him.

Chloe shed one last tear. *Don't save me; I'm not worth it.*

Seconds seemed to pass into minutes, minutes seemed to pass into hours. She continued to sit there, her body becoming sore and frozen, her wrists becoming raw.

The men in the warehouse only grew more antsy, while Lucifer only grew more crazed. Meanwhile, the three men continued watching her, the twins continuing to circle around her like a slow and broken clock as time crept on.

Chloe could feel the energy of the men change in the room, one by one, as the sound of cars started roaring closer, headlights illuminating the bleak, abandoned warehouse.

Looking down at her wrists, she could see trickles of blood flowing.

The twins stood on each side of her now, closer than they had stood, as Lucifer came to stand behind her.

The men all filed around the building, pointing their guns toward the massive door, with Lucifer's son standing in front of the line.

"You will await my orders. I have waited many years for this moment," Lucifer proudly ordered. "Today is the day we take back our city."

The door flew open, revealing many clean-cut men in Italian suits.

Tears brimmed her eyes. She could already feel the loss of him. *Lucca, don't!*

Gasps filled the air, and Lucifer's men started backing up. Some of them were practically shitting themselves in confusion.

"The Carusos! You didn't tell us it would be them!" was heard whisper-hissed around the room.

The intimidating suits split up, taking different sides of the room.

Her eyes grew wide when she saw Nero, Vincent, and Amo standing in the middle. They looked different to her. Stronger, older, scarier. They didn't even look like themselves.

When her eyes landed on Amo's, she could see the pain in them, and the regret he felt for putting her here.

When the three of them split, they revealed Sal, who was holding a chain in his hand that led to a man who no longer looked human. He was just skin and bones, covered in dirt, burns, and both new and old wounds.

She and the Lucianos stared at him with the feeling they knew him, but his matted hair and disfigured eyes made it hard for them to tell who it was, until it hit them all at once.

"Holy fuck." The men all took a step back.

She thought she was going to throw up from looking at him, seeing the finger that had once held his gold horseshoe ring was now gone . . .

She knew exactly who had made him this way.

When Sal pushed the tortured man down to his knees, Chloe's breath froze with her body, not thinking it was possible to feel any number than she had felt before his blue-green eyes met hers.

Lucca . . .?

Her eyes roved over him, never before seeing him like this. Lucca's hair and beard had been trimmed, and every part of the suit he wore was as black as night. His rough appearance now gone, in its place was something more menacing, frightening, and deadly. This was the darkness in its true form. The boogieman.

I'm going to save you, darlin', his voice whispered through her mind as their eyes locked. *Everything will be okay.*

The feeling they shared grew stronger, wrapping around her and protecting her. She had waited four long years for this moment, for the moment she would finally feel . . . *saved.*

A POWER THAT WENT BEYOND THIS WORLD OR ANY OTHER

Only one gun was held on the Caruso side, and it was in the hand of Lucca as he pointed it down upon the tortured man's skull.

Chloe held her eyes to Lucca's, too scared to look away from him, feeling safer with her gaze on his.

"Where's Dante?" Lucifer spat from behind her.

Three men came from behind other suits; the same vision as Nero, Vincent, and Amo, except older. Dante stood between Vinny and Enzo, the three men protected by their sons and the other suits.

"I'm willing to give you one chance, Luciano," Dante spoke with authority and confidence. "Trade me your man for the girl. No blood has to be shed." His eyes went over all their sons, and then their families. "We both have a lot to lose here."

"When did you become such a bitch, Dante?" Lucifer snickered. "I put the hit out on your wife, had her killed, and you are willing to let me walk away? You are a disgrace to this city."

I'm so sorry. Staring into Lucca's eyes, her heart broke for him. The man who had stolen her soul was responsible for stealing his mother's.

The feeling and bond between them made more sense.

Dante flexed his jaw, taking a step forward, his voice becoming more powerful as he said, "The girl for your man, Luciano."

Lucifer put his hands on Chloe's shoulders, squeezing her harshly. "What do you want with her? She is nothing to you, nor does she belong to any Caruso." He moved one of his hands, running a finger down the scar across her eye. "She has my mark. She belongs to me and me alone."

The devil's touch scorched her, but her eyes still didn't waiver, finding strength in the blue-green eyes that didn't move from hers.

"You took her from my home, my protection, and from my son." Dante paused, his ice-blue eyes growing colder. "She belongs to Lucca."

A creeping fear pulsing off the Luciano men filled the air the second he said Lucca's name. They had all taken a step away from her, not wanting to be near her. The only ones who hadn't moved were Lucifer and the twins.

"No! She's mine!" Lucifer screamed.

"Chloe is *mine*," a low, lethal voice filled the space, hitting the ears of every living thing in here until their blood ran cold, whispering over and over in all their minds. "Give her to me now, or I will blow his fucking brains out." He pushed the barrel of the gun against the man's head while the man kneeled, unmoving.

"There's not much of him left. He's better off dead." Lucifer laughed. "He serves no purpose to me anymore if he can't hold her precious body dow—"

POP.

Lucca had pulled the trigger, and the body fell forward to the floor.

Keep them to me, his eyes told her when she jumped from the noise.

"Kill them!" Lucifer demanded.

The room went silent. Lucifer's men looked around at each other, trying to decide what to do.

"What are you doing? Kill them!" Lucifer crazily screamed again, pulling his hands off of Chloe to back up and look around at his men. When he did, the twins stepped closer to her.

Lucifer's son, who stood in the front, hadn't yet moved. He had simply kept his eyes on Dante. But now he finally moved them to Lucca's.

"She's yours?"

"She's mine," Lucca told him with certainty.

"Step aside, Dominic. Let us take those who should be held responsible for their crimes, and no one else will have to die"— Dante paused—"today."

"I SAID, KILL THEM!" Lucifer was becoming deranged now.

Chloe's chest rose and fell with the force of her breaths while all the other Lucianos waited to see what Dominic would do.

Dominic slowly put down his gun, stepping to the side. The air felt like it had been sucked out of the room. Then they all followed suit, dropping their guns to the floor and stepping to the side. You could practically touch the shift of power from Lucifer to Dominic, from father to son. Now, the air that had been sucked from the room returned in a whoosh that felt different.

A stunned and crazed Lucifer went for his knife before going straight for Chloe. The twins immediately grabbed him, pulling him back and away from her.

It finally hit Chloe then. *They were protecting me … this whole time.*

Lucca took a step forward then, the only one in the room moving as he came toward her. The Carusos followed behind him with every step he took to her.

As the boogieman's blue-green eyes came closer to her, she tried to wiggle out of her bonds, tears falling from her eyes.

When he pulled out his knife, she didn't move an inch. Not even her eyes moved from his as he brought it close to her face, cutting the fabric wrapped around her face and head, letting it fall to the ground. Then the boogieman fell to his knees in front of her, cutting the rope away from her ankles.

Her heart was pumping out of her chest, the tears still falling, when he finally and carefully cut away the bloody rope that had bound her wrists together.

There was this split second, a moment in time that surely stood still. A moment so powerful it had been stopped by an equally powerful force when the two of them looked into each other's eyes. Only the two knew what was going to happen next, what they were thinking, how they were feeling. It was a power that went beyond this world or any other.

When time resumed, Chloe, who would have once run away, terrified of the dangerous being who stood before her, opened her arms and jumped into the embrace of the boogieman who kneeled before her.

It was beautiful.

"You saved me." She began to cry into his chest.

"I promised to save you, darlin'." Lucca held her to him with a tight force. "I will always save you."

Picking her up and cradling her, he stood as she held on to him, keeping her eyes closed and her face pressed into his neck as fighting and screaming replaced the beauty of their reunion with horror.

She never saw the moment when Sal decided the fate of terrified men by a simple point of his finger.

She never saw the real, true heartbreak on Amo's face when he had to watch Lucca pass by him, carrying out the girl he loved.

She never saw the daunting look Lucca had given Amo, promising to make true the threat he had given him.

Chloe never saw that the exact moment she had finally been saved was the exact moment Lucca had been saved from his own nightmares.

A SOUL THAT COULD ONLY BE RETURNED TO HER BY HIM

Lucca carried her up the steps and into the house, passing the doorframe where Drago's blood still stained the floors.

"Is he . . .?" Chloe swallowed, unable to say the words.

"We'll talk about it later, darlin'." Holding her tighter, he started packing her up the stairs.

She slammed her eyes shut, putting her face into the crook of his neck, her legs and arms wrapped tightly around him. Drago had given his life for hers, *something I will never, ever be able to repay.*

Reaching the top of the stairs, he smoothed his hand up and down her back, trying to comfort her while he took her into his room, passing through to the bathroom where he placed her on the vanity counter between the two sinks. When he stood between her legs, Chloe kept her eyes on his chest.

The softness in him seemed to disappear as he looked over her disheveled body, removing his black suit jacket from her shoulders. "Did he hurt you?"

"N-No." She found Lucca a little frightening. The darkness in him had yet to be released. "I-I did that to myself," she said when he pulled up her sleeves, exposing the raw and broken skin on her wrists.

"Did he touch you anywhere I need to know about?" Lucca growled, his possessiveness showing.

Knowing what he meant by that, she shook her head, hoping her answer would ease him just a little and shoo away the darkness. However, as she looked down at her lap, she could still feel the trails of fire where the devil had touched her.

Lucca put a finger under her chin, lifting her head and making her look up at him. "What is it?"

"I-I-I still feel him," she confessed. *All over me.*

He turned away from her then, and she didn't know if her confession had broken him or if it had made him more furious.

Leaving her on the vanity, he went to the glass shower and turned the water on before he returned right back to her. Then he pulled her off the vanity and to her feet, telling her, "You're going to let me help you."

"W-What?" She grew nervous, which made her body shake. She had felt like her frozen skin was finally beginning to warm, only to go back to feeling doused in ice.

"I will not touch your skin, nor will I join you, even though it kills me not to." There was slight pain in his commanding voice. "But you will let me help you undress and dress. I can't leave your side right now, Chloe. I just can't."

I don't want you to leave. She couldn't take not being with him, either, not after what had just happened. Slowly, she nodded her head.

When Lucca grabbed the hem of her sweater, gently removing it from her body, his eyes went directly to the scars on her arms. Then he gazed over the ones on her stomach he hadn't seen before.

Even though she wasn't able to look in his eyes, she could feel how hungry he was.

When he went to unsnap the back of her black bra, she became increasingly nervous. The scars on her body weren't her only insecurity. She had grown into her body early, having a womanly figure at a young age that she had never been able to hide. Her short stature didn't help; it only exaggerated her already overstated hips and breasts.

As soon as the bra fell away, she covered her heavy breasts with her arms, becoming embarrassed. *Why am I doing this?* The old part of her wanted to run, while the new side wouldn't let her.

Lucca could see her second-guessing and didn't waste any more time. He went to the hem of the black jeans around her hips, removing them and her thin underwear altogether.

"Shower," he gruffly ordered.

She ran to the safety of the shower as she held herself, trying not to die of embarrassment. When she closed the shower door behind her, the steamy warmth of the air gave her more privacy.

The second the water hit her skin, she felt like she could melt away. It was so warm, heating up her body that had been frozen for hours.

Lucca hadn't moved an inch from his spot, his eyes never leaving her silhouette behind the glass shower door. "Clean your wrists."

Listening to his command, she held her wrists under the water, watching the blood wash away and how the water turned slightly red before it cleared. Then she picked up the soap bottle and squirted some into her hands, lathering it over her body and trying to be careful not to get it on her sores.

Turning around to let the water run down her back and hair, she saw Lucca through the glass and froze in place. It was evident through his starving, fully blue eyes that he was in agony. Chloe could see how badly he hated that he had said he wouldn't touch her or join her. It was so bad that it looked like he was about to jump in here at any second.

Suddenly frightened that he would, Chloe quickly tried to finish, putting some shampoo into her hair and rinsing it out. Then she poured just a bit more soap into her hand and scrubbed at her face where Lucifer had touched her the most.

Get off, get off, get off. The feeling of him licking her still lingered, but with each scrub of Lucca's soap, the lingering feeling disappeared, replacing the devil's touch with Lucca's intoxicating clean mint smell.

When she was sure the devil's germs were no longer on her, she turned off the hot water and opened the shower door to grab the towel hanging outside of it. Then she hurriedly wrapped it around her body.

Lucca still hadn't moved.

"Come here," he ordered.

Hugging the towel around her, she shakily walked back over to him, her chest heavily rising and falling.

When he reached out, she didn't know what to expect; all she knew was that she completely and undoubtedly trusted him.

Lucca picked her up, placing her back on the vanity. Then he started pulling things out from under the sink, getting supplies to bandage her wrists.

While he began the process of taking care of her wrists, it was hard for Chloe to look at him. The pain of fighting the darkness back was so visible on him. And by the time he had fully bandaged her up, it was now killing her to see him like this.

"I-I'm sorry," she whispered. "I-I wish I could, but-but—"

"I want you so fucking bad, darlin'." He leaned down, resting his head on hers as he softened. "But I know you're not ready. I have waited over eight months for you, and I will wait forever if that's what it takes."

A single tear escaped her eye, feeling his emotions as her own.

She wrapped her arms around his neck and moved her head, positioning her face for him to kiss her.

Lucca looked down at her, wiping away the tear. "I've never seen you cry before today. Not even when you scream in your sleep."

"I-I haven't. I thought all my tears had dried up." In reality, they had just needed to be started back up again. They had needed a reason to run.

Leaning down closer, he claimed her soft lips with his, taking her in a passionate kiss that was most definitely not like the others. This kiss heated her from the inside, warming her low belly and then down to her femininity when he pulled her closer. Their breathing synced, both of them lost in one another.

"Open," Lucca rumbled over her lips when she wasn't getting the hint from his tongue.

Parting her lips from the vibration alone, she let his tongue enter her, creating a whole new sensation that she had never experienced before. She felt it hadn't lasted nearly long enough when he pulled his lips away.

Moving her damp hair behind her back, he placed light kisses from her jaw down her neck, his tongue picking up the droplets of water as he went.

Chloe quietly moaned when he licked at a sensitive part on her neck. She was burning up now.

He suddenly stopped and picked her up, holding her by her curvy ass as he carried her into the bedroom before setting her down on the edge of the bed.

Different emotions hit her—from confusion to neediness to worry—as she stared up at the dangerous, hungry being.

"I have to stop. Otherwise, there will be no forever if you need it," he strained to get out.

Her eyes grew wide, realizing she had been playing with fire.

He then hurriedly went to his drawers, grabbing one of his shirts, then returning in front of her. "Remove your towel," he demanded, staring down at her.

Biting her lip, her body obeyed, parting the towel and letting it fall to the bed, giving him a full view of her large breasts.

Lucca leisurely took his time placing his shirt over her head and down her chest while she raised her arms. His knuckles lightly grazed her peaked nipples so fast she wasn't even sure if they had or not.

The hunger was still there. The darkness right under the surface. He was a dangerous man even more so tonight, yet she still found herself safe in the boogieman's presence.

He's so beautiful, she thought, looking up at the haunting man who she was seeing dressed in a full suit for the first time. It somehow made him extraordinarily more handsome. It was a dangerous and scary thing for a man with his looks to look like that.

"You're staring, darlin'," he warned her, still trying to calm himself and keep himself from touching her.

She blushed, quickly looking away. "I-I'm sorry. I've just never seen you in a suit before."

"Do you like it?" he asked, placing a hand over her throat to get her to look back at him.

"Y-Yes," she nervously admitted, even though it made him look scarier and more intimidating.

"I guess I'll have to wear it more often for you then."

That sent another flame of heat to warm her body. Her eyes roved over his cleaned-up appearance, or cleaner, that was. He still had a beard, unlike the rest of the family; and his black-brown hair might have been shorter, mostly on the sides, but it was still just as wild, even when he slicked it back.

"You trimmed your hair and beard, too."

He smiled, his hand still firmly wrapped around her neck. "Do you like that, too, darlin'?"

That was hard to decide, since it was more permanent than putting on a suit. He was handsome no matter what length his beard and hair were. It just gave him a different effect.

"I-I like this length just as much as it was before." She licked her bottom lip, a bit nervous to say the next part. "You're very handsome either way."

By the wicked smile on his face, she was sure it wasn't anything he didn't know.

He placed a quick kiss on her lips before he released her throat to pull down the big comforter. "Get in bed before I change my mind."

Backing up from the dangerous being, she hurriedly got under the covers, pulling the thick material around her while she rested back on the bed. It had been a very long, painful day, and it all hit her just how tiring it had been.

When he started walking away, she sat up halfway. "W-Where are you go—"

"I'm just going to change. I'm not leaving you, darlin'."

Relaxing back, she watched him go to his dresser again. She wasn't able to look away when he pulled off the black tie then started unbuttoning his shirt. His dark Italian skin glowed in the dimly-lit room, highlighting the muscles all over his body.

Lucca had the body type every woman desired, and every man

dreamed of having. His arms, chest, shoulders, and upper back were the biggest part of him, having a tapered waist that had a strong six pack. She'd had a hint of what he might look like underneath just based on his black shirts hugging the top part of him, but never in her wildest dreams had she thought he would have been as perfect as she was seeing now. Everything about him truly put every other man to shame; as his lesser. Lucca was born right where he belonged. *The king of Kansas City.*

Turning her head away when he went to remove his pants, she pulled the comforter to her tighter and closed her eyes, trying not to picture the devil's face in her mind. She lay there like that for a few minutes until the bed moved and strong arms pulled her to a hard, warm body. The skin she felt was alarming, making her pull away to see it was his bare chest.

Lucca held her firmly, bringing her back to him. "I'm not naked, darlin', but I'm not going to wear a shirt, either."

Now that she could feel the thick material covering his bottom half, she eased back into him, yet still stiffly. It was strange to be held, feeling his skin all over her, but it was also strangely nice.

Both of their bodies held a cooling, minty scent between them, making her melt into him. She honestly felt she couldn't get enough of that smell. It called to her, soothing her.

The longer she lay with him like this, held by him against his chest, the faster the now faint trails of where the devil had touched her began to disappear. The memory, however, remained very much there, sending a shiver coursing through her body.

"D-Did you know that it was him who ...?" *Killed your mother.*

He rubbed his fingers up and down her back. "Yes, I always had the feeling he had something to do with her death, but I could never prove it."

"I'm s-sorry." She pressed closer to him, knowing how Lucca felt about his mother, though he never said it. "I'm sorry you had to wait that long."

His voice went dark. "I got him now, and that's all that matters."

Shivering at his words, her hair stood on end, thinking about the devil's wretched fate. It also comforted her to know he wouldn't be able to touch her again.

Beginning to fall asleep, the nightmares weren't as harsh while being in his arms, but she could still feel them coming for her, silently tormenting her.

Even though the devil's fate was fatal, she just wished her soul would have been set free ...

Every night for weeks, Lucca always had the same nightmare whenever he closed his eyes ...

Lucca could feel it suddenly hit him. It was like a change in the direction of wind—the feeling of dread that something terrible was about to take place.

His eyes went to her, knowing she felt it, too. The look of pure terror upon Chloe's face when the gunshots rang out through the mall would haunt him until the day he died.

He was so close, yet so far away from her again. The people running at him wouldn't let him push through to get to her. No matter how hard he tried to fight through the wave of what felt like thousands of people, he was still only one man.

She wasn't moving. She needed to mo——

"Chloe!" He singled out Amo's voice through the chaos.

He and Amo stood at equal distances apart, at equal distances away from her. The three made a triangle, with her being at the top.

He fought harder against the wave as he watched her take a small step toward Amo. He needed her to move faster and to him, knowing he would take the bullet for her if it came to that.

"Chloe, move!"

When she took a step again, this time toward him, his heart thudded in his chest, feeling like it was synced with hers. That's it, baby, come to me.

"This way, Chloe!" Amo's voice cut through again.

No! *"To me, Chloe!" He needed her. She needed him. He had to hold her. He had to save her. He had dreamt of this moment for months.*

If he saw her walk away with Amo yet again, he didn't know if he would be able to handle it, not for a second time.

Lucca could see the indecision on her face, the choice before her. It frightened him to his core, the thought that she would choose Amo, knowing it would be the wrong one. His and Chloe's souls were tethered together, twirling into one. He just hoped she could feel it.

Come to me and let me save you. I love you, Chloe.

When he watched her move toward him, he could have cried. She felt it!

Then he watched something change as she stared into his eyes. Fear. Fear of him.

He felt himself beginning to lose her when she looked back at Amo. It was like time had unfrozen while he watched in slow motion as she ran to the one she had chosen.

There was no heartbreak in this world that compared to his when she jumped into another man's arms. One who didn't belong with her. One who could never possibly love her the way he did. One who would never ever truly save her, because he didn't even know her soul no longer belonged to her. A soul that could only be returned to her by him . . .

Holding her now, he could close his eyes without the nightmares, knowing she had finally picked him. Knowing that her soul was finally in his possession. He just had to wait until she was ready, until she was ready to fully accept what she had always been meant to be. His.

AS YE SOW,
SO SHALL YE REAP

"**P**ut *the cigarette out, Lucca,*" Dante ordered, annoyed by the smell. They had been discussing the Luciano family's fate, and he was already furious enough as it was.

Lucca flicked the ashes off his cigarette, ignoring the order.

Dante's jaw flexed as he waved his hand in front of his face to get the smoke to dissipate.

A brief knock on the door interrupted the staring contest between the two men. The consigliere had arrived.

Vinny waited until the door closed behind him to say, "The Lucianos have requested a meeting."

Dante took a swig of his glass, his attitude unforgiving.

The consigliere knew his boss too well.

"I think we should listen to what they have to say. If war is inevitable, then so be it, but if it can be averted by the Lucianos making amends, should we not at least listen to their offer?"

"No." His father's pitiless gaze moved to Lucca's. "If she hadn't been there, I would have fucking lit that place up."

You mean, if I didn't care about her. Taking a bigger hit, he blew the puff of smoke in his father's direction.

"We might win the war, but there will be costs. Make sure you are willing to pay that price, Dante," Vinny told him with finality.

Lucca put his cigarette out in the ashtray. "I say we hear what they have to say."

After a few moments and a few sips later, Dante abruptly nodded his head.

Vinny opened the door, letting the three Lucianos enter. At least they were smart enough to keep their eyes down and respectfully bowed their heads to his father, while Dante's ice-cold eyes pierced each one of their souls.

"Mr. Caruso, we are here to beg for your forgiveness." Dominic took a step toward the desk, looking more disheveled than usual, which wasn't saying much. His brown hair was messed up as if he had been running his fingers through it repeatedly, his dark beard that usually successfully disguised his sinister expression only accented it, and his tattoos under his V-neck muscle shirt showed starkly against his olive complexion.

All three of the men appeared as if they hadn't slept.

Angel and Matthias' hands were in their jacket pockets, both wearing stony expressions. Lucca knew their pride was suffering from having to listen to Dominic come to beg Dante for their lives.

"Why should I give it? Your father broke the contract to keep the peace between our families." Dante slammed his fist down on his desk, causing the cigarette's ashes from the ashtray to fly up into the air. "He murdered my wife!"

Dominic now looked into the cold eyes. "We had no knowle—"

"I don't give a fuck!" Dante cut him off. "Lucifer and his men also broke into my home, took something that belonged to the Carusos, and almost killed one of my best men, who is still fighting for his life. Your father wouldn't have given the same consideration to my sons, to my family!" The ferocity in his depths grew, along with the disgust on his face. "He didn't even care if Sal would die trying to defend me. A son he didn't want to claim because of the embarrassment of fucking a drugged-out whore, even though the Luciano family name was becoming extinct. But why am not surprised? If he didn't care Sal was starving on the streets when he was a kid, why would he give a fuck when Sal was grown?"

Sitting there quietly, Lucca took out his lighter and began flicking it open and closed. They were to never speak about Lucifer being Sal's biological father, not even Sal himself. He had only ever heard Dante talk about it once.

"My father regretted his decision not to claim Sal, but it was too late. You had already taken him in. Angel, Matthias, and I never agreed with our father's decision not to claim Sal as his son. We are only soldiers trained to obey his orders. Lucifer insured loyalty through fear, you insure loyalty through respect. Sal was better off on the streets than being under our father's thumb."

Dante sat back in his chair, his ears seemingly attempting to listen. "As you and your brothers were?"

"Yes. Lucifer wasn't an easy man to live with, let alone have as a father." Dominic's grim face showed that this wasn't the first time he had begged for his and his brothers' lives.

"Are you trying to gain my sympathy? The Lucianos have been shown mercy once already by not having their name wiped out. Your father was left alive to continue the name, and he has betrayed the Caruso family, not once but twice."

Dominic shook his head. "We aren't in a war. Wars have two sides."

"You telling me the Lucianos won't avenge Lucifer and his men?"

Dominic gave a sarcastic, almost demonic, laugh. "Avenge them? You did us a favor."

Lucca stared down at his Zippo. "If you wanted your father dead, why didn't you take him out yourselves?"

"Lucifer knew I hated him. I wanted him dead, but not at the cost of one of my brothers' lives. He was careful to always keep one of the twins next to someone he trusted, someone who wouldn't hesitate to put a bullet in their head."

"He didn't trust you?" Lucca looked into Dominic's eyes to see if he was lying.

"No, Lucifer didn't trust any of his sons. He used the Luciano name to butcher and destroy anyone who was in his way, even at the expense of his own family. You weren't the only one killing the

Lucianos off. No one was safe from him. He wasn't the best choice to lead our family. What few of us are left only want peace and to rebuild our name."

Vinny moved from the side of Dante's desk to stand in front, the consigliere taking over the conversation. "And which Luciano has been chosen to lead?"

Dominic's gaze didn't waver. "Me."

Vinny and Dante shared a long glance, but it was Vinny who said, "You may carry the name, but will they accept you?"

"They already have." Dominic stared back at the two older men arrogantly. "They'll follow me; I'll make sure of it."

"How do you propose to alleviate Dante's anger?" Vinny asked.

"The Lucianos will give up another fourth of our profits until you see fit to go back to the original contract agreed upon."

Vinny didn't turn to Dante to see if he agreed. He knew, as well as Lucca did, that the ridiculous offer wouldn't deter his father's anger.

"Half." Vinny increased Dominic's offer to one that would hurt.

Dominic sharply nodded his head, his quick response showing he had expected his low ball offer to be refused.

Vinny hadn't become Dante's consigliere by being an idiot. His sharp gaze watched Dominic's expression as he dropped the next bombshell. "The Luciano men need help rebuilding their bloodlines. The Italian blood running through your blood is weak and diluted," Vinny spat out, his voice hitting the three like a whip with the insult. "A woman from the Luciano family who is at a marriageable consent will be chosen to wed one of the Carusos."

Lucca evilly grinned as he rolled his Zippo through his fingers. The show he had expected from Vinny was much more pleasing than he had originally thought.

Dominic clearly hadn't planned on that, and Angel and Matthias weren't able to hide their own horrified expressions.

"Which one of the women do you want? Which Caruso would she be expected to marry?" Dominic grated out.

Vinny shrugged. "Both will be up for Dante and I to decide. Whoever we choose from the Carusos will be able to see that the Luciano will live up to the contract this time. Trust will be earned, one child at a time, as the Caruso's blood mingles with the Luciano's. Maybe by the time we have four or five Carusos born, Dante will feel more forgiving. A child can heal a lot of wounds."

Dominic wasn't as quick to agree to the second term when he nodded his head. "Are we done?"

"Not quite." Vinny smiled. What they had thought was hard before wasn't going to compare to this. "Until Dante can find it in his heart to find forgiveness, one of the twins will be our insurance. If any part of the contract isn't enforced, one of your brothers will pay the price."

It just keeps getting better.

The twins looked at each other. Neither brother wanted the other chosen.

Angel stepped forward. "I'll stay."

Matthias moved to stand beside Dominic. "No, I will."

Both of them were trying to protect the other. Lucca guessed it wasn't the first time.

He studied the men. Opening his mouth, a name was coming to his lips, when Vinny spoke before he could.

"Angel."

Lucca took out one of his cigarettes from his pack. It was a no-brainer for Vinny to choose Angel. None of the Lucianos would ever be considered classy, but the twins looked like thugs. The number of tattoos and overblown muscles were more suited to the riffraff found in the dark alleyways of the old city of their heritage. The identical twins were mirror images. From what Lucca knew, everyone in the Lucianos joked that the only way to tell them apart was to stare at the images of their tattoos. The twins shared the same exact tattoos, even going so far as placing them in the same exact part of their bodies. The difference was, Angel's tattoos were the mirror image of Matthias'. Lucca understood what Vinny didn't. Angel was the twisted image of Matthias.

Lucca debated challenging Vinny's choice. Instead, he decided to keep quiet. He wasn't fooled by the attempts of the Lucianos to save their lives. They reminded him of a rabid dog that was just waiting for the right time to attack, ripping off the hand that fed them.

Dominic shook his head. "Matthias would be the better choice. I wouldn't do anything that would jeopardize either of my brothers' lives."

That Lucca believed.

Vinny raised his hand, stopping Dominic. "Angel is the younger one. The Lucianos have taken a protective attitude toward him."

Lucca lit his cigarette to keep from laughing.

Angel was lazy. He let everyone do his dirty work for him. Matthias would break bones if the gang bangers and drug dealers didn't pay for their protection. If breaking bones didn't work, that was when Angel would be sent in. When he was finished, the protection was paid for with interest.

Lucca had a better chance of controlling Angel than his own family did. He didn't want Angel to do anything to break the fragile peace that was being given to them.

Lucca remained silent, feeling a flash of respect for Dominic. The new boss of the Lucianos wanted a true peace for the first time in decades.

Lucca met Dominic's gaze. "I supervise the men. I'll find the perfect place for him."

Everyone in the room could see them size each other up as Lucca silently told him he wasn't fooled by Angel.

It was a strange thing but, for once, Lucca actually wanted peace between the two families. After his mother had been killed, he hadn't given two shits if they were in a war. He had begged for it to exact revenge. Chloe had changed that, however. He wanted peace to keep her safe.

It had taken years to fully understand the enormous responsibility his father held.

Dominic turned back to Vinny. "So, we good?"

"Dante?"

His father's expression was torn.

Lucca looked down at the glowing tip of his cigarette. He wanted peace for Chloe's sake, but it was Dante's wife they had killed.

"Dante,"Vinny repeated sadly. "Whatever you do will not bring Melissa back. If the Lucianos redeem themselves, then what have you lost? You already lost what was most important to you. A child born with Caruso and Luciano blood could accomplish what generations have tried to do—bring true peace."

Dante held out his hand to Dominic then, and the younger man took his hand in his firmly, agreeing to the terms.

A threat came to Dante's eyes and voice when he warned, "Don't you fucking disappoint me."

Lucca inhaled deeply, letting the end of his cigarette burn bright red. He remembered an old Italian proverb Dante had drilled into his head when he was younger. *Come semini, cosi raccogli.*

As ye sow, so shall ye reap.

NOT EVEN IN DEATH

Chloe *had stayed at the* house with Lucca for a week, not leaving, giving herself time to heal and for Lucca to make sure all threats were gone.

It was weird to think of the future, something she had pushed out of her mind for the past week, unsure of where exactly she belonged anymore.

Ever since her scars, she had no longer felt she belonged in this city because it had betrayed her, but she no longer felt she could belong anywhere without Lucca, and Lucca did belong in Kansas City.

She once thought she always belonged beside her best friend Elle, but it had been unrealistic for her to think it would last past college. Now, Elle had found her place in the city beside Nero.

The future was a scary, dark thing, especially when she felt the bond between her and Lucca so strongly and so soon. It scared the shit out of her, to be honest.

On one hand, she loved being protected by him. And the power he held made her feel as if she could never be hurt and always be saved. And yet, the little girl in her still believed it was too good to be true, that Lucca might get sick of her and toss her aside, just like her parents had.

So, when Lucca had asked her to pack her bags, a creeping fear had snuck in that it was already that time. Then he had brought her to the casino hotel, carrying her bags up to the top floor and heading down toward Nero and Elle's place.

Even though she was excited to see her best friend for the first time in a long time, she was also scared that Lucca was leaving her, dropping her off to become Elle's problem until she could go to Stanford, for real this time.

Getting to almost the end of the hall, Nero's door flew open and Elle ran out. Then she froze in place the second she saw Chloe, who was just as frozen.

A furious Nero came out of the door a moment later.

"Lucca, I tried t—" He stopped when Lucca raised his hand behind Chloe, stopping him. That was when Nero finally noticed the girls hadn't yet moved.

Not until Chloe saw Elle's face had she realized just exactly how much she had missed her. Then Chloe was the one to take the first step toward her, opening her arms when Elle closed the distance between them. They held each other tightly for a few minutes, their eyes becoming teary.

"I've missed you so much," Elle cried. "I haven't even been able to watch a movie without crying, wishing you were here."

Chloe giggled through her own cries. "I've missed you so much, too." She had been sure Elle would probably hate her guts for lying to her for over a month. "I-I'm sorry I didn't tell—"

Elle quickly pulled away from her then, going right up to Lucca's face and shoving him right in the chest as hard as she could.

What the—

"I told you that you couldn't have her!" Elle pushed him harder this time. Lucca didn't budge.

"What the fuck!" Nero yelled, running to get her away from him.

Lucca held his hand up, stopping him again.

"I told you that if you hurt her, I will kill you!" Elle hit his unresponsive chest again.

Chloe's mouth dropped to the floor.

Lucca stood there, taking the hits. "I promise you that if I do, I'll let you."

Elle, who was mid-hit, stopped, shocked by the answer. "Really?"

Lucca nodded. "Yes."

What Chloe saw next shocked her even more while it also warmed her heart.

Elle wrapped her arms around Lucca, hugging him. "Thank you for saving her."

"You're welcome, Elle." He accepted her hug, patting her on the back.

Aw … Chloe felt herself getting emotional again.

"I still don't like you." Elle composed herself, going back to pushing him. "You're not good enough for her. She deserves a nice boy. I know why you're so secretive at your place. All you do is fuc——"

Lucca reached out, grabbing her and covering her mouth with his hand. "Okay, you can fucking get her away from me now," he growled at Nero.

Nero, completely stunned, hurriedly went for Elle.

"W-What did she just say?" Chloe bit her lip.

Elle managed to get her mouth free when they transferred her. "Women. Probably hundr——"

Nero slammed his hand over her mouth. "I'm sorry, Lucca. I'll get her under contr——OW!" He jerked his hand from her mouth when she bit him.

"No, you will not. I'm still mad at you for knowing she was with Lucca this whole time!"

Chloe could see by Lucca's face he hadn't even known Nero had known.

He then pulled Chloe to the door opposite of Nero and Elle's and started unlocking it.

"Is this your place? Where she said you fu …?" She couldn't even think clearly.

"Yep! He answered the door, covered in sweat, with no shirt on. Me and Lake think he has a sex dunge——"

"Shut her the fuck up before I do it my-fucking-self!" Lucca yelled over his shoulder while trying to hurry up and unlock all his bolts.

"I'm trying, but she's fucking slippery!" Nero tried to push a fighting Elle back into his place.

"I-I-Is all that true?" Chloe started wringing her hands. *A sex dungeon?*

"She's just assuming, darlin'," he assured her as he started pushing her quickly inside, along with her things. "When she needs to look at who she's with."

"Fuck it." Nero quit worrying about Elle's mouth and just picked her up over his shoulder.

"Don't let him call you that. He calls every girl darlin'. You got to nip it in the bud like I did with Nero when he called me bab—"

Both doors slammed at the same time.

She wasn't even able to look up at him, not knowing what to think.

Lucca's ferocity simmered out at seeing Chloe's nerves, and he gently took her hand in his. "Come with me."

Following him, she looked around the space, noticing it was laid out just like Nero's, but mirrored. The styles, however, were completely different. Lucca's had earth tones of dark wood and greens, just like in his room at the house. It was modern, but not too modern. More traditional than the other penthouses she had seen. It was cozy, warm, and perfect, reminding her of the outdoors that perfectly sat in downtown Kansas City.

With it being a corner penthouse, it had floor-to-ceiling windows on two of the walls, really giving juxtaposition on the outdoors and the city.

A slight pain reached her heart, thinking about what Elle had said. It was hard to imagine Lucca in here with many women.

Pulling her close, he wrapped his arms around her, holding her tightly. "I'm not going to pretend I'm a virgin, when we both know I'm not."

"I-I know." She pressed her face into his chest, not wanting him to see the hurt on her face.

She knew he was far from a virgin, but it had stung to hear how he brought many other women here when this was her first time coming here. Admittedly, it hurt to even think about Lucca with a woman.

He leaned his head down, nestling into her neck. "But I can promise you, you're the first and last woman I have or ever will bring here."

Moving her head, she wanted to look into his eyes, almost not believing it.

"I've had this place for a long time now. I don't like letting anyone in here because it's my own personal space and a place for me to think. The only one to come in here, other than me, is Sal on occasion."

Chloe smiled, pressing her face back into his chest. For once in her life, she felt important. She took it as an honor for a man like Lucca to trust her in a space so special to him.

"Now, is there anything else that upset you?" he asked teasingly, bending down to bite her earlobe.

Biting her lip, she didn't know how to come out and say it, but … "I-I like it when you call me darlin', but …"

"You don't want me calling anyone else that," Lucca finished for her, smiling.

She nodded as she blushed from confessing how the darlin' thing worked on her so much so she didn't want him to stop calling her that.

He took another bite of her earlobe. "Then I won't, darlin'."

Leaning up, she gave him a quick kiss on the lips, wanting him to know how happy he made her.

When she dropped back to her feet, she couldn't help laughing. "So, what were you doing to get all sweaty?"

"I'll show you." Lucca took her hand again, leading her through his penthouse and going up the stairs that led off into the master bedroom. She could see a spiral staircase that hadn't been in Nero's, which he led her to, allowing her to head up first.

With each step, she became more confused. "How can it go anywhere? This is the top floor."

"You'll see." He helped her push up the top hatch in the ceiling.

Chloe looked down at her feet as she watched her step, finishing the climb up. Then the slight noise of the city greeted her ears, making her finally look up. When she did, she almost fell back on Lucca, the beauty taking her breath away.

He was silent, holding her up in front of him and keeping her steady as she took it all in.

"I-Is this real?" she whispered, blinking to see if it was heaven or just a mirage.

"Yes, darlin'."

Taking a step forward and spinning around, her eyes moved over the flowers then to the glass walls where she could see the city all around. It was a little greenhouse filled with many flowers on top of the building. The breathtaking view was unlike anything she had ever seen.

It took her a few moments of looking around before she turned to look into his eyes. "You did this?"

Lucca's eyes were now a fully bright shade of green. "For you, yes."

Another slight pain reached her heart. Except, this one was different.

When she turned back to him, it was like the wind had been knocked out of her to stare at someone like him, surrounded by something like this.

"It's so beautiful," she whispered.

Walking toward her, he wrapped his strong arms around her again. "I started working on it months ago, to keep myself busy so I wouldn't come for you. I haven't been with a single woman since I first saw you. I couldn't. None of them were you. Every time I wanted you so fucking bad, I would come here to keep myself sane."

The pain in her chest only grew stronger, consuming her whole heart. The heavy, old chains on her soul were beginning to rattle.

"I didn't think I would ever be capable of love, until you." He lightly tugged her hair down, forcing her to look into his eyes. "I love you, Chloe. You're the only person I've loved, or ever will love."

The chains broke free, her soul feeling freedom for the first time in four years. Freedom that only lasted a second before it was claimed again as lighter, tighter chains took hold, claiming her as his.

These chains might hold her captive, but they were ones she could live with. Chains that didn't weigh heavily on her body, mind, or soul. Chains that were more permanent. Chains that could never be broken … Not even in death.

I am yours forever.

A TASTE OF YOU IS . . .
WORTH A LIFETIME IN HELL

"*thought you brought me here* to have me stay with Elle," Chloe admitted nervously as Lucca helped her down the last step of the winding staircase after spending hours in the greenhouse.

Lucca lost his smile at her words, stopping to stare down at her bowed head. "Chloe, look at me."

She made herself look up, seeing mixed emotions on his face.

"I once promised you that, when the semester was over, I would let you leave. You don't have to be afraid of Lucifer ever again. You don't have to be afraid of anyone anymore." He ran a tender finger down her cheek, watching her lip tremble at the love glowing in his eyes, making them look greener than she had ever seen them before. "I can't keep that promise, though. I can't let you leave and walk out that door, because now I know what it's like to have you."

"I don't want you to let me leave," she breathed helplessly. *Ever.* "I gave myself over to you. I said the words."

Lucca raised his hand to her throat, his eyes now turning back to blue-green. "Say the words, darlin'."

Her chest rose and fell with a force, knowing exactly what she was about to do.

Setting her fate in stone, she said. "I am yours … forever."

He squeezed her delicate throat under his grasp a little tighter. "Again."

She looked at the frightening being, unafraid, her heart swelling. "I am yours forever."

His eyes flashed blue for a split second before he lifted her up and carried her to his bed, where he was going to prove he owned her body the way she had always known he had.

Chloe buried her head in his shoulder, nervously imagining the things he was going to do to her. Shockingly, she didn't feel any of the fear she had always expected. Instead, she was more nervous that she would disappoint him. He had waited months for her, for this moment.

"You won't be disappointed if I get it wrong the first time? I mean, you've been with a lot of women …"

"Darlin'," Lucca set her down on the bed, then started tearing his clothes off. "That would be fucking impossible."

She wanted to look away when he unzipped his pants, but she couldn't. His arousal was so evident her body wouldn't allow her to. It wanted to see all of him.

When his long, thick length was set free, she didn't know if she gasped or moaned.

Lifting her up from the bed, he wasn't giving her time to decide which one it was. He took her clothes off just as fast as he had his own. Then he slammed her ass back down onto the mattress, causing another gasp to escape her.

Leaning down to press a quick kiss to her lips, he brought his hands to her shoulders, pushing her farther down on his bed.

Chloe could feel the fire between her legs as he braced his hands on the bed next to her and began kissing the side of her neck, working down until he was kissing the cleft between her breasts.

She stiffened, the fire wanting to simmer when he went lower, kissing the scars across her abdomen.

"Beautiful," he murmured as his tongue wiped every memory of Lucifer inflicting them on her. "I'm never going to let anyone hurt you again, baby."

Chloe's breath hitched at the sight and the words he had spoken. *How does someone like him exist?*

"I know you won't." Her trust in him was unbreakable.

The fire burned hotter than ever when he slid his mouth lower until his bearded lips hovered over her center.

"I'm going to have to go to confession," he told her. "God is going to damn me to Hell for what I'm about to do."

"W-Wha—"

With the tip of his tongue, he parted her flesh and swiped up and down her slit.

Chloe jumped at the startling sensation, her head falling back and her legs beginning to shake.

He pressed his arm into her hips, holding her still. Groaning, he then pressed his mouth closer. "A taste of you … is worth a lifetime in Hell."

When he increased the pressure of his mouth against her, Chloe felt him sliding his tongue inside of her in quick licks, and then deeper as he became more demanding, more hungered.

Lifting one of her legs over his shoulder, he plunged his tongue into her writhing body.

Oh my God. She began panting. "Take me with you."

Her admission had him tightening his grip on her thigh, his mouth working harder, becoming more ravenous.

The fire inside of her blazed stronger, each lick exposing nerve endings that had lain dormant until Lucca had set them off.

"Lucca!" she loudly moaned. Her nerves had reached their breaking point, sending her to an abyss that she hadn't seen before and didn't want to come back from.

As she tried to come back, she felt Lucca lower her leg to the bed before his arousal went to where his mouth had been.

Her breaths became haggard, her nerves coming back. "I-I might need to catch my bre—"

His hand went to her throat as he stared down at her with fierce eyes that silenced her. Then she felt his arousal start to slide inside as he wrapped his other arm around her.

Chloe winced at the slight pain, writhing to adjust herself.

"Stay still, Chloe," he demanded as he took her bottom lip between his teeth. "It won't hurt for long."

She wasn't so sure.

The hand on her throat tightened slightly. "Which one do you think is tighter: my hand or your tight pussy?"

At his words, her eyes wanted to roll to the back of her head and a rush of wetness hit her that made him move more easily inside of her.

Without warning, she felt a hard thrust deep inside as he loosened his hand around her neck. When his length started to retreat again, his hold on her throat then tightened. Chloe couldn't regain her equilibrium, becoming lost in the repetitive motions. He was playing her body like a musical instrument, like a violinist that made breathtakingly beautiful music with his hands.

The now familiar curling sensation was coming back, making her grab Lucca's broad shoulders as she tightened her legs around his hips, thrusting herself up as he thrust down.

Lucca kept his eyes intently on her scarred face, reading every expression. "You like that, darlin'?"

"Yes!" Chloe cried, shocking herself. She couldn't believe she enjoyed him holding her throat as much as when he rocked inside her body.

Now as he alternated between holding and releasing her throat, it was tighter, rougher, forcing her to look into his blue-green depths.

"I love you, Chloe."

She witnessed something different in him as she looked deeper into his eyes. Chloe had thought she needed him, that she depended on him more than he ever needed or depended on her. But that wasn't it at all. Lucca needed and depended on her just as much as she did him. Their need and dependency were equal. The relationship between them was just as equal. One was not more important than the other. They both needed one another to survive.

The chains that had captured her body, mind, and soul didn't mean Lucca owned her. Now she could visibly see he carried his own chains around his body, mind, and soul. The same chains that held her, held him. They were held together … as one.

That feeling, that bond they shared between them, she was now fully able to understand.

We're soulmates.

Chloe felt a tear escape, running down her scar. "I love you, Lucca."

His eyes turned a striking shade of green as he tightened his hand around her throat and plunged into her tightness harder.

"Again," he ground out.

"I love you!" she cried out as he gave a thrust that had her screaming as she fell into the abyss that was waiting for her. And Lucca was, too. It was like a beautiful nightmare she never ever wanted to awake from …

REBORN

Now *that Chloe and Elle* lived right across the hall from each other, they were making up for the time they had missed over the past month.

It was like a dream come true. For the first time in her life, Chloe felt like she truly belonged, which was right beside Lucca and only a few steps away from her best friend, the girl who had protected her with her own life.

Chloe had already applied to the university here in Kansas City so she would start next semester. She was still trying to figure out what to major in. At Stanford, she had taken a bunch of different classes, trying to figure out what exactly she wanted to do. Lucca had assured her, however, that in time, she would know what it was. If that was to stay in her greenhouse all day, that was okay by him.

The truth was that Chloe had never thought much about a future, because she never really felt like she had one. The only thing she had ever wanted in her future was to leave Kansas City, and college was the best way to do it.

Even now, she didn't know what the future held for her, but she knew, as long as it was with Lucca, then everything was the way it was meant to be.

Her friend, however, still didn't think that.

"You know what it means, right? To be with Lucca . . .?" Elle asked.

"I know," she tried to assure Elle. Then she looked over at her strangely. "You do know who you're with, right?"

"Yes, but Nero isn't the underboss."

Has he not told her?

"Um, you do know he can be, right? When Lucca becomes the boss?"

"Yes, but he will never *be* the boss." Elle's big blue eyes drilled into her. "And if Lucca has a son . . ."

Chloe swallowed the huge lump that had suddenly formed in her throat. She couldn't believe she had never thought of that. *Oh, shi—*

Lake came storming through the door, slamming Nero's door shut behind her.

"What's wrong?" Elle asked as their attention went to the tall, furious brunette.

Lake fell onto the couch, crossing her arms. "I've told Vincent a million freaking times to make Lucca find him somewhere else to work. He says he has, but I think he's lying to me." She threw a pillow at a laughing Elle. "I don't know why you think it's so funny. Nero's working down there, too!"

Having dodged the pillow, Elle tried to sound confident when she said, "Nero promises he doesn't watch the women."

Women?

Lake rolled her eyes. "They aren't blind!"

"I don't think he's lying," Elle said as she shook her head, but her confidence seemed to be leaving.

"Trust me; they are."

"Maybe it's important they watch the women," Chloe said. Lucca had told her they were like bouncers protecting the workers.

Lake huffed. "Yeah, it's *real* important that Nero, Vincent, and Amo watch the women with skimpy outfits give lap dances."

What? "I thought it was an underground casino?"

"It is. One where the dealers are all women in slutty outfits."

That's why Amo loves it down there. Wait . . .

"H-How do you know so much about it?" Chloe asked, confused.

Elle busted out in laughter.

Lake paused then dodged the question. "That's beside the point. The point is that Nero and Vincent are down there right now, in a sea of practically naked women!"

Elle's laughter quickly died, which made Chloe burst out in her own.

"You shouldn't be laughing. Lucca practically runs it," Elle snapped at her.

Her laughter started to die. "H-He does?"

"Yep." Elle stuck her tongue out. "Lucca isn't so perfect, now, is he? Bet his greenhouse ain't so freaking grea—"

"I trust him," she said without a doubt. "He said he hasn't been with a girl since he met me nine months ago. I don't have a reason not to trust him."

Elle and Lake stared at her, blinking.

It was Lake who spoke first, practically fanning herself. "I'm sorry, Elle. I can't pretend anymore that I'm not team Lucca. Are you sure the greenhouse isn't a sex dungeon?"

"Team Lucca—What? No!" Chloe stared at the girls, who appeared a little warm.

"Oh my God," Lake whispered, her eyes getting a weird look to them as she looked over at Chloe, and then to Elle. The two of them looked like they knew what each other was thinking.

Elle scooted closer to her. "I've changed my mind. Lucca is good for you."

I don't like where . . .

Lake scooted closer to her, too. "He will do anything for you, right?"

Leaving Nero's place, she was beginning to think being so close to Elle *might not be such a good thing.*

When one of the guards by the elevator door shifted his feet, it had Chloe turning.

Amo's dejected expression remained lowered, not looking her way, showing her he knew she was in the hall.

Biting her lip, she tried to decide if she should talk to him. Then, taking a deep breath, she walked down the hall toward him, stopping a few feet away and not getting close enough for him to touch her.

"Amo, may I talk to you?"

He kept his head straight forward, not looking at her. "I'm working."

"I-I thought you worked downstairs ..."

She could tell by the look that flashed across his face that he hadn't realized she knew what that meant.

"I have been moved up here."

"Oh." She figured Lucca had taken the job he loved away *to punish him.*

Seeing how much Amo was hurting, it hurt her to know she had done that to him. Regardless, there was nothing she could do. Her saying something about it to Lucca would probably only hurt him more, since Lucca was still very upset with him.

Seeing the cast on his hand, her heart broke a little more. "I-I'm sorry about your hand."

Amo's jaw flexed, the heartbreak and damage she had caused him so evident in his eyes.

Realizing how much of a bad idea this was, she nervously turned to walk away, wanting to cry for what felt like the loss of a great friendship.

She was halfway down the hall when she heard his yell.

"Chloe!"

Once upon a time, she would have kept running, but now she

stopped, turning around to watch him walk up to her.

"I'm sorry." Amo raked his hand through his hair. "I'm sorry for so many fucking things that I wish I could take back. I was the one who led the Lucianos to you. I was the one to call you a freak and not once take up for you in high school——"

"Please, stop punishing yourself, Amo." She had to stop him, unable to bear his regret. "I don't blame you for any of that."

Amo looked at her, letting her see the pain in his eyes. "I have to. That's the only way I can live with you choosing to be with him after he fucking kidnapped you. If he hadn't, we would have been more than friends. You know that deep down."

"I left, Amo." Her eyes started to water. She hated the way he always made her break his heart even more, but it was the only way she could ever get him to understand. "I was leaving you behind."

"I would have come for you." Amo took a step toward her. "I was coming for you. I did come for you!"

She had to look away from him. "I know, but it was too late."

"No, it's not. It's not too late, Chloe …" He took another step toward her, the hope in his eyes growing. He prayed she would change her mind and choose him.

"It wouldn't have been real between us. You changed around me, and I never changed around you." She took a step back from him, looking him straight in the eyes. "We were just never meant to be. I know that, because I feel it in my bones. I'm meant to be with him. I am meant to be with Lucca."

Amo's eyes became glossy, his vision going toward the ground.

"I will always care about you, Amo, but as a friend … The same way I feel about Elle."

His fists began to curl at hearing the word 'friend.' "I fucking hate him for taking you from me."

Chloe shook her head. "Don't blame him. Blame me. It's not Lucca's fault I'm not in love you."

Amo didn't see the silent elevator doors sliding open, but Chloe did. Her eyes pleaded with the man getting off. *Please don't!*

When Lucca didn't move, she looked back at Amo. "Do you like gardening?"

"What?" Amo gave a frown of distaste, wondering why she had said that. "No."

Chloe gave a shaky laugh. "I do. I didn't know I did, but I do now. Lucca taught me how."

Lucca's harsh face relaxed while he remained silent by the elevator.

"I have always loved looking at flowers, but I never realized how much work goes into creating a beautiful garden. You have to pull out the weeds to give the flowers' roots room to grow. Lucca sat with me for hours upon hours, just helping me pull weeds." Chloe tucked her hair behind her ear, letting her beautiful, scarred face show proudly. "One by one."

Amo looked up at her, his eyes travelling down her scars, seeing the difference in her now. She had changed.

This was it. The moment when she would make her final choice once and for all.

"I didn't fall in love with Lucca because he kidnapped me. I fell in love with him because … he set me free."

Amo's tight fist loosened. The heartbreak was still there, but that little bit of hope in his eyes shattered to where the hope was gone. It was to the point where she didn't know which one was worse: *to have some hope or none at all.*

"Good-bye, Chloe," he said with finality, telling her in unspoken words that their friendship was over.

It broke her heart to see him end it, yet she understood, seeing the pain it caused him to even look at her.

"Good-bye, Amo."

Amo turned, coming face-to-face with a frightening Lucca yet again.

She held her breath for a brief moment, hoping he would listen to her pleas and wouldn't do anything.

Lucca continued staring at a frozen Amo before he passed him, hitting him with his shoulder. "Back to work, soldier."

Thank you. Chloe let out her held breath as Lucca walked toward her, taking her hand. She pressed herself into him, letting him take her weight as they walked into their place. By the time he had closed the door behind them, she had fallen into him, sobbing.

Packing her upstairs and to their bed, he let her cry into his chest as he ran his tender fingers down her back and twirled her tendrils of black hair.

When the tears no longer continued to shed, she whispered into the room, "Why does it feel like he died?"

"In a way, he did," he told her regretfully. "But he will be reborn when he finds his new purpose."

Chloe raised her gray eyes to his blue-green ones.

"It happens to every made man once. I thought it happened to me when I first became made, then when my mother died, and then when I saw you for the first time. But that wasn't when it happened, either."

"W-When did it?" she asked when he didn't continue.

Lucca rubbed his finger down her scar. "Maybe I'll tell you one day, but not today, darlin'."

She snuggled back into him, letting Lucca heal her broken heart. "I love you."

"I love you, too, darlin'." Twirling a strand of her hair, he then dropped it to hold her close. "Is there anything I can do to make you feel better? I can cook you something."

A slow smile appeared on her lips. Raising her head, she looked back into his eyes playfully. "Anything?"

Lucca stared hard into the two men's eyes before him, *the future of this family.* He took a hit of his cigarette, letting the end burn bright, "You two owe me."

Nero and Vincent gave a sharp nod to their heads.

"We three have the same problem." He flicked his ashes into the tray.

"What's that?" Vincent asked.

Nero's emerald eyes narrowed knowing exactly what it was,

"Our women are not Italian."

Lucca smiled, seeing the wheels turning in their heads. "They will give you an ultimatum; they will make you choose between the family and your girl. Our fathers have done it to others who will hold lesser power than us, and *they will* eventually make us choose."

Both Nero and Vincent's jaws squared knowing it to be true.

He could see the two men torn; one side of them who lived and breathed the Caruso family, and the other side finding true love. To make a man choose like that will surely kill him, no matter the choice.

"I gave you both the girl of your dreams, and in return you will choose them when the decision has to be made." An evil glow cast over his face. "As will I; then the Caruso future will be destroyed."

Nero grinned, "So you turn the tables and give them the ultimatum?"

"An ultimatum with only one choice they can live with."

"Thank you, fucking God. I've been waiting for the day when you would finally fuck over my father," Vincent began praying, a tear looking like it was going to stroll down his cheek. "And what's even better… I get to help you do it."

Lucca stared at the blond dumbass who thankfully at least had his good looks going for him. "If you think you are going to be my consigliere, you are shit out of luck."

"I'll be your consigliere," Maria chimed in, smiling as she flipped her magazine and tapped her high heels.

Vincent scoffed, "Like he would choose you over me."

"Over you, I would," he told him with certainty, hurting his pretty-boy pride.

"On one condition." Maria smiled. "That I don't have to be with a man of Italian blood, either."

Taking a hit, he blew the smoke at her, "No."

Her expensive heel stopped tapping the ground, "We'll see."

THIS IS YOUR
FINAL PURPOSE

Maxwell *poured another generous portion* of liquor into his glass. He didn't even look to see what he was drinking. As long as it gave him enough of a buzz to hide from the wretched mess he had made out of his life, it didn't matter.

He should have put a bullet through his head long ago, but he was too much of a coward. He also could have divorced his bitch of a wife, and not cared about the political power he had enjoyed the last few years.

"Maxwell?" A woman's sharp voice had him lifting his head from the desk he had been slumped over.

"Wh-What?" He tried to focus his gaze on his wife as she walked into his office. *Fucking bitch.* "Is it dinner time?"

Elaine curled her lips in disdain. "We had dinner four hours ago."

Maxwell tried to remember what he had eaten, but drew a blank. "I'm not ready for bed. You go ahead."

"Don't flatter yourself. I don't care when you go to bed."

"Then what do you want?" Maxwell reached for his glass, finding it empty. He started looking for the bottle of liquor, squinting his eyes as he looked around his desk, not seeing it. Then he searched where he must have left it after filling his glass.

"Maxwell, can you give me your attention for one second?" His wife came to the side of his desk, picking up the bottle from the floor.

"Go ahead. I'm listening." He took the bottle from her and started unscrewing the top.

"I just received an interesting phone call."

"Tell the telemarketers to call in the morning. Lana can answer their calls."

"It wasn't on the house phone. It was on my cell phone."

"Then I don't see what it's got to do with me." He poured another full glass, waiting for her to leave before drinking it. It wouldn't be worth the bitch session if he drank it in front of her.

Elaine moved the drink away. "Will you listen to me, you drunk?" Seeing she finally had his attention, she said, "I just received a strange call. The caller asked me if I knew where my daughter was."

"If she wanted to talk to Chloe, why didn't she just call her?" he asked stupidly.

"It was a man," she revealed. "I told him she was at college."

"So?" He just wished she would leave. "Did he say what he wanted?"

"No, he said, 'wrong answer' and hung up." Elaine gave a slight shiver, though she was practically made of steel.

Maxwell shrugged. "If you care so much, look at your recent calls and call him back."

"I did. No one answered, and it went to voice mail."

"I don't know what the big deal is. It's a fucking telemarketer. Block their call."

"It was just strange, and I did block him," she snapped back. "I'm going to bed."

Her irritating high heels clicked on the hardwood floors as the bitch left him in peace.

Finishing his drink, he slumped back down in his chair, dozing off.

The urgent need to take a piss had him jerking awake. He unsteadily left his office to go to the powder room, almost not making it. When he was finished, he splashed cold water on his face. He was getting old. His heavy drinking was beginning to affect his appearance.

Unable to stare at the man in the mirror any longer, Maxwell exited the powder room, going back inside his office.

Throwing the empty liquor bottle into the trash can beside his desk, he went to the liquor cabinet for another one.

He was reaching for the brandy when his cell phone rang on his desk. Taking the liquor with him, he picked up the phone, seeing it was an unidentified number. He almost didn't answer, but the thought of another pesky telemarketer calling Elaine if he didn't had him hitting the accept button.

"Hello …?" he slurred out.

"Do you know where your wife is?" The male voice sent a chill down his spine.

Trying to fight through the self-induced alcohol haze, Maxwell asked, "Who is this? *Do I know where my wife is?*" Maxwell snorted sarcastically. "She's in her fucking bed. Next time, ask me if my refrigerator is running." Maxwell ended the call. He thought prank calls had gone out of style decades ago.

Pouring his drink, he was about to sit back down in his chair when he heard Elaine calling his name from the kitchen.

He almost didn't respond to her, thinking it was just the prankster calling her now. She would never shut up about it. However, after downing the glass of brandy in one swallow, he walked toward the kitchen.

"Is it another tele—" Maxwell blinked owlishly at the man standing in his kitchen. "What are you doing here?"

"Shut up and sit the fuck down," Lucca ordered.

Paling, Maxwell went to the table and clumsily sat down before turning to look at his wife, who was sitting next to him.

Her normally styled hair was in disarray, and it took him a few drunken moments to realize that each of her hands were zip-tied behind her back.

"Why the fuck is she tied—?"

Maxwell lurched forward when a hard hand pressed against his back before it twisted his hands roughly behind his back. When he would have tried to stop him, Lucca punched him in the side of his face.

Dazedly, Maxwell started to fall out of the chair, but Lucca held him upright as he zip-tied his wrists to the arms of the chair.

He nearly pissed himself when Lucca tugged the chair away from the table and started zip-tying his ankles to each leg of the chair. Then he began crying.

"Tell me what you want. You want more money? I can get it for—"

"This isn't about money," Lucca said as he stood up, pushing Maxwell's chair back toward the table when he was done. Then he moved to the other side of the table to stare at them.

"Then what do you want!" Maxwell cried.

"Shut up, Maxwell," his wife hissed. "Lucca, we have a profitable relationship with the Carusos—"

"The Carusos will no longer be doing business with you. Your dealings with Lucifer voided any promises we made."

Maxwell started sobbing as he stared at the boogieman's heartless, frightening eyes, knowing he was fucked.

Lucca's cold voice cut through his tears. "I got a new dog, and he told me a story about how you sold your daughter's soul to the devil. That he would get her when she reached the age of eighteen."

Maxwell's crying sobs turned into whimpers.

"Shut the fuck up!" his wife screamed at him, her chair nearly tilting sideways. "You're going to get us killed." Then she turned her attention to Lucca. "I told Lucifer he could have Chloe when she left for college. I would have given her to you if tha—"

Lucca backhanded her across the face, effectively shutting her up.

"Not another fucking word out of your fucking mouth unless I address you," he sneered.

You could see Elaine's fear now as she realized she would not be able to talk her way out of this.

Lucca walked over to the counter, picking up a briefcase and placing it on the table in front of them. Then he adjusted his arm, making his black suit jacket rise up as he looked down at his watch.

Staring at the demon in front of him, who was dressed in an expensive, black Italian suit, Maxwell felt the impending doom. *I'm going to die.*

Lucca set a cell phone down on the table in front of the briefcase. "Before I forget, where do you keep your chili recipe?"

"Huh?" Maxwell stared at him, not sure he was hearing him right.

"Your chili recipe. I want it. Now," he demanded from Elaine this time.

Maxwell stared in horror as Lucca grabbed a fistful of Elaine's hair and slammed her head down onto the table when she didn't answer fast enough.

"I don't know!" A trickle of blood ran out of her nostrils. "I don't do the cooking anymore!"

Maxwell lost control over his once again full bladder, and he pissed himself when Lucca turned toward him.

"Lana's recipes are in the cabinet by the stove."

As Lucca walked away from them, Maxwell twisted his neck to see Lucca take the recipe box out of the cabinet. Then he watched as the boogieman went through the recipes until, with a smile of satisfaction, he found the one he was looking for, putting the rest of the recipes back in the box and leaving it on the counter.

When he returned to stand next to them, tears were burning

Maxwell's face. Even his wife started crying when Lucca cut one of the zip-ties off one of her arms, then turned to do the same thing to one of Maxwell's.

"Listen up; I'm only going to speak my instructions once." Lucca moved to the side, opening the briefcase.

If he hadn't already pissed himself, Maxwell would have then at the sight of what was inside the case. His wife was crying as hard as he was now.

Lucca pushed a button, triggering a light to go from red to green. Closing the briefcase, he then twirled the tiny numbers on the handle. "You have five minutes to get yourselves loose. Then call Chloe; she has the combination. If you don't have enough time to get all the ties off, Chloe is your only chance." He set a disposable phone on top of the case.

Neither of them turned to look at Lucca when he left with the recipe. Maxwell had already started struggling to get the tie off his free hand. When he did, he quickly lunged toward the phone, still zip-tied at the ankles.

Grabbing the phone, he dialed Chloe then held it shakily up to his ear. He heard one ring after another, wondering if she would ever pick up. *Fucking answer!*

Finally, when the phone was answered, they both screamed her name, "Chloe!"

A deadly voice came through the line, making Maxwell lose control of all his bodily functions. "Sorry, Chloe's busy."

His eyes went to the suitcase as flames engulfed his skin.

Maxwell had sold his daughter's soul to the devil to escape Hell, only for the boogieman to send him straight to Hell in a ball of flames.

The naked man in the corner of the room sat up slowly, using the pipe he was chained to and grimacing as he did.

Lucca stepped closer to the bloodied man, his eyes scanning the hundreds of knife cuts that had been given to him.

Every single mark he had given to Chloe meant fifty for him.

"You did it, didn't you?" Lucifer's black eyes took in his attire. "You killed her parents."

Lucca nodded. "You were right; they did give her to you."

Lucifer's maniacal laugh had blood spitting out his mouth before his ominous gaze went back to his. "Did it help?"

"Some," Lucca admitted. "But we both know it never gets satiated."

"No, it doesn't. Not for men like us." Lucifer smiled evilly, clearly remembering a fond memory.

Looking at the scar that had almost taken out the devil's eye, Lucca admired how he had gotten closer than he thought he could without actually taking it.

"I still remember it like it was just yesterday—the day you proved yourself and became a made man. It was the first time I saw you in a suit." Lucifer smiled, wiping the blood away from his mouth and causing it to smear across his lips. "At first, I thought Dante was crazy to let you try to get the information out of that rat who had stolen our money. But then, when I looked into your eyes, I could see it … The darkness lurking behind them. You put on quite a show for only being seventeen."

"Imagine how fast I could get him to speak now," Lucca said.

Seeing this was going to take longer than expected, he pulled out a cigarette, lighting the end.

"Do you know what I thought when you were done with him?" Lucifer asked.

He exhaled deeply, smoke filling the room as he asked, "What?"

"*I wish he were my son*," the devil revealed. "We could have ruled this city together."

Lucca smiled as he squatted down, stopping at eye level with the crazed black orbs. "I do … with your son."

"Ah, the great Salvatore!" The devil raised his hand like the name was on a billboard. "The son your father stole from me."

"You mean, the son who would have fucking starved to death if he had waited for you to realize he's a genius."

Lucifer shrugged. "He doesn't have our trait, though. Me and you, we could have done some great things together if you had just been born on the opposite side of the tracks."

The burn from the cigarette glowed off his face when he inhaled harshly.

Black eyes blazed back at him. "How does it feel to know you could be me someday?"

"You know that's not true. Not anymore." Lucca stared at the demented man before him, knowing it could have very well been a mirror between them, showing him what he would have looked like many years down the road *if I hadn't met Chloe.* "I met her before I walked down that path alone for too long ... Unlike you."

Lucifer's maniac face changed into one of jealousy. "I made her beautiful!"

"No, you just framed her beauty for me to see."

The jealousy grew worse in his eyes. "I still touched her fir—"

Grabbing his face, Lucca held the devil's mouth open as he shoved his smoking cigarette down his throat, making him swallow it.

Lucifer coughed, puffing out smoke while the hot, burning stick slid down the inside of his body. Then the maniacal laughter came back.

"When will you do it? When will I serve the boogieman's purpose so you can finally send me to Hell?"

Lucca was now the one to throw his head back in maniacal laughter as he stood up from the ground.

"Take a look around, Lucifer." He spanned his arms out. "You're in Hell, and this is your final purpose."

For the first time since coming here, the black, soulless eyes finally showed an ounce of fear as he watched the boogieman walk away.

Pulling back the huge sliding metal door, Lucca walked through it, putting himself on the other side. When he then spoke, it made the devil himself turn cold as the metal door started sliding back into place.

"And we are just getting fucking started."

OFF INTO THE BEAUTIFUL
DARK ABYSS

When *Lucca came up the* stairs, Chloe's heart jumped at seeing him in his all-black suit. So much so that he literally took her breath away.

"Y-You're back early," she said, holding the music box securely in her hand.

"I finished early." Closing the distance, he kneeled in front of her, staring at the cracked gold box. "You've never showed me this, darlin'."

Chloe opened the delicate box, showing him that it no longer played. "It belonged to my aunt. She birthed me for my mother, but ... she died in the process." She remembered the words she had once heard her mother say to her father: *You can thank your daughter for killing her.*

"I'm sorry you were never able to meet her, darlin'." He pushed her hair back so he could see her face better. He seemed like he had already known what she was telling him.

Me, too. "I think she must have been really sweet. I think my father was in love with her."

"I'm sure she was." He smoothed his hand over the crack in the box like he always did to her scars. "How did it break?"

Taking a deep breath, she told him the truth. "My father broke it one night after he had too much to drink. I used to listen to it every night, over and over and over, letting the lullaby sing me to sleep, like a mother would her baby."

Lucca stayed silent, still rubbing the box with his fingers as he let her finish the story.

"I searched forever, trying to find another one so I could hear the tune again. Then one day, I finally did. So, I went to the little shop and was able to hear it once more." Chloe put the box in his hands. "Now I'm happy he broke it, because it led me to you."

Leaning in, Lucca gave her a hard kiss, swiping his tongue along her bottom lip before he pulled back.

"I want you to have it now." She told him the reasoning behind why she had pulled it out.

"Are you sure, darlin'?" he asked, already holding the box like he cherished it, like how he cherished her.

"Yes." She pressed her forehead against his. "Besides, I have the one you gave me."

"I missed having the box sitting on my desk." He revealed where it had sat for those seven months as he carefully placed the box on the bed before he picked her up.

She twisted her legs around his waist. "Where are we going?"

"I need a shower, and you're going to join me." He carried her into the bathroom and put her back on her feet as he grinned down at her. "Did you do what I asked?"

"Yes." Chloe blushed, her cheeks burning red. "It wasn't easy. I've never shaved myself bare before."

He leaned down to her short stature, taking a bite of her lip. "Next time, I can help."

Um, no. "That is never going to happen. Ever."

"We'll see." He winked at her before he started shrugging out of his suit, setting his watch on the vanity. "Get undressed."

A fire immediately started burning inside of her from his demand.

Her body obeyed, pulling the black clothes away from her skin. Then she stood there, vulnerable in front of him, as his dark eyes caressed her porcelain skin then to her cleanly shaven pussy. Chloe was able to see the pleasure he found just looking at her when his hardness grew.

The man before her hadn't been satiated enough from the first time; that she knew. Tonight, her body, mind, and soul hoped to help satiate his hunger.

Lucca gave her a scary smile as he opened one of the vanity drawers and took out a bottle of mousse. Then he wet a cloth under the water.

Coming toward her, he then pulled her into the shower and urged her down onto the bench before kneeling in front of her.

She was confused that he hadn't started the shower, and even more so when he revealed he also carried his lighter and a hair tie.

"Tie your hair back."

Chloe pulled up her long mass of hair, securing it with the band.

"What are you doing?" she asked curiously when he made her lean back until her abdomen was more level.

Her question went unanswered as he sprayed the mousse into a small heart shape on her belly. Lucca then flicked his lighter open, weaving it between his fingers and causing the flame to dance.

"Do you trust me, darlin'?"

Staring at the mesmerizing flame, she answered with, "Always."

"Stay still," he ordered while he drew the flame close to the mousse.

Chloe's mouth dropped open when the flame danced right above her skin, following the pattern of the mousse. It was somehow even more mesmerizing than watching the tricks he could do with his Zippo. She guessed this was how he felt when he would touch his fingers to the flame. All she could feel was a small tingle of warmth.

"Did you like it?" he asked as he drew the flame close again, lighting the same pattern once more. Except it burned out much quicker this time.

"Yes," she breathed when the flames had disappeared.

Instead of lighting it back on fire, he took the damp cloth and wiped away the mousse. Then he drew an even bigger heart on her stomach with the mousse. The top curves of the heart were closer to her heavy breasts while the bottom point rested on her shaved pussy.

"Now do you trust me, darlin'?" His green eyes flashed while he spun the lighter through his fingers.

"Always," she repeated the word without hesitation.

The flame drew closer, and she could already feel herself practically panting. When the heart-shaped pattern went up in flames, her head fell back, resting on the glass. She moaned as the flames licked between her thighs.

Holy fu—

Lucca kept it going, relighting the mousse over and over until it burned no more.

Her heart raced when Lucca wiped away the design, letting the cold, damp towel linger over her warmed skin. Then he turned the water on after he had moved the nozzle, waiting for it to warm before he put it back in its normal position.

Lucca's impressive body stalked up to her. He brought his hand to her hair, releasing the hair tie and letting her hair wildly fall back down. Then he slid his hand down to one of her huge globes, wiping away a trickle of water that rested on her nipple with his thumb, making it peak.

"Do you still like it after I set you on fire?"

"Yes …" Her body became putty under his hands. "I'm not afraid of anything you do to me."

"Darlin' …" He twined a wet strand of her hair around his finger. "Those are dangerous words to use around me." He tugged the dark strand down, forcing her head to lower and sending her a silent message.

Chloe's gray eyes grew as she stared down at his enlarged cock.

"Are you sure you want to trust me? I never——"

"I'll take my chances."

Lucca groaned when she dropped to her knees and took his arousal into her hand, inexpertly stroking his length. He stared down at her with fierce eyes as she leaned in closer.

"You're killing me, darlin'," he told her, on the verge of a growl.

Biting her lip, she started to jerk away, but his grip on her hair stopped her.

"Don't you dare stop." The low growl finally escaped. "Open your mouth."

She timidly opened her mouth and took him inside. It was the most beautiful thing imaginable, seeing she pleased him. You could tell Lucca thought the same thing as he looked down at her with intense eyes. It cleansed away the ugliness of his world, just like when he had first looked upon her scarred face, her face that mirrored the scars he had carried inside his heart for his mother.

Lucca started slow, giving her time to adjust before he couldn't hold back and started pumping into her mouth faster. The feelings that arose inside of him were so intense that he had to jerk himself out of her mouth, afraid he would come.

The want and need to be inside of her was evident on his face when his hands went to her ass, lifting her up until he placed his arousal where he wanted it. Then, when he pushed her against the glass, soaring deep inside of her in one thrust, she screamed out, feeling on the edge of pleasure and pain.

"Lucca!"

Pounding into her, he didn't hold anything back, giving her all of him.

The roughness and ferocity of him scared her, but only a little, as she allowed the boogieman to take what he wanted from her. He had been starving for too long, and she wanted to see the darkness still.

"Harder ..." she moaned.

Lucca's mouth covered hers, delving his tongue into her mouth as his hard length delved harder into her spasming center. Then he bit her bottom lip before slowly pulling back until he released it.

"This what you want, darlin'?"

"Faster ..." she moaned when the orgasm began to claim her body, sending her into a beautiful nightmare.

The boogieman had kept his promise as she began to beg him not to stop.

He sent her off into the beautiful, dark abyss over and over until the beautiful nightmares replaced the devil's nightmares, *one by one.*

THE CHAINS THAT
HELD THEIR SOULS

Lucca cradled her unconscious body in his arms. He hadn't been able to look away from her face since the moment she had drifted off to sleep.

It killed him that he had to put her to sleep. What he was about to do to her killed him. She wasn't going to understand for a long while that he had to do it to save her and to set her and his mother's souls free.

Sitting down on the bed, he held her for just a little longer. This was the last time he was going to be able to touch her for a long while.

He began talking to her, hoping that somehow, when she woke up, a part of her would remember the things he had said.

"He was coming for you. He was going to take you away. He gave me no

choice, Chloe. He tried to take you in the mall, and if I had let you walk ten steps farther, Lucifer would have had you."

Lucca stood, placing her slumbering body on the bed before he sat back down beside her, wanting, needing one more moment with her.

He raised a finger to her porcelain face, stroking the scar he had dreamt about touching for seven months. Smoothing his finger over the mark, the darkness in him rumbled then stilled, becoming slow, steady, finding its purpose.

He had thought he had already found his true purpose when he had seen her for the first time, but that had been only the half of it. His purpose was saving Chloe Masters, but his true purpose was them saving each other.

Every day, he had felt himself become more insatiable. The darkness in him was walking a path of no return … And then he had touched her, and the heinous being inside that had been desolate and alone finally found hope. He was reborn.

The boogieman had found another the world viewed as a freak, as a monster.

Lucca smoothed his finger over her scar for just one more final moment. "I love you, darlin'. Please remember that when you wake up …"

Chloe pressed herself closer to Lucca, wanting to feel the warmth from his body, as she rested her head on his shoulder. The light dusting of snowfall in January was so beautiful to look at under the lighted gazebo. It took her breath away every time, almost as much as when she looked into Lucca's fully green eyes.

She looked around, seeing the changes she and Lucca had created back here and the changes she had made within herself.

Lucca took her hand in his, pulling it onto his lap. "Do you know what day it is, darlin'?"

She raised her head to look into his green eyes, her breath once again being taken away.

Unable to find words, she simply shook her head.

"You met me right here for the first time … a year ago today."

Her heart swelled at the fact that he had remembered.

"I can't believe—" Chloe's eyes drifted to her left hand as Lucca slid a diamond ring onto her finger.

"It was my mother's," he told her bittersweetly.

"It's beautiful," she whispered, a single tear running down her scar as her gray depths took in the glittering diamond that was held by an intricate design.

"Do you know what I had to tell the shop owner to talk her into selling me the music box?"

Chloe shook her head as more tears fell from her eyes.

"The day we first met under here, I went back after only knowing you existed for a week, and I told her I loved you." He said it with such a fierceness that she felt the chains that held their souls together rattle.

"I love you," she breathed with all her being, sending her own message to their souls.

Lucca leaned in, bringing his lips closer and closer to her scarred ones. "Marry me, darlin'."

CHAINED

My body is chained, weak, and afraid.
      My mind is broken.
      The man who put me in these chains
Owns me.

My body is chained, tough, and brave.
My mind is stronger.
The man who put me in these chains
Will not own me.

My chains are old, weak, and afraid.
They are broken.
The man who put me in these chains
Can no longer hold me.

Sarah Brianne

Please, if you or someone you know ever needs help,
follow this link to get more information and help.
YOU ARE NOT ALONE.

www.victimsofcrime.org/help-for-crime-victims
/national-hotlines-and-helpful-links

Made in the USA
Monee, IL
29 August 2021